PRAISE FOR CAROLYN BROWN

Hummingbird Lane

"Brown's (*The Daydream Cabin*) gentle story of a woman finding strength within a tight-knit community has just a touch of romance at the end. Recommended for readers who enjoy heartwarming stories about women overcoming obstacles."

—*Library Journal*

Miss Janie's Girls

"[A] heartfelt tale of familial love and self-acceptance."

—*Publishers Weekly*

"Heartfelt moments and family drama collide in this saga about sisters."

—*Woman's World*

The Banty House

"Brown throws together a colorful cast of characters to excellent effect and maximum charm in this small-town contemporary romance . . . This first-rate romance will delight readers young and old."

—*Publishers Weekly*

The Family Journal

HOLT MEDALLION FINALIST

"Reading a Carolyn Brown book is like coming home again."
—Harlequin Junkie (top pick)

The Empty Nesters

"A delightful journey of hope and healing."
—Woman's World

"The story is full of emotion . . . and the joy of friendship and family. Carolyn Brown is known for her strong, loving characters, and this book is full of them."
—Harlequin Junkie

"Carolyn Brown takes us back to small-town Texas with a story about women, friendships, love, loss, and hope for the future."
—Storeybook Reviews

"Ms. Brown has fast become one of my favorite authors!"
—Romance Junkies

The Perfect Dress

"Fans of Brown will swoon for this sweet contemporary, which skillfully pairs a shy small-town bridal shop owner and a softhearted car dealership owner . . . The expected but welcomed happily ever after for all involved will make readers of all ages sigh with satisfaction."

—*Publishers Weekly*

"Carolyn Brown writes the best comfort-for-the-soul, heartwarming stories, and she never disappoints . . . You won't go wrong with *The Perfect Dress!*"

—*Harlequin Junkie*

The Magnolia Inn

"The author does a first-rate job of depicting the devastating stages of grief, provides a simple but appealing plot with a sympathetic hero and heroine and a cast of lovable supporting characters, and wraps it all up with a happily ever after to cheer for."

—*Publishers Weekly*

"*The Magnolia Inn* by Carolyn Brown is a feel-good story about friendship, fighting your demons, and finding love, and maybe just a little bit of magic."

—*Harlequin Junkie*

"Chock-full of Carolyn Brown's signature country charm, *The Magnolia Inn* is a sweet and heartwarming story of two people trying to make the most of their lives, even when they have no idea what exactly is at stake."

—Fresh Fiction

Small Town Rumors

"Carolyn Brown is a master at writing warm, complex characters who find their way into your heart."

—*Harlequin Junkie*

The Sometimes Sisters

"Carolyn Brown continues her streak of winning, heartfelt novels with *The Sometimes Sisters*, a story of estranged sisters and frustrated romance."

—All About Romance

"This is an amazing feel-good story that will make you wish you were a part of this amazing family."

—*Harlequin Junkie* (top pick)

Meadow Falls

ALSO BY CAROLYN BROWN

CONTEMPORARY ROMANCES

The Devine Doughnut Shop
The Sandcastle Hurricane
Riverbend Reunion
The Bluebonnet Battle
The Sunshine Club
The Hope Chest
Hummingbird Lane
The Daydream Cabin
Miss Janie's Girls
The Banty House
The Family Journal
The Empty Nesters
The Perfect Dress
The Magnolia Inn
Small Town Rumors
The Sometimes Sisters
The Strawberry Hearts Diner
The Lilac Bouquet
The Barefoot Summer
The Lullaby Sky
The Wedding Pearls
The Yellow Rose Beauty Shop
The Ladies' Room
Hidden Secrets
Long, Hot Texas Summer
Daisies in the Canyon
Trouble in Paradise

CONTEMPORARY SERIES

The Broken Roads Series
To Trust
To Commit
To Believe
To Dream
To Hope

Three Magic Words Trilogy
A Forever Thing
In Shining Whatever
Life After Wife

HISTORICAL ROMANCE

The Black Swan Trilogy
Pushin' Up Daisies
From Thin Air
Come High Water

The Drifters & Dreamers Trilogy
Morning Glory
Sweet Tilly
Evening Star

The Love's Valley Series
Choices
Absolution
Chances
Redemption
Promises

Meadow Falls

CAROLYN BROWN

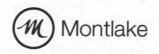 Montlake

Published by Montlake, Seattle

www.apub.com

Amazon, the Amazon logo, and Montlake are trademarks of Amazon.com, Inc., or its affiliates.

ISBN-13: 9781662514326 (paperback)
ISBN-13: 9781662514319 (digital)

Cover design by Leah Jacobs-Gordon
Cover image: © Delcroix Romain / Shutterstock; © HTWE / Shutterstock;
© Monica.E.Tan / Shutterstock; © MaxyM / Shutterstock;
© Eugene_Photo / Shutterstock; © Leonardo Baldini / ArcAngel

Printed in the United States of America

In memory of my granny, Bessie Chapman.
She helped raise me like Mandy did Celeste and Angela
Marie in this story,
and I'm so grateful for everything she taught me.

Chapter One

"Don't treat me like I'm an old woman, Angela Marie Duncan." Mandy crossed her arms over her chest. "I'm only ninety-seven on paper. I'm barely sixty in my mind. I want to walk to the cemetery for Harrison's funeral, and I want to think about him while I take each step. He wasn't perfect, but he did what he was supposed to for Meadow Falls."

Thinking about my father was the one thing I did not want to do. Being dead didn't make him an angel, and my memories were not good ones.

"But, Mandy, it's freezing cold, and the wind is blowing," I argued.

She shot me one of those looks that I recognized from childhood, through my teenage years, and all the way through every one of the thirty-five years of my life. Then it dawned on me that she'd called me by all three of my names. She'd only done that a handful of times in the past.

"Everyone is parking their vehicles out here in the front yard and walking to the cemetery, and we will be doing the same thing. Don't argue with an old woman," she scolded.

"You just said you weren't old," I reminded her.

She tipped her head up and said, "Get me my cane, and help me put on my good funeral coat and my hat with the wide brim. We *are* walking, and the discussion is over."

I should have known better than to hope that she would change her mind. One of the first lessons I'd learned as a child was that Mandy's word was the law. *No* meant *no*, and never—not one time—had it meant *maybe* or *try again later*. As my nanny, she had a power that superseded all others, including my mother and father.

When we got outside, I looped her free arm into mine to keep the north wind from blowing her all the way to the private Duncan family cemetery. Even though she was short and built tiny, she had always been a force to reckon with. That morning, she had tied a black silk scarf around her head and knotted it under her chin. She had on the same black dress she had worn to every funeral she'd attended for the past fifty years.

"You look nice today," Mandy said. "I'm glad you showed respect and wore your good black dress instead of jeans and a sweatshirt."

"I didn't want to disappoint *you*," I told her.

For the most part, my father had barely acknowledged me as a daughter. I've heard that indifference—not hate—is the opposite of love. I don't think my father hated me, but there was no doubt that he was indifferent to me. As his daughter, I was simply a person he tolerated because he had to do so. I just hoped the preacher wouldn't try to preach Harrison Duncan into heaven. That would take so long that our bodies would be frozen before he got the job done.

When we walked through the gate into the cemetery, an eerie feeling settled over me, not totally unlike the one I'd had when I held the results of a paternity-confirming DNA test in my hands. I hadn't felt like this when my mother died, so why today?

The bitter wind shook the lone scrub oak tree's limbs, but that was the only sound over Meadow Falls. The marble tombstones seemed to throw coldness out from them in waves. Dark clouds hung low in the sky, threatening rain or snow any minute. Folks who had braved the weather to attend the service huddled together like crows sitting on a telephone wire. A few nodded at me and Mandy as we took our seats in the two chairs in front of my father's oak casket.

The wind picked up even more, stirring dead leaves into miniature tornadoes that blasted the tombstones in vain and then fell into piles against their bases. In life, my father had been a hard, austere man, who'd had no trouble letting everyone know he was disappointed that his only offspring was a daughter and not a son. In death, his name— etched onto his own personal slab of polished marble—reminded every- one that a bunch of leaves would never be a match for a hard headstone. I was living proof that even a human being seldom had the nerve to go up against Harrison Duncan.

The big marble stone standing in the middle of the small graveyard was six feet tall and almost as wide, with the name *Duncan* engraved on it. Headstones lined up in neat rows behind it announced the names, births, and dates of death for the various members of the family, from babies to young adults to elderly folks. Next week, or maybe the one after that, someone would put the dates on this one—1962–2023—to signify the years of Harrison Duncan's own birth and death.

I was more mesmerized by the stirring of the leaves than with what the preacher was saying about what a great man my father, Harrison, had been and how saddened the community was by his passing. I turned slightly to see the folks behind me nodding in agreement, but I could relate to the leaves more than I could to my father, who had been one of the most prosperous peanut farmers in the whole state of Texas. The leaves and I had a lot more in common; we had both butted heads with Harrison—and nothing had worked.

I was so angry that I didn't want to hear what a good man Harrison Duncan had been. He'd left me with a mess to clean up. He had never had to worry about hiring a foreman. Back in the first years of Meadow Falls, Raymone had been the foreman. When he died, his son, Martin, took over, and when Martin retired, his son, Luis, was given the job. Luis passed away two years ago, and his nephew Thomas stepped into the role. After harvest this past year, Thomas got married and moved to Mexico.

Now, since my father had been too busy with his social life to hire the next foreman before he died, the job fell on me—just like everything else.

Harrison didn't plan to die, the niggling voice in my head said.

No, and I didn't plan to be running the biggest peanut farm in the Texas Panhandle until I was thirty-five, either.

Beside me, Mandy wiped away a tear with a lace-edged handkerchief that had been ironed and folded into a perfect little square. A box of tissues sat on the chair beside me, but I didn't need a single one.

Who would have thought that he would drop dead of a heart attack before he was even sixty-two years old? I had expected that Mandy would go long before my father. A lump grew in my throat at the idea of her passing away. Had it been Mandy's funeral, the story would be altogether different. She had been my nanny, surrogate mother, and father all rolled into one—as well as my friend and confidante—for all the years I'd been on this earth. If her great-granddaughter, Celeste, and I had been sitting in these cold chairs and staring at *her* casket, I would have used every tissue in the box. Growing up, Celeste had been my best friend, and she and Mandy were my rocks.

A daughter, especially an only child, should be able to at least cry for her father, shouldn't she? But there were no tears—not that morning. I was sorry that he was gone, but the peanut business would go on in his absence. He'd taken care of the social side of Meadow Falls for years, leaving me to worry with the actual work.

Was something wrong with me? Was there no warm blood in my body? Had I grown as hard as my father and now had no emotions? I shivered from my head all the way to my toes, as if the universe had answered me. Guilt wrapped its chilly arms around me, and despite the black hat that Mandy had insisted I wear that day—and the warm socks and leather boots on my feet—I couldn't shake the coldness surrounding me and encasing my heart in ice.

I had sweated over the planting, the watering, the harvesting, and everything that went into making a profitable crop. Every year, by the time we had finished a season, the harsh sun had turned my skin a deep, dark brown. My father didn't have even a hint of a farmer's tan because he spent all his waking hours driving around in his fancy pickup truck, which one of the hired hands washed every evening. In his mind, he was the king of Meadow Falls, and he had a reputation to live up to that had been passed down to him for generations. He was always dressed to be seen, wearing starched and ironed white shirts, black dress jeans, and boots that were shined each evening. Mandy had told me more than once that he had an image to uphold when he attended all kinds of meetings for the peanut co-op and went to lunches with other farmers in the county.

I took care of the books, so I knew how much he'd spent on those *business* lunches, and I was glad I knew how to run Meadow Falls. But why, I'd often wondered, didn't he ever take me along to some of those meetings so I would be trained for the social side of running the biggest peanut farm in this part of Texas? I'd never been to a lunch with him and had no idea if everything he did was to promote our business or if it was really for his own gratification. Did I even need to learn that side of things on my own now that he was gone?

The preacher was reading something from a psalm, and I heard a few long sighs behind me. A vision of my father getting ready to leave the farm flashed through my mind. I saw him walking out to a spotlessly clean white pickup truck, which he would trade in for a brand-new model every two years. Always white, always sparkling clean, always with the vanity tag on the back that said MEADOW. In my vision, he was wearing his signature white shirt, shiny black cowboy boots, and jeans that he wore only once before throwing them into the basket in his room.

I would take them to Polly Jackson, the lady who did his laundry and ironing, and then pick them up at the end of each week.

I hated his white shirts—always starched, creased down the sleeves, monogrammed with *HCD* on the collar and cuffs, and perfectly tailored to fit his tall, lanky body—because they signified a man who had no time for me, other than to tell me that I needed to finish my meal and stop wandering off in my thoughts because our foreman, Luis, would be waiting for me. Before I even started going to school, he'd insisted that I begin to learn the peanut business. That took up all my time, every day after school and all summer long. I guess my father had thought if he couldn't have a son to pass his king's crown down to, he would be sure that his daughter could carry on with what needed to be done—with or without the crown.

I loved Celeste like a sister, but I envied her, too. She didn't have to get dressed in bibbed overalls and boots and go out into the fields. She got to wear whatever she wanted, stay in the house with Mandy, dust furniture, and learn to cook. I would have gladly signed away the whole farm to her if we could have changed places.

We were only thirteen months apart, but I'd almost hated her when she got to choose what she wanted to do after graduating from high school. She'd joined the air force with her boyfriend, and the only thing that saved me from running away that year was knowing that I had only twelve more months on the farm. After that, I would go to college and figure out what I wanted to do with my life.

Plans are often like pie crusts—made to be broken. I'd seen that as a meme once, and it stuck with me through the years.

I glanced over at my mother's headstone: Sophia Mendoza Duncan. 1967–2005. She fell sick when I started my senior year. Mandy and I cared for her. Mandy never complained, but I certainly did—not to anyone standing in front of me, but at midnight, when I was working on the computer, I said words that could have blistered the paint right off the walls.

Mother was so beautiful that she could have been a model. Tall, slender, and carrying herself like she had a diamond crown settled onto her jet-black hair, she was every bit as much the queen of Meadow Falls as my father was the king. For a small town that had fewer than a thousand people in it, she managed to stay involved in everything: a member of the Chamber of Commerce, on the board of directors at the local bank as well as that of our small library. She was on several committees at the church, and we never missed a Sunday-morning service—the only time she and I actually spent much time together. On those days, she made sure I was wearing a pretty dress and my curly red hair was fixed nice. She threw dinner parties at least once a week, and when she wasn't socializing, she was in the office, taking care of Meadow Falls' financial reports and doing bookwork in general. That left practically no time for a daughter who was constantly getting in her way.

The preacher finally said a prayer, and folks began to walk past the casket, lay a rose on the top, and then pause to offer condolences and shake hands with me and Mandy. When everyone had gone, Mandy picked up her cane and slowly made her way to the casket. She dropped the cane onto the frozen earth, laid both hands on the oak, and just stood there for a few minutes with tears running down her wrinkled cheeks.

"My sweet boy," she groaned. "You weren't supposed to go before me. Why couldn't you have kept that attitude that you had when you were a little child?"

I made a mental note to ask her what she was talking about. The only time I'd ever seen my father smile was when he was in a group of men about his age. So where did a different attitude come into play?

When I stood up and joined her, everything seemed surreal. Guilt still lay in my chest like a heavy rock because I couldn't shed tears. My father and I had lived in the same house together my whole life, and yet I felt as if I had just attended a stranger's service. I had cried hard two years ago when Luis passed away—but for my father, not a single tear.

Mandy grieved for the little boy whom she'd been a nanny to and raised with her own daughter, Emma. I couldn't even begin to imagine my father as a baby or as a child. To me, he had never been a little boy who ran barefoot in the freshly plowed fields or shook a few peanut plants to see if the crop was ready to harvest like Celeste and I had done as little girls.

"Oh, Harrison, I . . ." She broke down and buried her face in a hankie.

I patted her on the shoulder. "We have to tell him goodbye, Mandy, and get you back to the house, where it's warm. You could get pneumonia out here in this cold weather."

She stepped closer to the casket, kissed the rose in her hand, and laid it on top of the others. "I loved you. Tell my Emma hello for me, and it won't be long before—"

I butted in before she could finish. "Don't say it, Mandy. I need you to be here with me. You're all I've got left."

"I'm almost a hundred years old, my child, and I'm wearing out," she said as she looped her arm through mine once more. "We'll have to say goodbye before too many years. My mama named me Amanda, not Methuselah."

"We'll cross that bridge when we get to it," I told her and led her away so the men, who were waiting in a warm truck, could lower the casket and fill in the hole with dirt. The sound of the first shovel of soil hitting the casket filled the air behind us, and all I could think was that the dirt covering kings was the same as the dirt thrown into the graves of paupers.

The folks who had gathered for the service had hurried back to their vehicles to finally get warm again, so we were the only two on the path back to the house. Mandy walked slowly, so the five-minute trip took double that.

"I wish Celeste could have been here." Mandy's breath sent a fog out into the air as if she'd just blown out smoke.

"Me too," I answered. "Maybe we'll get to see her in the spring."

"She hasn't been home for six months. That's the longest she's ever been gone. I can hear something in her voice when she calls on Sundays. I'm not sure if she's keeping something from me or if she's just homesick," she said.

"I've noticed that, too, but I guess she'll tell us when she's ready."

Celeste had never been one to talk about her problems, so if she did have issues with something, she would analyze it to death before she ever said a word.

"Think we should come right out and ask her tomorrow when she calls us?" Mandy asked.

"No, let her figure things out first."

The house on Meadow Falls was visible at least a mile away, coming east toward Meadow, Texas, or going west away from it. It was a big white structure that rose like a silent sentinel in the distant flat countryside, where earth seemingly met the sky when the sun came up in the morning and set in the evening. Nothing but dirt now, but later, acres and acres would be covered with peanut plants. A wide porch wrapped around three sides of the house, offering rocking chairs and shade in the evenings during the hot summer months. Each of the eight bedrooms on the second floor opened out onto an upstairs porch. Mandy called it a sleeping porch, but my mother had said that I had to call it the balcony because that sounded more sophisticated, and we certainly would never sleep out there.

It was by far the biggest house in the county and had been on the cover of various agricultural magazines through the years. Like my father's truck, the outside was kept every bit as spotless as the inside, which looked more like a museum than a home. Even though I was convinced that we lived in the dustiest part of the whole wide world, I could never remember seeing dirty windows or even a speck of dust on the white clapboards. The royal family, the Duncans, had to keep up their image in all things—my father's words, not mine.

Even though the house was set off the road at the end of a lane lined with pecan trees, the wind carried the sound of the cars and trucks passing on the highway. Several of those would probably have been vehicles carrying the folks who had come to pay their last respects back home.

"We should have put out a brunch spread for the people who were kind enough to come out in this miserable weather. We could have served hot coffee and desserts, and they could have warmed up in the house," Mandy said. "Folks will talk about you not doing what was proper. Duncans have to live up to the name, you know?"

A few bits of sleet stung my face, and I picked up the pace just a little. "I wasn't ever a princess, and I refuse to put on airs. I'm not interested in all that social crap. I'll just raise peanuts, like I've always done."

"I want to see you settled down with a family before I slip on over into eternity," she said as we stepped up onto the back porch. "You need to get busy, Angela Marie Duncan. You've got a legacy to uphold."

"You never use my whole name unless I'm in trouble, and you've used it twice this morning." I opened the door and stood to the side to let her go in first.

"You will be in big trouble"—Mandy shook her finger at me and unbuttoned her long black coat—"if I don't get to leave this old world knowing that there's a baby on the way and that Meadow Falls will go on for another generation."

"Hello?" someone yelled from the foyer. "The door was open. Did I miss the funeral?"

"Celeste!" Mandy squealed and froze right there in the middle of the kitchen. "She's here, Angela Marie!"

Then something hit the floor, and for a split second, I was afraid Mandy had just breathed her last because of the shock of Celeste coming home unannounced. Another layer of guilt crept over me when I thought of the walk to the cemetery and back in the cold wind being too much on her fragile body and heart, and then I realized that the noise I'd heard was her cane hitting the floor.

Celeste is really in the house. Surely we were both wrong. Someone else had popped in. Someone whose voice sounded just like Celeste's. We'd just been talking about her, and she was on our minds. That would explain why we mistakenly thought it was really her. Mandy was going to be so disappointed.

Mandy moved faster than I'd seen her go in over a year. She even beat me across the kitchen and into the dining room and was already hugging Celeste when I made it to the middle of the foyer.

"The snow in New Mexico slowed me down." Celeste bent to hug her great-grandmother a second time. "I got here as fast as I could, but the roads were slick. I wanted to be here for y'all for the service, but I was too late. I can't believe that Harrison is gone. I thought he would live forever."

"So did I," I said as I hugged her. "Welcome home." I didn't want to let go of her for fear that I was dreaming. A couple of deep breaths seemed to help my heart settle into a regular beat. "This is a surprise. Why didn't you call? How long can you stay? Are you okay? Is something wrong?"

"I wanted it to be a surprise, for more reasons than one." Celeste shivered as she removed her jacket, hung it on the hall tree in the foyer, and looped her arm through Mandy's. "I could sure use a cup of hot coffee. That wind feels like it's coming off ice. It chilled me all the way to the bone. Once I get warm, I'll answer all your questions."

"Well, you sure enough surprised us." Mandy patted her on the arm.

"Remember what Mandy told us when we were little girls and wanted to drink coffee?" I led the way back into the kitchen.

"I told you girls lots of things," Mandy said.

"She told us that it would make our toenails turn black." Celeste held Mandy's hand and walked slowly. "Did you ever check yours to be sure?"

"Oh, yeah," I said with a giggle.

Having Celeste there was like a breath of fresh spring air after a class 5 tornado. Suddenly, everything was better, and my heart was lighter than it had been in the past three days.

"I'm starving," she said when we reached the kitchen.

"There's food everywhere," Mandy told her.

"I'll make a pot of coffee if you'll get in the refrigerator and get out one of those pies that folks have brought in. There's half a dozen to choose from," I offered. "Did you drive straight through from California?"

"No, I made it halfway before I got too tired to go another mile. This morning, I left a cheap hotel somewhere over in New Mexico before daylight and haven't eaten since lunchtime yesterday." Celeste settled Mandy in a chair, kissed her on the forehead, and then opened the refrigerator door. "Is that chicken and dressing?"

"Help yourself, if you'd rather have that than pie," I told her. "There's also mashed potatoes and a sweet potato casserole in there."

"And dozens of other casseroles, plus a couple of sliced hams," Mandy said. "We've got enough food that we won't need to cook for a couple of weeks. How long can you stay this time? Are you on your way to another deployment?"

"I didn't reenlist," Celeste said with force as she filled up a plate.

"But you've only got two years until you retire." I couldn't believe that she would quit with that short a time to go.

"That's right, but there are more important things in life than a twenty-year retirement. I've been so homesick that I could hardly bear it." She added a slice of homemade bread to her plate and carried it to the table.

"I'm glad you are home," Mandy said. "When does Trevor get here?"

"He isn't coming," Celeste replied, her voice turning downright chilly.

A long pregnant pause settled over the room like a dense fog.

"I signed divorce papers a few days ago," she finally said with a long sigh.

She had to be joking with us—and yet Celeste would have never joked about something that serious. Not after eighteen years of marriage to her high school sweetheart.

Mandy's smile faded, and her face looked like stone. "Did I hear you right? You didn't mention that when you called us on Sundays. When did all this start?"

I am so guilty of letting my mind wander when I should be listening that I figured I hadn't heard her right. But the expression on her face and the slight quiver in her chin said that she was not kidding: she and Trevor had gotten a divorce.

They had been my role models. To me, they'd had the perfect life, one that I'd always been so jealous of. Someday, if I ever married, I wanted a husband just like Trevor—or so I thought. Evidently, I didn't know a thing about men.

"He cheated on me two years ago." Celeste swallowed hard a couple of times before she went on. "I didn't tell y'all because I wanted our marriage to work, and I didn't want you to have bad feelings toward him. I blamed myself for not making enough time for him, anyway."

"And?" Mandy asked.

"Please tell me you are teasing," I whispered.

"Sorry, darlin', but it's the truth," Celeste answered.

"You could have given us some warning," I scolded. "I just now almost had a heart attack."

"I practiced ways to tell you and Granny all the way from California, but I couldn't figure out anything other than to just blurt it out."

"That sorry sucker," Mandy growled. "I'd like to get my hands on him right now. I wouldn't even mind sitting in a jail cell if I could just work him over with my cane."

"Why did you stay with him?" I was still having trouble believing that their marriage had gone down the drain and that we were just now hearing about something that had been going on for two years.

"He begged me for a second chance, and I caved," she said, "with the understanding that it would be his last and he would never get another one."

"And he did it again after that?" I asked.

"Last month, just before I was going to sign the new re-up papers, I found out that he had never broken it off with the other woman and that they have a year-old son together. He managed to keep it all a big secret because she lives in Georgia, and he was sent over there to teach classes every few weeks," Celeste explained. "He's the one that filed divorce papers. I got them at work while he was halfway across the United States."

The expression on her face was still serious, but her tone was flat, as if she were reading a poem that she didn't like. All the respect I'd had for Trevor flew out the window. Just like Mandy, I wanted to do him bodily harm, only my fists and temper would do a better job than a cane. I studied Mandy for a few seconds. She didn't seem to be too badly affected, other than sadness in her eyes.

"How can you be so calm?" I asked.

"Divorce isn't the worst thing in life," Mandy said. "Fix me a plate, please. We'll have a brunch with just the three of us. I'd like a spoonful of dressing, some of the sweet potato casserole, and a little cranberry sauce on the side."

The microwave timer dinged, and Celeste removed the plate. I wondered what could be worse than the day we'd just had, but it wasn't the time to ask Mandy what she meant.

"You go on and eat while your food is hot," I told Celeste. "I'll fix Mandy right up."

"Thank you," she said. "Down deep inside, I knew that Trevor hadn't been happy these past two years. He volunteered for too many extra duties and was gone as many nights as he was home. He was always eager to leave and sad when he got back. I tried to tell myself that if I was a better wife, he would be happier to come back to see me.

Now I know that he was living a double life. Spending time with his family in Georgia every minute he could."

"Did *she* know about *you?*" I asked and wondered if the day's roller coaster of emotions—or lack of them—would ever end.

Celeste shrugged. "I'm not sure, but I figure he was probably spinning her a tale about why he couldn't divorce me. She might have finally forced him to make a choice."

"Trevor wouldn't be forced to do anything," Mandy growled. "He did what he did of his own free will, and not one bit of this is your fault, so I won't be hearing any more of that kind of crap." She paused for a breath. "You are home now. You are still young, and the good Lord willin', you have a long life ahead of you, so don't look back, and live the days you get with happiness."

Mandy's plate went into the microwave, and I fixed mine while hers heated.

"We should have split up two years ago," Celeste said between bites. "Our marriage was really dying in its sleep then, and I grieved for it at *that* time. I thought it was like one of those phoenix birds that could rise from the ashes. It was so dead that there weren't even any ashes left to resurrect."

"I'm not all that surprised, but I prayed every day that he would always make you happy. I wish I'd been wrong," Mandy said and shifted her gaze over to me.

"Wrong about what?" I asked as I removed her plate from the microwave and set it before her, then filled two glasses with sweet tea and one with milk.

"He had wandering eyes, always looking at other women," Mandy said. "I hoped that marriage would settle him down."

"Why didn't you tell me that, Granny?" Celeste asked.

"Would you have listened? You were sixteen when you started dating him, and then y'all got married right out of high school and joined the air force," Mandy reminded her. "You thought you knew everything back then, and I was just an old great-granny that had rocks for brains."

"I've grown up a lot since then," Celeste whispered.

"Haven't we all?" I muttered as I took the glass of milk to Mandy.

"Okay, then," Mandy said with a long sigh. "Enough about this today. It's the past, and we can't undo it or change it—but right now, we are having a brunch for Harrison."

I bit back a smart-aleck remark about my father wanting something much more posh than three people sitting around the table, having leftovers for his memorial brunch.

"This might not be an open house for everyone in the area to come and visit about Harrison," Mandy said, "but it wouldn't be right for us to just bury him and then forget he ever existed. We should each have something to say about him while we eat. It's the right thing to do. But first, Celeste, I'm glad you're home for good. I want to have my two girls close to me in the last years of my life. If I can live to be a hundred, then I won't fight the good Lord when he comes to take me away. And you know you've got a home here with us as long as you want it."

"Thank you, Granny," Celeste said, and then glanced over at me. "Want to hire me to help with the books, Angela Marie? Or I can clean house or whatever else you need done."

"There's always room for an extra hand here at Meadow Falls," I answered. "We'll get you on the payroll this week."

I took my food to the table and sat down across from her. My father had never been home at lunchtime, and I would usually just run in from the barns for a quick sandwich and to check on Mandy. She had the beginning signs of dementia these days, and the time would come when I'd need to hire someone to watch over her. She was so independent that I hated to even think about having to do that.

Now that Celeste was home, that worry had ebbed, but that wasn't the only reason I kept glancing at her to be sure I wasn't imagining things. A song that had nothing to do with my father's funeral service,

"Everything's Gonna Be Alright," came to my mind. I didn't hum it, but the message was there, loud and clear—Celeste was home, and she wasn't leaving again.

"I'll go first with a memory about Harrison," Mandy said after she'd taken a long drink of her milk. "His birth was a big day here on the farm. His mama, Inez, had lost five babies before he came along, so to have a big, healthy baby boy was quite the time for a celebration. Inez was worn out from all the miscarriages and the stillbirths, and she still had to help Clifford in the office, so I became his nanny. My own daughter, Emma, was about ten years old that fall when he was born, and she thought she'd gotten a little brother. The next few years were really good, and even though things got rough after that, I like to remember the first ones. So today, I'm going to remember those times when he was *the baby* and Emma and I doted on him as bad as his mother and father did."

I wondered what she meant by things getting rough and tried to envision my father as a baby. The idea of tough times was a lot easier than ever seeing Harrison Duncan as a newborn, or even as a little boy. I made a mental note to make Mandy tell me details about the past before she . . . I couldn't make myself even think of the day when she would be gone.

"You go next, Celeste," Mandy said after a minute had passed and neither Celeste nor I had said a word.

Mandy had always said that we shouldn't speak ill of the dead. My father had seen to it that I learned the business. He had given me a place to live and put me on the payroll when I was seventeen. He had never done anything evil that I knew of, but I couldn't remember a single good memory, and I knew my turn was coming.

"When I graduated from high school, he handed me an envelope with a thousand dollars in it and said, 'I'm proud of you,'" Celeste said, but there was a pained expression on her face that told me she was hiding something. "He never talked to me, but I caught him staring at me from time to time through the years. I always wondered what was on his mind, but he was *Harrison Duncan*. There was no way I'd ever ask him a question."

They both looked over at me, but all I could do was shrug. My father had never told me that he was proud of me. He hadn't even come to my high school graduation. He said that he had to stay with Mother, which seemed strange since days went by when he didn't even go into her bedroom to talk to her. Mandy went with me and told me I'd done a good job of delivering my valedictorian speech.

"You've got to have one good story to tell us about him," Mandy pressured.

Story!

That word stuck firmly in my mind. Mandy had always had a story to tell me and Celeste when we were little girls. One of my favorites was a tale she'd woven about a princess who came all the way from a foreign land to the Texas Panhandle to live on a peanut farm with her handsome prince. Her husband felt so bad about taking her away from her beloved home near a huge waterfall that he had one made on the land, and then he built her a castle.

We had a few months of cold weather and lots of long evenings left before the busy planting season began. It was the perfect time to get Mandy to tell me what she remembered, and I intended to write every bit of it down in a journal—or better yet, I could record it so I could listen to it and hear her voice later.

"Angela Marie!" Mandy's voice sliced into my thoughts.

I blinked several times and left my wonderings behind. "Yes, ma'am?"

"What's your memory?"

God, give me something so I don't disappoint Mandy, I prayed.

The only thing that came to me was a flash of him in his monogrammed white shirts, so I blurted out, "He always looked so put together in his white shirts."

"I made sure of that until I couldn't iron anymore," Mandy said with a smile. "Then we sent all his clothes out. Last week, Polly told me that we were going to have to find someone else to take care of Harrison's laundry because she was retiring. Funny how that worked out, isn't it?"

"Yes, it is," I finally answered.

Chapter Two

A few years ago, my father had wanted to put Mandy in a nursing home and employ someone else to supervise the hired hands who cleaned the house and did the cooking, but I convinced him that I could add her job to my list of responsibilities. She wouldn't have lived six months away from Meadow Falls, and by then, she was my only link to anything that resembled a mother and/or a friend. After a day's hard work, sitting on the porch swing or in one of the many rocking chairs with Mandy and listening to her stories and whatever gossip she'd heard on the phone that day or at church on Sunday morning was my escape.

My father and I had argued for the first time in my life that evening. I'd told him if he kicked Mandy out of Meadow Falls, I would leave with her. I could always find a job on another peanut farm since I knew the business so well. The only other time I'd argued with him was when I wanted to move her into the downstairs bedroom. He'd said hired help didn't belong in the house, and I reminded him of all she had done for the Duncan family. I'd won both arguments, but I never had occasion or nerve to press my luck a third time.

Everything that Mandy had helped me through—during both good and bad times—and whatever had caused that expression on Celeste's face earlier in the day were on my mind that night when I drifted off to sleep.

I didn't dream about her or Celeste. What plagued my subconscious was a dream of my father. When I awoke, the dream was all gone, but there were tears in my eyes. I tried to remember what had caused me to cry, but nothing came back to me. I hadn't even cried when the doctor had come out into the hospital waiting room four days ago with *that look* on his face. I'd known that my father was dead before he asked me what funeral home he should contact.

The next morning, the smell of bacon wafting up the stairs awoke me. "Good Lord!" I muttered as I threw back the covers, hurriedly slipped on my well-worn pink-and-black-plaid flannel robe, and tucked my cell phone into the pocket. The last time Mandy had tried to make breakfast, she'd fallen, and we were lucky she hadn't broken a hip. She had scolded me when I fussed at her and said the milk that she drank with every meal kept her bones strong.

I ran down the wide staircase, across the foyer, and into the kitchen to find Mandy sitting at the far end of the table with a cup of coffee in her hands. She was wearing the pink sweat suit I had given her for Christmas and the fluffy slippers Celeste had sent her.

"Slow down, Angela Marie. You didn't oversleep."

"Good mornin'." Celeste was whipping up eggs in a bowl. "Looks like that snowstorm I had to drive through finally reached this part of Texas."

"I'm glad you got here before the storm hit," I said breathlessly. Everything was going to be all right—Celeste was here to help me. My heart must not have gotten the message, because it kept doing double time in my chest even after I'd poured a cup of coffee and taken a sip.

"It's good for the ground," Mandy said. "We'll gripe about the cold and the snow, but it'll make the soil rich for the peanut crop. And come July, when it's hotter than the barbed wire fences in hell, we'll be wishin' for some cool weather."

I patted her on the shoulder with my free hand as my pulse eased. "That's right—and thanks for diving right in and cooking breakfast, Celeste. What can I do to help?"

"Not a thing," Celeste answered. "I'll just scramble these eggs, and then we'll be ready to eat. I was a financial manager in the military, which is a fancy title for an accountant. I expect I can find a job around here somewhere with that skill set. Or I could help you with all the ranch bookwork. I'll even do it for room and board; you don't have to put me on payroll."

I shook my head. "If you do the work, you get a paycheck. And yes, ma'am, you can have the office, and I appreciate you taking over."

"Then consider it done," Celeste said.

"But . . ." I paused. "While we have breakfast this morning, I want Mandy to tell us a story like she did when we were little girls."

Mandy beamed. "What do you want to hear?"

"I want to hear about the prince and princess," Celeste answered as she set a platter of bacon and eggs in the middle of the table and then brought another one filled with hash brown potatoes and steaming-hot biscuits.

My father had told me to hire a full-time cook when Mandy moved into the house, but I couldn't take everything from her. So the compromise was that I would fix breakfast, she would set out sandwiches or leftovers for our noon meal, and then we'd fix supper together. That plan had gone well for the past two years, but now that Celeste could take over the office, I wouldn't have to rush through supper and work until midnight on the books.

"Oops, I forgot to get the butter and jelly." Celeste brought them to the table and then sat down.

My father had been gone four days now, and yet I could still feel his eyes glancing over at me from his place at the head of the kitchen table. Before my mother got sick, we'd had breakfast at the formal dining room table, but when she couldn't get out of bed anymore, he had decided that we should have it in the kitchen. Mandy had joined us whenever we ate in the kitchen, but in the evenings, when he insisted that he and I eat in the formal dining room, she could not sit with us. I had always been glad when he had somewhere else to be in the evenings so Mandy and I could have our meal together in the kitchen.

"This all looks and smells wonderful," I said as I laid my phone on the table and hoped that Mandy hadn't seen me press the record button. "Are you ready to tell us a story?"

"Do you want to hear the real story or the one I told you girls when you were little?" Mandy asked.

"Tell us the real one," I answered. "Was the princess story based on Wyatt and Victoria's story?"

"Yes, it was," Mandy replied. "The prince and princess in the story that I told you when you were little girls were your great-grandparents, Angela Marie—Wyatt and Victoria Duncan. You got your red hair from Victoria. I wish I could tell you where you got your blonde hair and green eyes from, Celeste, but your mama never would tell me who your father was. Roxy had dark hair and brown eyes, so I suppose you got your looks from your secret dad."

That same expression I'd seen when we were coming up with a memory about my father passed over Celeste's face now. I wasn't sure if it was anger or pain, but I intended to find out.

Wyatt and Victoria's picture hung above the fireplace in the formal living room. As a child, I had avoided even looking at the painting because I felt like Wyatt's eyes followed me around the room. When I'd asked about the mean man in the picture, my mother told me that they were my great-grandparents. I remember asking her if he was the first king of Meadow Falls. She had laughed and said that he probably felt like he was.

Mandy took a sip of her coffee and began. "I came to the farm to help in the fields—and I did for a day or two, but then the cook quit on the spot. I guess my Edward had been bragging about what a good cook I was, because Clifford came out to our makeshift home in the back of our truck one evening and asked me to come to the house and cook the next day."

"Wait, what kind of home?" Celeste asked.

"Folks who followed the peanut crops for work in the early fifties took a tent with them." She smiled. "With the kids in the family all riding in the back of the truck on top of their tent. All those kids scrambling out onto the ground as the harvesters arrived was quite a sight. My precious Edward built a hutch on the back of our old pickup truck, and that was our home. It was kind of like what y'all would call a camper these days. To get back to the story, Inez and I became really good friends when I went to work as the cook," Mandy said. "She seemed to adore Emma more with each of the babies that she lost in the next few years. Then she finally carried Harrison to full term. In those days, when women were down to the last few weeks, they didn't go out much, especially ladies who were kind of . . ." She paused.

"Well-to-do?" Celeste suggested, finishing the sentence for her. "I'm confused. I thought you were telling us a story about Victoria, the princess who named this place Meadow Falls."

"Victoria was Inez's mother-in-law, and she was already gone when I came to live here. From what Inez told me, the woman was a saint to have stayed with Wyatt," Mandy said. "He loved her just like in the fairy-tale story I told you about them, but he was *the boss*. That wasn't so unusual in that time, but it sure didn't make for a happy home."

"Wyatt and Victoria were the ones that came from a far land, right?" Celeste slathered a biscuit with butter and added a spoonful of jelly.

"That's right." Mandy smiled. "I don't reckon I need to start with *once upon a time* with this one. So I'll just tell it to y'all like Inez told it to me one afternoon when we had lemonade on the back porch. Wyatt was . . ." She frowned. "He must have had some strong genes, because from what Inez said, Clifford was just like him. They ran the farm well, but . . ."

"They were 'the kings,'" I offered, using air quotes, "and no one crossed them." I thought of my father's attitude and realized that it had been passed down to him from at least two generations back.

Mandy nodded and went on. "Clifford didn't take too well to his wife being friends with the hired help, but he didn't argue with Inez about visiting with me if we didn't sit on the front porch."

"That was mean," I gasped. "I need to get this straight: Wyatt was the first king of Meadow Falls. Then Clifford was his son."

"That's right. Then Harrison stepped into Clifford's place when he died. You would have been about a year old when Clifford had a heart attack and Harrison inherited everything. You girls need to remember that society was different. Way back then, Wyatt and then Clifford had control. Each man felt like he had an image to uphold, just like Harrison did," Mandy said in a stern voice. She went on: "Now, let's go all the way back to the beginning. A hundred years ago—in 1924, to be exact—Wyatt Duncan married Victoria Bisbee. She had grown up on a peanut farm somewhere in Georgia, and Wyatt was a war hero from World War I. Her daddy had inherited this land—where Meadow Falls is still in operation today—from his ancestors, who'd been given the acreage back when Texas became a state. Victoria's father gave it to her as a wedding gift. Wyatt's folks then gave the two newlyweds enough money to get started; his folks had plenty."

"I wonder how much money that was back then," Celeste said.

"I have no idea, but it must've been a goodly amount," Mandy answered.

"Did this house come with the land?" I asked.

"Oh, no!" Mandy shook her head. "The little house Wyatt and Victoria took up housekeeping in is the one out back where I lived. It was real modern for the day, though, with an indoor bathroom and electricity and even a refrigerator. Victoria loved living there, but she didn't love this flat land. She missed her family and the waterfall at the back side of the farm where she grew up. That picture that hangs in the dining room is one that she painted and brought with her when she and Wyatt moved to Texas. Sometimes Victoria would sit and stare at it for hours and hours. I did the same thing when I first came to work here. After a long day of work, I would spend a few minutes sitting in front of that picture. I imagined that I could hear the water as it tumbled down to the pool and that I was soaking my swollen, aching feet in the cool water."

Celeste and I both leaned back in our chairs far enough that we could see the picture. To think that it had hung there for a hundred years, and I hadn't ever known that my great-grandmother had painted it. Looking at it now, I could well imagine what a culture shock it had been to leave a place like that and come to the Texas Panhandle, where the wind blew every day and, most of the time, kicked up some dust along the way. From planting to harvesttime, I always came in from my work on the farm with a layer of mud, made by dirt and sweat, everywhere it could find a place to hide—on the back of my neck and even in my ears.

Had Victoria resented all the hours that Wyatt spent out in the fields? Had she ever thought of throwing up her hands and going back to Georgia?

Mandy finished her breakfast and went on with the story. "Like I've said many times, things have changed since back then. Women had only been given—no, that's not the right word. They had only *earned* the right to vote a few years before, and that didn't include all women. It was a lot longer before Black women or any women of color got that right. There were different rules for women and for men. Men went out to work; women stayed home, kept house, and raised babies, for the most part. And I even heard of a few men who told their wives which way to cast their votes at the polls."

"But *you* shook peanuts?" Celeste argued.

"For a little while—and I was the hired help, not the royalty. There were different rules for my people and the Meadow Falls kingdom," Mandy said. "But that's a story for another day. Wyatt loved Victoria and tried to make her happy. He built this house for her and let her furnish it just the way she wanted. I suppose everything in this place would be considered antiques these days. He had come from a big family, and Victoria had a couple of older brothers, so they wanted lots of children. That's why there are eight bedrooms."

"Did Clifford have brothers and sisters?" Most of the bedrooms had been empty in my lifetime. I couldn't imagine kids running and playing in the hallway or sliding down the staircase banister. Siblings were something I'd wanted my entire life but never got. A big, huge family that filled every one of those bedrooms—that would be the first thing on my bucket list if I had one.

"No," Mandy answered, slid her chair back, and stood. "I need another cup of coffee. All this talk has got me so dry, I'm spittin' dust."

"I'll get it for you," Celeste said and then raised an eyebrow at me when she noticed the phone was recording.

"Later," I mouthed.

Mandy sat back down into her chair. "Where was I? Oh yes, the house. Wyatt wanted Victoria to be the queen of the whole area, so he made sure he built her the biggest house around these parts."

Celeste set a fresh cup of coffee in front of Mandy, and she took a sip. "Thank you, darlin'. Did I tell you how happy I am to have you back home with me? Well, if I talked through a whole pot of coffee, there wouldn't be enough words to make you understand that I'm glad you are here. What you had to go through to get here wasn't right, but I believe everything happens for a reason."

"Ditto," I agreed. "We are family—and, Mandy, you've been a part of this place longer than either me or Celeste, so this is where you belong."

I wondered about my own family, all of whom were gone now. Was there something in Mandy's stories that would help me understand who I was? I'd always felt like a big rock that couldn't be moved, but I wanted to be more like a bubbly stream that could go anywhere it wanted. That was something I had never voiced. But I had a responsibility to Meadow Falls, so there was no use in wishing for something I couldn't have.

"Angela Marie!" Mandy said in a sharp tone.

"I'm sorry," I said. "What were you saying?"

"That you had to fight with Harrison to make it happen, didn't you? A hired hand living in the house with him was *not* his idea of keeping up his image, was it?"

I didn't want her to get offtrack before she finished the story of Wyatt and Victoria, so I chose my words carefully. "You are *not* a hired hand, Mandy, and some things are worth fighting for. The way my father thought that his image in Meadow was the be-all and end-all was always a thorn in my side, so I didn't really care what he considered his rights as king of the farm. Now, tell us more of the story."

For once Mandy didn't give me a lecture on my father having good points, and after taking a drink, she continued. "The house was finished a few months before Wyatt and Victoria had Clifford, and he was supposed to be the first of lots of children. But . . ." She paused.

"But what?" I pressured, hoping she wasn't having one of her "forgetful moments," as she called them. Suddenly, I felt a desperate need to really pay attention to her stories. If I understood, Meadow Falls wouldn't seem like an albatross hanging on to my heart with heavy chains. Maybe I could learn to love the farm and not just do my duty to the land.

"But if you go out to the cemetery, you'll find four little graves of more sons who were born to Wyatt and Victoria and didn't live more than a day or two," Mandy said. "Your grandma Inez told me the land was cursed, because Wyatt and Victoria only had one baby that lived, and she and Clifford only had Harrison."

She took a drink of her coffee and paused for several minutes. "I get sad just thinking about the grief both of those women went through every year when they stood out there in the weather, whether it was bitter cold or blistering heat, and watched another child being buried. Parents are not supposed to outlive their children. We're born with the ability to grieve when we have lost a mother, a father, even a husband"— she picked up a paper napkin and wiped tears from her cheeks—"but never a child. It doesn't matter if it's a baby or a full-grown woman with a child of her own, like my Emma was when she died. The grief is unnatural, and that business of seven or five or however many steps it takes to get closure is nothing but a bunch of horse crap."

I could count on the fingers of one hand the times I had seen Mandy cry. Yesterday had been one of them, when she'd shed tears over my father, and then today, when she mentioned her own daughter's early death.

"But they had Clifford," she went on. "Victoria doted on him, but Wyatt was a strict father, as men were in those days. I remember how my own father treated my five older brothers, and I imagine that Wyatt was the same—only maybe even a little worse. After all, my folks were itinerant laborers who followed the cotton and peanut crops all over Texas, then holed up in whatever house or barn they could find through the winter months when there was little work to be had. Like the men in the Duncan family down through the ages, Harrison was born with the old proverbial silver spoon in his mouth, and he often referred to his grandfather as the original king of Meadow Falls."

She stopped and took a drink of her coffee, then frowned so hard that the lines in her forehead deepened. I was afraid she'd forgotten what she was talking about for a while there.

"You need to understand something about your father, Angela Marie." She hesitated for another sip of coffee.

Celeste's jaw worked like she was chewing gum, but she didn't say anything. Did she know something about my father? Could he have cheated on my mother, like Trevor did her?

Mandy went on. "Clifford had to be tough on Harrison so that when he grew up, he would do right by what his grandfather and father had built up here at Meadow Falls. But as some sons—and daughters—do, Harrison rebelled. Oh, he worked hard, all right; Clifford made sure of that. But he liked to party—as you kids call it—just as hard. It didn't help that he was a good-looking young man that the women all flocked around like bees to a honeypot."

I wondered if Mandy had slipped into a bit of dementia. I couldn't imagine my staid, controlling father ever being a rebellious child or a player. Not Harrison Duncan!

I glanced over at Celeste to see a smug smile on her face. She knew something, and I would pry it out of her.

Mandy seemed to ramble, going from one generation to the next, so I was glad I was recording the story. Later, I would make a chart and write it all down in a journal, but remembering everything she was saying about Wyatt and Victoria, then Clifford and Inez—all my ancestors whom I had never met—wasn't easy. Not when my mind wanted to figure out what Celeste knew that I didn't.

"Was there ever really a waterfall here on the farm?" Celeste glanced over at the painting again.

"Inez said that there was," Mandy answered, "but it was gone before she married Clifford. Remember where I took you girls to play in that shallow little creek way out at the back of the farm?"

Celeste and I both nodded.

"That's spring fed, so the water is always clear and cold," Mandy said. "Wyatt had some of the hired hands dam it up with rocks so that there was a little waterfall back there, and then he had a gazebo built so Victoria could take one of her beloved books out there to read and listen to the sound of the stream as it tumbled down over the rocks. Inez said that Victoria told her it was the only place she could find peace after she lost each baby."

"What happened to it?" I asked.

"A tornado came through this area and smashed up the gazebo and stream," Mandy answered. "Victoria's health had begun to fail by then, so nothing was ever rebuilt."

"But she wouldn't have been old," I said.

"Like I said, things were different back then." Mandy finished off her coffee. "A baby or a miscarriage every year had taken its toll on her body." She pushed back her chair and picked up her cane. "Now, time is getting away from us. The cleaning ladies will be here soon, and we need to have things ready to offer them some cookies and tea on their break. That new girl, Mallory, has to be watched every minute or else she forgets to dust all the furniture in the spare rooms properly."

I patted Mandy on the arm and said, "Our cleaning crew got full-time jobs and won't be coming around anymore. Celeste and I need to hire someone new to take care of the house."

"I forgot all about that," Mandy said. "My old mind isn't what it used to be."

I turned the recorder off.

"We'll get the kitchen cleaned up, Granny," Celeste said. "If I get you another cup of coffee, can you tell us another story?"

"Not today," Mandy answered. "I'm going to the living room to spend a little time with my Bible. When I face Saint Peter, I want to be able to answer any questions he might have."

She left the room, and I noticed that she was leaning on her cane a little more than usual again. "I should have driven her down there in the work truck," I mumbled.

"What was that?" Celeste asked as she stacked the dishes and carried them over to the sink.

"She didn't want to ride down to the cemetery yesterday. She wanted to walk with all the other folks who came out to the graveside service," I explained. "That and the cold walk back to the house was too much for her."

"I noticed that you were recording her." Celeste set the dishes down in a sink full of hot, soapy water. "Why were you doing that?"

I started washing the plates. "Did you know all that about Wyatt and Victoria?"

"No, but I liked the story better when they were the prince and princess, and this was the castle."

"Castle?" My tone was colder than the north wind. In my experience, this house had never been anything but a big, empty showplace that didn't have a bit of warmth in it.

"You lived here, Angela Marie. I lived in the little house out back. To you, it was just home. To me, it was a castle, and you were the lucky princess who got to live in it," Celeste said as she rinsed, dried, and put the dishes away.

"To me, you were the lucky one because you got to go home with Mandy, and I had to stay here. I bet she either read to you or told you bedtime stories. Pretty often, I snuck out of my bedroom at night and hid in the shadows while my folks entertained their friends. You know that credenza at the end of the foyer? If you hide at the side of it, you can see into both the dining and the living room. Even back then, it made me angry to see how much attention they gave all those people and how they smiled and talked to them," I told her. "I was so jealous of you that I wished I belonged to Mandy, and you had been born to my folks."

"And in those days, I would have traded places with you in a heartbeat," Celeste said with a wistful look in her eyes. "But that was just little-girl thinking. I'll confess that as much as I wanted to live here in the past, I'm not comfortable staying in this place now. It's so big and so . . ."

"Empty?" I finished for her.

She nodded. "I'd rather live out in the house where I was raised, if you don't mind. I could move Granny back out there with me, and she could live out the rest—"

"No!" I raised my voice higher than I'd intended. "I want you both to live here with me. This place is so big, and"—tears welled up in my eyes—"it was empty-feeling when it was just me and my father. I can't imagine how it would be with only me. Please don't go back to the other place."

When she didn't answer, I swallowed the lump in my throat and said, "I've never been comfortable here, either, Celeste, but it got better when I moved Mandy into the downstairs guest room—and now that you're here, it's even better than before. You and Mandy are the closest thing to family I've got, and you were always a sister to me, whether we shared DNA or not."

"And you were to me." She smiled, but it didn't reach her eyes. "The hardest thing about leaving Meadow after I graduated was seeing you standing on the porch and waving until I couldn't see you in the rearview mirror any longer."

"I cried for a week," I admitted.

I didn't tell her that my father had told me to suck it up and get on into the office with my mother. I had things to learn about the financial end of running a ranch while she still had the energy to teach me. That was the day I learned my mother had been diagnosed with cancer and only had a year—at the most—to live, and that I would not be going to college.

Chapter Three

"While Granny is sleeping, I'd like to go see Harrison's grave," Celeste said as we washed up the dinner dishes that afternoon.

"I bet that'll be okay. I hardly ever leave her alone, but she never wakes up before two o'clock. We probably won't be gone more than half an hour." I set the alarm on my phone to be sure that we were back home in plenty of time. "Why do you want to go out there in the cold? He wouldn't have known if anyone came to his funeral or if anyone visits his grave."

"I need closure," she answered. "And on another note, thank you for all you've done for Granny. I had no idea that you were carrying such a heavy burden."

I gave her a quick sideways hug. "There is no burden if there is love."

She raised an eyebrow. "And if there isn't any love?"

"Then you just bear the burden, but it's a lot heavier."

We finished up the dishes, put on our coats and stocking hats, and braced ourselves against the cold wind. An inch of a mix of sleet and snow made a crunching sound with every step we took as we followed the path to the little family cemetery.

The ornate cast-iron gate put up a fight when Celeste tried to open it. "This thing is frozen, Angela Marie."

"Maybe that's a sign that we shouldn't be here. The universe is saying we need to turn around and go back," I told her.

"The universe does not control me," Celeste declared. "Help me push on it. I want to at least see Harrison's grave since I couldn't be here for the service. Maybe that will make it seem more real."

We put our shoulders against the gate, and finally, the ice around the hinges broke with a long creaking noise. It swung open. The roses that had been laid on my father's casket, and the other dozens of floral arrangements, lay frozen on top of a hump of fresh dirt. In time, the dirt would settle, and the flowers would have to be gathered up and thrown away. But today, covered in a thin layer of ice and dusted with snow, they looked as fresh as they had the day before.

"Even standing here looking at this, I can't believe he is gone," Celeste whispered. "How's that going to affect the business? How much more are you going to have to do?"

"Not nearly as much, since you are home for good and have offered to help me," I answered.

"I'm glad to be here—but I'm tired, Angela Marie." Celeste's tone matched her words. "I'm tired of doing everything I could to save a drowning marriage; tired of worrying about not being here to spend Granny's last few months or years with her; and more than anything else, I was tired of the job I was doing. The last two years, all I could see when I closed my eyes at night was Meadow Falls."

"And yet you offered to take over the bookwork?"

"That's a minor thing compared to the responsibility I had in the service," she said with a long sigh. "And besides, I'm here with you and Granny. I feel like I can breathe again. Like I'm free."

How could Meadow Falls make her feel free when it had the exact opposite effect on me?

"When I close my eyes at night, all I see is Meadow Falls, too. Only I am seeing it in the rearview mirror of our old work truck as I drive away so fast that there's just a trail of dust behind me."

"The grass is not always greener on the other side of the fence," she muttered. "And sometimes you have to . . ." She stopped and gave me a hug.

"Have to what?" I asked.

"Just find closure wherever you are," she said.

I gave her another side hug. "I bet what you were feeling out there on the West Coast was my wishing you were here with me. My heart was calling out to you to come home."

"You are probably right," she agreed. "We've always had a connection— but then, we were raised together. Let's go on out to the other cemetery, where my great-grandfather is buried. But don't tell Granny that we visited Grandpa Edward's grave, or she'll fuss at us for not taking her along."

I checked the time on my phone and saw that we didn't have to rush back. Mandy could sleep through a class 5 tornado and wouldn't be ready for her afternoon snack for another little while.

Celeste was six inches taller than me, but she slowed her stride so that I didn't have to do double time. Other than our matching eyes, we were as different as night and day—as the old folks said. My hair was so red that it was almost burgundy; hers was blonde. Roxy would never tell—not even Mandy—who had fathered Celeste, but I wondered if he had been a blond-haired guy with green eyes or if those had been recessive genes passed down from Mandy's side of the family.

The Meadow Falls cemetery was about a hundred yards on down the well-beaten path from the Duncan family cemetery. There was no fancy gate or even a fence around it, but I had always seen to it that the grounds were free of weeds and looked nice. The tombstones were all sizes and shapes and had different surnames on them. We stopped at the one for Luis Lopez. A tear escaped and traveled down my cheek. He had taught me so much and been so patient with me. I reached up to touch the gold necklace with the pendant of Saint Isidore—patron saint of farmers and day laborers—hanging from it, which he had given me for my high school–graduation present, but then I realized it was under several layers of clothing.

"Luis was a good man," Celeste said. "He always mowed our yard for us and kept the weeds out of the picket fence. That was after he had worked from dawn to dark on the farm. Granny oftentimes gave him a pie or invited him in to have supper with us since he wouldn't take pay for what he did."

"He taught me almost everything I know about peanuts but also about working hard." I brushed the tear away with my gloved hand. "He had the patience of Job. Looking back, I think he understood my frustrations."

"And he had the wisdom of Solomon," Celeste added. "One of the things I remember the most was him telling me that I should listen to my heart and do what was right."

"He told me the same thing." I kissed my gloved hand and pressed it to his headstone. "Rest in peace, Luis—knowing that you touched a lot of lives in your time here at Meadow Falls."

Celeste did the same and then sighed. "He might not have had children of his own, but he sure was a role model to both of us. Let's go pay our respects to Grandpa Edward's grave, and then we'd better head back to the house."

Edward's grave was a couple of rows back, and like all the others, it had a fine sheen of ice covering it. From the dates on his gray granite tombstone, he'd been only twenty-eight when he passed away. When Mandy talked about him, there was so much love in her voice, it wasn't a surprise that she had never remarried. For the past seventy years, she had been a widow, and I don't think she ever looked at another man.

"Did she ever tell you the story of her life?" I asked.

Celeste shook her head. "I think it was too painful for her to talk about him very much—but when she did, it was so sweet. Every Sunday after we got home from church, we would walk out here, and she would sit down in front of his grave and bow her head. I didn't know if she was praying or talking to his spirit, but after a little while, she would stand up and we'd go home. Sometimes we would gather wildflowers along the way and scatter them on his grave. One year at Christmas, she brought a sprig of mistletoe and put it on top of his tombstone and then blew kisses up in the air toward the sky."

"We need to get her to tell us about him before her dementia gets worse," I declared.

"What are you going to do with the recordings you are making?" Celeste asked.

"I'm writing the stories down in a journal," I answered, "and then I'm transferring them all over to an external hard drive so we can listen to them later."

"Can I copy the journal? And if I buy a USB drive, will you make me a copy of the recordings, too?" Celeste asked. "I have often thought of her stories and wished I could remember all of them."

"I'm happy to share with you, but don't buy anything. I've got a couple extra ones in the junk drawer," I answered.

"I've had enough cemetery today," Celeste said. "I'm ready to go back to the house."

"Just one more stop—please." I laid a hand on her shoulder. "I want to go down to the creek to see the place where Wyatt made a waterfall for Victoria."

"Okay," Celeste agreed. "But after that, let's go back. It's freezing cold out here. It will take me a while to acclimate to this weather after living in California for six years."

"Deal," I agreed.

We set out on the path again, walking a little faster than we had been. We passed the equipment barn on the way, and Celeste must have heard my sigh.

"What's on your mind?"

"Spring and all the work that I'll have to do on the machinery," I answered. "There won't be much time for days like this for long walks."

"You need to hire someone with mechanical experience," she suggested. "I've got a good friend who is about to retire and move back to Texas. You should talk to him."

"No!" I said and then clamped my lips together. I didn't have the time or the patience right now to teach anyone the peanut business. And besides, it would confuse Mandy even more to have strangers on the place.

"Don't be so stubborn." Celeste's tone went cold, like it did back when we had childhood arguments. "You need help; Devon will need a job. You could at least talk to him."

"I said no!" My voice was just as chilly as hers. I hated it when we argued, even as little girls and teenagers. "Is he your boyfriend? Is that the reason you weren't so upset about the divorce?"

"Devon is my *friend*," she said through clenched teeth. "He helped me get through the tough times. He is not my boyfriend, and I did not cheat on Trevor."

I threw up my gloved hands. "Okay, okay."

"I told Devon to stop by and see me on his way home." Her voice was still icy. "If that's not all right, I can always meet him in town for lunch."

"Your friends are always welcome here," I said. "I guess I'm just a little jealous that you have a friend to invite to stop by. When can we expect him?"

"Don't know," Celeste said. "He's got the address. Maybe if I lived out in the old house, this wouldn't be an issue."

I shivered and wondered if I had slipped involuntarily into the role of queen after all when my father died. "No," I said again, but this time there was no anger involved. "I'm sorry that I made you feel like that. It's just that . . ." I paused. "Luis was the foreman all those years, and then his nephew Thomas stepped up to do that work when Luis passed away. I know we need help, but the idea of a stranger being here is more than I can deal with right now."

"I'm sorry that I snapped at you," Celeste said. "Just remember that I'm here and willing to help. We are two strong women. We can always take Granny with us out to the barns and do the jobs ourselves," she assured me with a quiver in her voice. "I really, really don't like this cold weather."

"Me either, but it's the price we pay for living in this part of the world," I agreed. "I always liked summers better when we were growing up because then the work crews were here and there was always some-one to visit with. I loved coming out to the RVs and their communal picnics."

"Me too," she said. "Other than school, we were pretty much iso-lated in the winter months. But remember something, darlin': the work-crew folks were strangers, too."

"Yep, but they became family before the end of summer. I used to daydream about going with them when they left." I stopped under a weeping willow tree not far from the edge of the shallow creek, which was frozen solid. "Poor little fishes are nothing but ice."

Celeste smiled and then giggled. "If those little fishes could talk, what kind of stories could they tell about us?"

"Their ancestors would have passed down the story about a young girl who lost her virginity out there in the creek about eighteen years ago," I confessed.

Celeste gasped. "You didn't!"

I nudged her on the shoulder. "Don't tell me you didn't ever go skinny-dippin' in the creek."

"I don't kiss and tell." Her cheeks turned even more scarlet than what the cold wind had caused.

I poked her in the arm. "Was it Trevor?"

"Nuh-uh. You first," she said.

"His name was Abe, and he'd come here with the work crew from somewhere over in Arkansas that hot summer. Ever heard the old song 'Strawberry Wine'?"

"I've heard it, but I thought it was written for me—and my skinny-dippin' experience was when I was fifteen, with a hired hand named Jake. I was terrified that I'd gotten pregnant and swore to God and the whole universe I wouldn't do that again until I was married. I didn't want to make Granny sad, like she was when she told me about how wild my mother had been," Celeste admitted.

I was still trying to take in the story about my father being wild. He had always been so serious that it was hard to imagine him as a rebellious teenager.

"Well, whoever wrote the lyrics must have known Roxy and both of us back then. My little rebellious fling started right after you left home. It might have been *because* you left, but most likely it was because my father told me I wouldn't be going to college, that I could get all the education I needed right here on Meadow Falls. Abe told me that I was beautiful and that my kisses tasted like the Boone's Farm Strawberry Hill wine he'd shared with me, is what I remember," I said, then asked, "Did you keep that promise to not have sex again until you were married?"

"No, I didn't, but I got on the pill before Trevor and I got involved," she answered.

"I never thought about getting pregnant," I whispered. "I just wanted to make a few choices of my own. Mother was sick, and Mandy and I had to take care of her; plus, I had to learn the financial part of the business. Did Mandy know you were on the pill?"

"Lord, no!" Celeste gasped. "Trevor drove me over to the health department in the next county to get them. I guess we both had dysfunctional families."

"Yes, we did," I agreed. "I feel a cold chill that has nothing to do with the weather. It's like Victoria's spirit is here, still grieving for her lost sons."

"Hadn't thought of that," Celeste answered. "Those little frozen fishes could probably tell more stories than we could even imagine."

I was glad that we had gotten past the argument. But then, we'd always had a bond that let us do that. Like real biological sisters, we bickered and we made up—in the same britches we had gotten upset in, as Mandy said.

"Maybe their stories could make me understand that my father—like his father and his grandfather—had been groomed to be the prestigious owner of Meadow Falls, and no doubt, he wanted to do the same with his offspring. And they could even shed some light on who your father is."

"Maybe so," she said as she shivered again.

I took a deep breath, let it out slowly, and went on. "I wish my father would have at least explained his reasons for treating me like he did. The only time I got to dress up like a girl was for school and for Sunday services. But even at church, I was always walking in my beautiful mother's shadow. More than once, I heard whispers about how much I didn't look like her or wouldn't it have been nice if I'd been pretty?"

Celeste draped an arm around my shoulders. "I remember when Granny used to let us play dress-up in your mother's old dresses and shoes before they were donated to a charity. I couldn't believe that she only wore such beautiful outfits one time."

"She and my father had an image to uphold—but looking back, those were some of the best memories. Mandy would tell us how lovely we both were and then tell us a story about two little princesses growing up to be the belles of the ball." That put a smile on my face. "And these two belles of the ball are about to freeze, so we should start back. My toes are beginning to ache from the cold."

"My nose is about to fall off," Celeste said with half a giggle. "Granny will fuss at us if we have blue lips and red noses when we get back."

We left the solitude of the creek behind us. When we reached the Duncan cemetery, I saw that we had left the gate open. "You go on," I told Celeste. "I want to go visit with my mother a little more before I go back to the house."

"I'll get a pot of hot chocolate going for our afternoon snack. Granny likes that with her cookies," she said and waved over her shoulder.

I went through the open gate and straight to my mother's grave. Somehow, staring down at the dates on the headstone created questions that didn't have answers—unless Mandy knew.

What did Grandfather Clifford and Grandmother Inez think of their only son, the heir to their kingdom, marrying a Latine who was younger than he was? Did they put up a fuss, or were they hoping to fill the house with grandchildren—preferably sons of any ethnicity—the oldest of whom would be next in the royal peanut line?

I knelt, not caring if the knees of my jeans got wet, and tried to brush away the frozen leaves on the top of my mother's headstone. Her name was blurry through the icy covering, but I would have needed a chisel to scrape that off for a better view. "Before you passed away, I wish you would have told me stories like Mandy did—or at least told me how you and my father met and why you married him."

There were no answers, but as I knelt there and tried to make sense of my whole existence, I wondered why they hadn't tried again for a son. I might never know, but I intended to ask Mandy about it.

A cold chill that had nothing to do with the north wind blowing through the bare trees danced down my spine. I touched the cold dates on my mother's tombstone. She hadn't even been forty when she died. Had I inherited that tendency? Would I die young? Even if I married next week and had a baby in nine months, I would leave behind young children if I died at fifty. Or maybe the genes from my father would give me a massive heart attack in my early sixties.

If either was the case, what would happen to Meadow Falls? I didn't have a child to leave the farm to, and I sure didn't intend to marry just for that reason.

Chapter Four

Mandy's memory had holes in it the next morning, but that was no surprise after what had happened the day before. The doctors had warned me that any amount of stress could cause relapses, and her condition would gradually get worse. Hopefully, her remembrance of the past wouldn't always cause her to have bad days. I was grateful that until now, Mandy hadn't gotten angry when she couldn't remember what happened yesterday or five days before.

I could sympathize with her because I'd felt like all the unknowns in my life were smothering me until I learned to put them in a box and store it away in the back corner of my mind. Somehow, since my father had died, that crazy box had popped open. I couldn't go around it, and it was too big to step over. There didn't seem to be anything I could do but open it and try to figure out the answers.

Mandy spent most of the morning in the living room with one of her beloved romance books. Celeste finished unloading her car and unpacked in the room next to mine, so neither Mandy nor I saw much of her from breakfast until lunchtime.

We were having cherry pie for dessert when Mandy frowned and stared at Celeste. "When did you get here, and how long can you stay?"

Celeste looked at me for answers. "Two days ago. Remember, Granny?"

"Lots of repeating," I whispered for her ears only.

Mandy shook her head. "My forgetting disease is acting up. Tell me again how long you can stay."

"I'm home for good."

"Did you tell me that when you called to wish me a Merry Christmas—or was it Happy Thanksgiving?" Mandy asked.

"It was Christmas, but I wasn't sure what decision I would make back then," Celeste answered. "I had a little while longer to make up my mind about reenlisting or not. I kept telling myself that I only needed two more years to make it to twenty and that it would be crazy not to re-up at this point. Then I would go home to Trevor and see how miserable we both were. He was the reason I was in the military and the reason I'd reenlisted in the past." She paused to take a breath. "And then Harrison died, and you didn't need even more stress. I wanted to tell you, but I just couldn't."

Mandy tilted her head to the side—a sure sign that she wasn't tracking too well. "Why was Trevor miserable, and where is he?"

"Trevor filed for divorce, Mandy. Celeste told us all about it when she came home," I told her. "And, Celeste, having you home is a blessing, not stress."

"But if I'd told you that I was coming back to stay and getting a divorce, you would have been worried about me," she shot back. "And you had enough on your plate with your father's sudden death."

"I remember now," Mandy said proudly. "You said that you really wanted to come back to Meadow Falls. I'm glad you did. Some marriages aren't worth trying to save. Polly proved that with her first and second husbands."

"Polly Jackson's been married more than once?" I asked, trying to veer the subject off Celeste.

"Yes, she has, and she can tell you all about it someday when she comes for the laundry. But right now I want to know why you"—she fixed her gaze on Celeste—"didn't tell us that you were going through such terrible times."

"I didn't want to disappoint you, Granny. My mother was so wild and didn't even know—or at least, she wouldn't tell—who my father was. That had to have broken your heart. You were always bragging on me for being such a good girl."

"I *am* proud of you," Mandy said. "Go on and tell me the rest again. No, I remember most of it now. Did that woman move to California to be with him? Are they living in your house and using your things?"

"He filed for a transfer to Arkansas and moved most of our things with him. His new woman will join him as soon as they can legally be married," Celeste answered.

Mandy fidgeted with a tissue she had pulled from the pocket of her sweater. "That's too close to Texas. He might figure out that he wants to leave her and try again with you. He could be here in a day's drive."

"His chances are all used up," Celeste assured her.

I finished the last of my pie. "You should have called me."

"It had to be solely my decision to reenlist or not, and you would have begged me to come back to Texas. I don't want to look back with regrets, so I thought about it long and hard."

I gathered up the rest of the dessert plates and cleaned off the table, then poured us all a cup of coffee. "Did you feel like my father's death was an omen for you to trash the re-up papers, because down deep in your heart, you knew we would need you?"

"It seemed like the old proverbial straw that broke the camel's back," Celeste said. "Once I made the decision, I was at peace. I'm just sorry I didn't make it in time for Harrison's funeral service. I wanted to be here to support both of you."

"Don't worry about that," Mandy said. "Why didn't the two of you have any children?"

Celeste took a sip of coffee before she answered. "The time never seemed right, but . . ." She frowned. "We argued about it pretty often. He wanted to get out of the service after the first six years and start a family. His dream was for me to stay home—or maybe work at a job I could do from home—and raise a family. But I thought we needed to save more money before we had children. Truth is, not knowing who my father was . . ." She stopped and took a long breath. "I was afraid I wouldn't have any parenting instincts. My mother left me, and my father was . . ." She seemed to be trying to find the right words. "Out of the picture."

"Did you talk to anyone about all this?" Mandy asked.

Celeste shook her head. "We saw a marriage counselor two years ago, but"—another shrug—"Trevor missed more meetings than he attended."

"Well, that's all cleared up in my mind now," Mandy said. "The papers are really signed?"

That reminded me of all the papers I had put my signature on when my father made out his will a couple of years back. Celeste had mentioned closure; could I find that when it finally sank in that Meadow Falls was now mine and I could do with it whatever I wanted?

"Yes, ma'am, and sixty days from the time I signed the papers, I will be legally divorced," Celeste answered. "That time will be up at the end of next month. Trevor can marry his new wife then."

"That's good." Mandy sighed. "I hear a vehicle driving up out front. I hope it's not Trevor, coming around to beg you to put the divorce aside. God *could* be busy today with so many souls trying to get into heaven, that me and Angela Marie might have to help Him out with a little vengeance."

"I am ready, willing, and able," I declared as I pushed my chair back and stood up.

Taking care of someone—especially Trevor for treating Celeste badly and for disappointing me—would feel really good right then, just to get some of the anger out of my body. It seemed like since we had put my father to rest, I'd skipped the first few steps of grief and dived right into the deep waters of anger. Hitting Trevor a couple dozen times might just relieve part of that.

My left hand had already knotted into a fist when I opened the door, but it relaxed when I saw that our visitor wasn't Trevor. The man standing in front of me wasn't much taller than me and was wearing a camouflage jacket and pants. My first thought was that a hunter had gotten lost and needed directions.

He removed his stocking hat to reveal black hair. "Hello, I'm Devon Parker. Is this where Celeste Butler lives?"

I opened the screen door and stared into his crystal-clear blue eyes. I blinked after a split second and fought a blush creeping up on my neck. I couldn't be attracted to this man—or any other one, for that matter—when I had so much to take care of. And besides, I still wasn't completely sure that Celeste didn't have a crush on him.

"Yes, it is. Come on in out of the cold," I answered. "Celeste, you've got company," I called out. Even after eighteen years, it always seemed strange for someone to call her Celeste Butler. To me, she would always be Celeste Murphy.

She came out of the kitchen and into the foyer, then squealed, "Devon Parker! I wasn't expecting you for another week or so."

"Paperwork went through faster than we thought it would." He opened up his arms, and she walked into them for a hug. There was definitely a sparkle in her eyes when she took a step back.

I didn't like the feeling, but a dose of pure green jealousy filled my heart that Celeste had a friend like Devon. From her reaction, I could easily see their relationship going from friends to lovers.

"I hope not," I whispered under my breath.

"Take off your coat and hang it on the hall tree," Celeste said. "Come on into the kitchen and have some lunch. I'm sorry, where are my manners? You surprised me so much, I'm practically speechless. This"—she pointed at me—"is Angela Marie."

He turned to me, removed his coat and gloves, and stuck out his hand. "Pleased to meet you, Angela Marie. I feel like I already know you and Celeste's grandmother. She talked about y'all all the time."

I shook with him, and sparks danced around the foyer like thousands of falling stars. I let go, and guilt replaced the vibes. This was Celeste's friend and possible future boyfriend.

Celeste led the way from the foyer to the kitchen. "We've just finished lunch and are having coffee. Have you eaten? Can I get you anything?"

"I had a burger on the way," he answered. "But I wouldn't say no to a cup of coffee or a glass of sweet tea."

"How about a slice of cherry or chocolate cream pie?" Celeste asked.

"I never turn down pie—and chocolate is my favorite, next to pecan, peach cobbler, and cherry," he said.

Luis had taught me to never believe in first impressions, to never be impulsive, and to always wait before judging. I failed all three tests that morning. I could have counted all my past hasty decisions on one hand, but that morning I decided I liked this man as I followed along behind them.

Mandy was still sitting at the table. Celeste laid a hand on her shoulder and said, "Granny, I want you to meet Devon Parker. We were stationed together in California, but he just retired out."

Mandy stuck out her hand, but instead of shaking with her, he bent low and kissed her knuckles. "Celeste tells me you are the uncrowned queen of this place. I'm honored to meet you," he said and then straightened back up.

"A true southern gentleman, and I can tell by that drawl that you are a Texas boy." Mandy beamed. "Pull out a chair and make yourself at home. Where are you from, Devon?"

Celeste took a step toward the cabinet, but I put a hand on her arm. "I'll take care of this. You sit down and visit with your friend."

"I grew up in Post, not far from here," Devon answered as he sat down. "But my folks moved all the way across the state to Jefferson to live near and help with my mama's folks while I was in the air force."

"He just finished up his twenty years, Granny. He did four overseas tours and is the finest mechanic I know." Celeste shot a look over at me, but I just gave her my best dose of stink eye.

I put a slice of chocolate pie on a plate, added a fork, and set it in front of him, "Coffee, tea, or both?"

"Coffee, please, Miz Angela Marie," he answered.

"So, what are you going to do now that you're out of the military?" I took an empty mug and the coffeepot to the table. After I filled his, I topped off all three of the others.

"I'm looking for a job," he answered as he took a bite of the large slice of pie. "I'm not one to sit still and let life go by. I want to be busy." His biceps stretched the knit of his dark green T-shirt. His voice was deep and smooth, kind of like a shot of Jameson—my favorite whiskey—with a little bit of honey in it.

"What other skills have you got?" Mandy asked.

"I grew up on a little peanut farm—nothing like this place, but my grandparents managed to make a living at it," he replied. "They retired about five years ago, sold the farm, and bought a small house in town. Grandma is happy because she's close to her church and friends; Grandpa says that he's content because he can go to the senior citizens' center and play dominoes with all his old farmer friends. He's whispered to me that he misses getting his hands dirty and the joy of bringing in a good crop."

I sat down beside Mandy, and she poked me sharp on the thigh with her hand.

"What?" I whispered and wondered if chocolate was smeared on my chin or cheek.

She gave me one of *those looks*, but I ignored it. Devon was a stranger, and he had only been in the house a few minutes.

"What kind of mechanic are you?" Mandy asked.

"If it's got wheels, I can fix it or maintain it," Devon answered.

"Angela Marie needs to hire someone to get all the farming equipment ready for planting season," Mandy said.

One impulsive decision a day—make that a year—was the limit for me, but now Mandy had put me on the spot, and I couldn't think of a thing to say.

Devon stopped eating, looked across the table, and locked eyes with me. "I just came by to see Celeste." His eyes never wavered or blinked. "But if there's a job opening here, I might be interested."

"You could go to work here after you go see your grandparents—and Meadow is only an hour's drive from them, so you would be close by," Mandy said.

His eyes stayed on mine. "Sounds like an ideal job for me. Is this just for a few weeks, or would it be permanent?"

"We always need help in some form on the farm, either mechanical or planting and harvesting," Mandy answered.

I finally blinked and glanced over at Celeste and Mandy, who were both smiling.

"Just like that"—he snapped his fingers—"I've got the possibility of an ideal job."

I grimaced at Celeste, but then I remembered the old adage *You can't fight city hall* and added Celeste's and Mandy's names to the saying. I reminded myself that the job could only be temporary—over as soon as harvest was finished.

"If you want it," I answered and imagined Luis turning over in his grave at me making such a fast decision about something so important. I hoped that Celeste was right about Devon being a good man, because I would be the one working with him. "But before you make an instant decision, you might want to take a walk out to the equipment barn with me and see if you even want to work on tractors and all the other machinery that we use to plant and harvest our crop."

"I know all about that kind of heavy equipment," Devon said with a broad smile. "But I've never worked for an operation that had more than one tractor, one digger, and one picker."

"Meadow Falls has ten tractors and that many diggers and pickers," I told him. "When the peanuts are ready for harvest, everything has to be in full working order. We hire a full crew to bring trucks to help get them out of the ground, bagged, and hauled to market, but the mechanic is the most important man during harvest season. It's long, hard, hot work. You sure you want to even think about the job?"

"Texas can't hold a light to Afghanistan when it comes to heat," he chuckled. "I'd love to see your machinery. I remember when Grandpa would pray hard every day and night that it didn't rain right before harvesttime because the peanut plants don't need to lay on wet ground. I can still hear him saying that we need to start out with good working machinery and clean it up every night, and then service it once it's been in use fifty hours. Harvest is a dusty business, and dirt can clog up the eight million pieces on a digger and a picker. If you don't maintain your equipment, then you won't have anything to use for very long. That's from the Gospel of Grandpa."

"You are hired, if you want the job," Mandy said. "If you can remember all that after being away from it twenty years, your grandfather taught you well."

I could almost hear Luis laughing in the background, and for some strange reason, it brought me a lot of comfort.

"Yes, Grandpa did." Devon flashed a brilliant smile across the table. "It's a lot like riding a bicycle: you can be away from it for years, but then when you get back on it, you just know how to do it. Y'all will start testing the soil and then plowing it to make a good seedbed pretty soon, I expect, right?"

He knew his business, for sure, and he reminded me of Luis as a young man—though not so much in looks. Luis had been a scrawny little guy with thin hair and enough wrinkles on his face to bury an army tank in. Devon looked like he could bench-press an Angus bull.

"You'll have to ask Angela Marie about all that. I've been away from here for eighteen years," Celeste said. "I drove a tractor for harvest from the time I was thirteen. I could keep it right on course, but when it comes to anything else, I'm afraid I'm lost."

"Angela Marie!" Mandy said, raising her voice. "Stop your wool-gathering and join the conversation."

"Sorry about that," I whispered and took a sip of coffee. "We'll take a soil sample after the last frost and decide how much fertilizer and what kind we need to add. We could probably use another hand to do that when the time comes, but we'll worry about hiring someone else another day." I still couldn't believe Mandy had hired him on the spot. When my father was alive, Mandy would have never done something like that.

"I'll need to go visit my grandparents, but I can be back Sunday evening or early Monday morning," he said.

"That sounds great," Mandy declared with a broad smile. Had the power at Meadow Falls shifted from my father to Mandy, bypassing me along the way, or was this simply another symptom of her dementia?

I kept sneaking quick little looks at Devon. If Celeste wasn't just a little bit interested in him, then Trevor had hurt her worse than I thought he had. I needed to think about something other than the niggling idea that maybe Celeste already had someone on the side when the divorce came about. After the way Trevor had treated her, I wouldn't blame her, but I didn't want those thoughts in my head, so I forced myself to study the faded yellow daisies on the wallpaper. I asked myself what the kitchen would look like if it had some *cosmetic help*, as they called it in the magazines. If I ever had it redone, I would definitely install a dishwasher.

When I tuned back to the conversation, Devon was saying, "I'm sure glad I stopped by to see Celeste. This is almost too good to be true. I don't suppose you've got a trailer or a bunkhouse for the hired help, do you?"

Devon living on the farm would make it easier for Celeste if she felt the vibes that were radiating through the room.

Mandy gave me a gentle kick under the table. "Angela Marie."

"Don't you want to think about this job situation overnight?" I focused my attention on Devon without looking him in the eyes again. "We haven't even discussed salary or wages, and you haven't looked at our equipment."

"Nope," Devon answered. "My grandma says that when opportunity knocks, you invite it in for chocolate pie and coffee. That's much easier than chasing after it when it's a mile down the road. I'll take the job. It's in the wheelhouse of my skills, and if it's mine, then I don't have to worry about someone coming along this evening and snatching the opportunity right out from under me. Besides all that, I like the peace I feel in this house."

My brain froze up. Was he in the same house I was sitting in at that very moment? I could vouch for thirty-five years of tension in Meadow Falls. I didn't realize how hard I was frowning until the daisies on the wallpaper started blurring into yellow blobs.

"You can have my house," Mandy said. "No one is using it anymore. It's not fancy, but it's furnished with everything you'll need, and you can take your meals with us."

I couldn't very well tell Devon we weren't offering room and board with the job after she'd already done it. Thank goodness Celeste knew him, but I'd be damned if I had to like what had just happened.

"That's the icing on the cake," Devon said. "Before I get on down the road, I *would* like to look at the rest of the farm and the barns, if you don't mind, Miz Angela Marie. Mainly, so I can tell my grandpa about it."

I nodded and pushed back my chair. If things didn't work out, I could always fire him—even if it upset Celeste. The first time my father had made me fire a hired hand, I'd stressed over it for a week, but after that it got easier. If someone didn't do their job, or if they caused trouble with the other folks, they were gone by the end of the day. We had enough stress on our nerves—and by *our*, I meant *my*, now that my father was gone—from the middle of May until the end of October that we didn't need problems with the folks who worked for us.

Chapter Five

I like that boy," Mandy said out of the clear blue sky as Celeste drove us to church on Sunday morning. "What did y'all think of him?"

"He knows his way around a peanut farm," I answered. "He checked all the tractors; took a long, hard look at the other equipment; and then said that the barns probably needed some repair work. I miss Luis. He took care of all that. But it would have been nice if we'd had a family discussion before you hired him, Mandy."

"Why?" Mandy asked. "He was qualified, and I liked him. Never doubt the first impression of an old woman. That boy is one of the good ones."

"Because he kissed your hand?" I asked.

"Don't you get sassy with me, Angela Marie," Mandy snapped. "You've needed help since Luis died. Thomas just did what he had to do to get by."

"If Devon doesn't work out, you can fire him, then."

"I will." Mandy's voice was still edgy. "And I won't even blink when I do it."

"Of course I like him—but, Granny, you don't have the authority to fire anyone. And you should have consulted Angela Marie before you hired him. She's the boss at Meadow Falls now," Celeste replied, probably trying to defuse the tension between me and Mandy.

"She needs help," Mandy said. "And if she can't see a good deal in front of her face, then I will help her. If he turns out to be a dud, I'll put him running in a heartbeat."

"He's not a dud," Celeste said in Devon's defense. "I worked with him, and he's been my close friend for a long time. He was the first person that I talked to when I was having trouble deciding what to do about reenlisting. He has always been like a brother to me."

Mandy cut her eyes to Celeste. "Some relationships start out as friends. Edward and I were best friends before we realized that we were in love."

Celeste pulled her SUV into the parking lot and snagged a spot not far from the front door of the little white-clapboard church. "Not with us. He's like a brother, not a boyfriend. Besides, I'm not even officially divorced, and I'm not ready to dive into another relationship. Maybe in five years, I'll think about it. Then in another five, I'll get serious about someone." She paused. "That's if I ever do, and that's a real big *if* right there."

"Methinks the lady protests too much." I unfastened my seat belt, opened the back door, and walked around the front of the vehicle.

"Just making it clear that I'm not interested in anything more than friendship with Devon Parker—and not to be whatever it is that's socially incorrect about tall women and short men, I'm just flat-out not attracted to him that way," Celeste said as she got out of the vehicle, hurried to the porch, and held the door open for us.

Then where were those vibes coming from? the voice in my head asked.

"I've learned that I don't need a man to define me any more than you did when Grandpa Edward passed away, Granny," Celeste went on. "We are strong, independent women who can take care of ourselves."

"Those are your words, Mandy," I said as I helped her out of the SUV. "That's what you've always told us."

She reached over the seat and picked up her cane, then slammed the door shut. "Yes, I did, and I meant every one." Mandy shook her finger at both of us. "And don't either of you ever forget it. If you will remember, I told you to look in the mirror and repeat those words to yourselves every day."

"I remember and wish I had done that more often in the past few years," Celeste said as we left the ever-blowing cold wind behind and stepped into the warm foyer. She helped Mandy remove her coat and hang it on one of the empty hooks that lined the wall, then did the same with hers. That morning, she wore a slim-fitting denim skirt and a bright green sweater; I'd dressed in a denim skirt and a lighter green sweater. Proof again that we could be related to each other—but then, Mandy had raised both of us, so that wasn't any big surprise.

"Did I tell you that Polly is coming home with us for Sunday dinner and maybe a movie or some dominoes this afternoon?" Mandy asked. "My forgetfulness is acting up this morning, and I can't remember what I did or didn't do yesterday."

"But you remember hiring Devon without even giving me a chance to have a word about it, and then you gave him your house?"

She slanted a glance at me. "Of course I do—and you are being sassy again, Angela Marie. Now, about Polly . . ."

"Yes, you told us, and I'd love to have a visit with her," Celeste answered. "I haven't seen her in years. How old is she getting to be?"

"It's not polite to ask a woman's age or weight, but she probably doesn't tip the scales at more than a buck twenty, and she was eighty-seven on her last birthday." Mandy led the way into the sanctuary. "Omens have been happening around here. First, Harrison passed away the very week that Polly said she wasn't going to iron anymore. He was buried on the first day of the year, which kind of seemed to me like the right time to pass the farm down to Angela Marie. And then Devon just drops in, and we get an experienced hand. It's all signs that there are good days ahead."

"Were those signs sent from God, fate, or the universe?" I asked.

"All of the above," Mandy replied.

The sanctuary seemed more peaceful that morning—but then, it was the first time I'd been to church since my father passed away. A center aisle separated two rows of well-worn oak pews that had been polished to a sheen from years and years of use. The pulpit was straight ahead, with the choir area and baptismal behind it. The old upright piano had been sitting in the same place over to the right ever since I could remember. Polly had played it at one time, but when I was a teenager, she gave up her bench to a younger woman. Two or three pianists had come and gone in the past twenty years, and now the preacher's wife played for the services.

The walls were covered in the same aged-pine paneling as the living room at Meadow Falls. Rather than closing in on me like the ones at home often did, they seemed to say that God was ageless and brought peace to all who entered there.

Mandy took a few steps down the aisle, where people who had left Sunday school classes and the ones who were just arriving moseyed around like they had nowhere to go and half a lifetime to get there. She weaved through them, stopping to talk with several about my father's sudden death.

"I've got a confession," Celeste said as we made our way to the pew where Polly was already seated. "I knew Devon was going to stop by, but after our argument about hiring someone, I didn't—"

"Y'all had an argument?" Mandy asked.

"We did, and *you* settled it," I answered.

"Glad I could help," she said cheerfully.

I didn't realize I had been holding my breath until it all came out in a whoosh.

"What was all that about?" Mandy asked.

"Nothing," I said as I stood back and let Mandy go first so she could sit by Polly. I motioned for Celeste to follow her, then brought up the rear and sat at the end of the pew. Usually, my father would be right next to me, all dressed up in his white shirt, a bolo tie, creased jeans, and one of his Western-cut sports jackets. The thought of his clothing brought on the idea of cleaning out his closet, and my chest tightened. Thank God that Celeste was there to help me.

I closed my eyes and tried to remember the last time I had even been in his bedroom, and not a single memory popped up. For as long as I could remember, my mother had always had her own room, and I had been in it a few times as a child. After my mother had gotten too sick to go to the office or hold social events, I went into her room every day to take care of her. The last couple of weeks, hospice had come daily, but for the most part, Mandy and I took care of her until she passed away. My father's bedroom, right across the hall, was like that inner room in the tabernacle we learned about in Sunday school. Only the cleaning lady Mandy trusted the most had been allowed in there. I wouldn't have been surprised if that woman had to sign her name in blood, declaring that she would never tell anyone a single thing about Harrison Duncan's bedroom.

I could feel the wrinkles in my forehead deepening as I tried to remember going into his room as a child, but no memories of such occasions came to mind. Mandy would check my room every night before she and Celeste went home. Besides, I'd been more afraid of my dad—or of Mother's anger rising to the top if I knocked on their doors—than of any storm that blew through the area.

Celeste leaned over and whispered, "I promise I'm not interested in Devon as anything more than a good friend. I'm not going to desert you again."

"I've never been in my father's bedroom," I blurted out.

"What's that got to do with Devon?" Celeste asked.

"Nothing, but that's what's on my mind," I answered. "But I believe you about Devon, and I'm glad. You need to heal from everything you've been through before you start something new."

"So do you," Celeste said. "I have been in Harrison's room many times. Granny and I cleaned it on weeks when we didn't have enough ladies to do it. For the most part, it's just like all the other bedrooms, except the bed is bigger."

"I have got to go through his things," I whispered.

"I'll help you do that," she said. "Just let me know when you are ready."

"Thank you." Just knowing that she would be there with me meant more than words could ever explain.

❖ ❖ ❖

"You get in the front seat," Mandy told me when we had shaken the preacher's hand and headed out across the parking lot toward the vehicle. "Polly and I will take the back so we can visit on the way to Meadow Falls."

"Yes, ma'am," I said and winked at Celeste.

The two elderly women were about the same height, and both had gray hair cut in a chin-length bob. Their eyes were different—Polly's were almost black, and Mandy's were crystal blue. At one time, Polly had had dark hair, whereas Mandy claimed Irish heritage and had had red hair back in her youth. I'd always thought that I could have passed for her great-granddaughter better than Celeste could.

They chatted about all the latest gossip in the county all the way back to the farm. By the time Celeste parked in front of the house, we knew who had recently died—besides my father—and what funerals were coming up in the next few days. They discussed which funeral dinners they needed to send a cake or casserole to, how many folks in Terry County would be getting married in the next few weeks because they were in "the family way," and who was cheating on their spouse.

With all that covered, I wondered what on earth they would visit about all afternoon. They were still talking when we got them settled in the living room. For the first Sunday in my whole life, we were setting the kitchen table for dinner.

After my mother died, it had only been me and my father for Sunday dinner. He sat at the head of the big dining room table, which could seat a dozen people, and I sat to his left, just like I had from the time I could remember. Mother's place had been to his right. After I'd insisted that Mandy move in with us, I also decided that she would be joining us, no matter where we took our meals. I still got a knot in my stomach thinking about how I had worried over the argument we would have. I had stood my ground when he set his jaw and glared at me that day. Finally, he had said, "I don't care anymore. Do whatever you want. You will when I'm dead and gone, anyway."

Mandy had always sat right beside me at the big table on Sundays, and other than a few words between us, we ate in silence. My father had never had anything to say to us. He ate and then left the room.

Celeste broke into my thoughts. "Do they still take an afternoon nap?"

"Right after lunch, one of them claims the sofa and one takes the love seat. And they'll still be talking when they fall asleep. Most of the time, it's all about the past." I took the plates that we used for every day from the cabinet—the china ones were stored in the glass-front cabinet in the dining room—and set the table. Then I took a gallon jug of sweet tea and a bowl of marinated vegetables from the refrigerator.

Celeste moved the salt and pepper shakers over to the table, then added the butter dish and a small jar of strawberry jam that Mandy had made the summer before. The aroma of baking bread filled the house and reminded me of my father sniffing the air when he came in from the living room on Sunday and sat down at the table. He never commented on it, but he'd seemed to enjoy the aroma.

That's a good memory. My mother's voice was in my head for the first time, and it startled me.

"Do you ever hear voices in your head? I'm talking about ones that you recognize," I asked Celeste.

"Oh yes," she said as she filled a basket with hot rolls. "Granny pops into my head on a regular basis, and sometimes I hear Luis whispering to me when I'm trying to make a decision. I used to pretend that he was my father, even though I knew that he was way too old for Roxy to have been attracted to him. I wonder why he never married."

I finished putting the food on the table. "When I asked him that question, he told me that he had a longtime girlfriend over in Ropesville, but neither of them were interested in getting married or ever having kids. He wasn't the kind to cheat on a woman, so there's no way you were his daughter."

"I know, but I needed to dream about someone back in those days, and he was kind to me and you." Then she raised her voice and called Polly and Mandy to dinner.

The two elderly ladies sat down at the table and visited even more between bites. "If it wasn't so cold, we'd walk down to the cemetery so I could pay my respects to Harrison," Polly said. "I had a terrible headache the day he was buried and couldn't get out to the service. That reminds me, I've got five of his shirts ready for y'all to pick up. His white shirts were the last thing on my list to get done before I retired that day. I got them all finished by early afternoon and then got the phone call from Elsie Landers that Harrison had died. Who'd have thought he would go before us, Mandy? And him only sixty-one years old."

"Would you just take them to the church, please? The clothes closet committee could distribute them to people," I said. "I'll pay you for the work before you leave today, but we don't need to bring them back to the house."

Polly nodded. "I'm on that committee, and we'll be glad to have them. Are you going to donate the rest of his things, too?"

Mandy looked across the table at me. "That would be a good thing to do with them, wouldn't it? No sense in them just fading or turning yellow with age sitting there. Why don't you girls take care of that while me and Polly get our nap? She's got a key to the closet down at the church. So when you take her home this evening, you could take a load with you."

"And this may sound strange, but we always need underwear and socks at the closet," Polly said. "People think they can't donate things so personal, but down-and-out folks appreciate having them."

My chest felt like someone had just dumped a load of rocks into it. I wasn't sure I was ready to open that can of worms just yet. My father had been gone just over a week. I still expected to see him at the breakfast table every morning and hear him telling me what needed to be done on the farm that day. But getting his things out of the house would take a load off my mind, so I might as well get it done.

You are the boss now. My mother's voice was back. *You make the decisions. You've always been smart. You never did need your father to tell you how to run this place. Luis did that for you.*

"Why didn't my father ever ask Luis to have lunch with us?" I blurted out.

"Times were different back then," Mandy answered. "There was a line between the hired help and the boss."

"Folks around here always said that your mother straightened Harrison out—and I guess she did in some ways, but she liked being the queen of Meadow Falls. Royalty doesn't eat with the peasants," Polly explained. "Mandy can tell you more about how things were than I can."

"I told you that things were different in the generations before Harrison came along, and he was raised to think like his granddaddy and his daddy did," Mandy said. "Luis told me that this big house intimidated him. It's up to you to change things or keep them the same. You are the boss now. Have you thought about what you're going to do different?"

She had voiced the same words out loud about me being the boss that the memory of my mother had whispered to me earlier. "Not really."

"Yes, you have," Celeste protested. "You're going to run the business end of the farm the same as it's been done for years, but you started asserting your power when you argued with Harrison about Granny living here in this house and having her meals with y'all. *You* aren't your father, or grandfather, or even great-grandfather. You are Angela Marie Duncan, and you *will* do things your way."

Polly shook her bony, veined finger at me. "And don't you forget it for one minute, young lady."

"Yes, ma'am!" I couldn't have forced the smile off my face if I'd been sucking on a raw lemon. Mother had never told me I was smart or pretty or paid me any kind of compliment. Maybe the voice in my head was nothing more than my imagination, but I was going to choose to believe that she meant what I'd heard her say.

Chapter Six

I would never have believed that my father's death could change my emotions, my life, *and* Meadow Falls—maybe only in baby steps, but I could feel a slight shift in the way I felt these days. When my father had told me that he'd made out a new will, I hadn't thought about him dying at such a young age. Harrison Duncan was supposed to live to be a hundred and drop dead on a freshly waxed floor without getting a bit of dust on his white shirt. He wasn't supposed to have a heart attack before he was even retirement age.

"Are you still kind of in shock that Harrison is gone?" Celeste asked as she and I went up the wide staircase side by side that Sunday afternoon.

"I'm still trying to figure out how I feel. The only way I can describe it is that it's like I'm stepping out onto the tip of an iceberg called Meadow Falls. I know there's more under the water, but I can't see it," I answered. "I guess if I'm totally honest, it would be somewhere between numb and indifferent. He and I were never close, but you already know that. We shared a house, worked in different areas of the farm, and pretty much stayed out of each other's way. That was easy in a place this big. I only confronted him twice, and both of those times had to do with Mandy. Maybe I should have forced him to tell me why he was so nice to other people and so distant with me, but . . ." I shrugged. "Time ran out."

"When the iceberg rises up and you are on top of it, that's when you'll have closure," Celeste said.

"Did you feel like this when your mother died? How did you handle it?" I asked her.

"There's a lot of difference in losing a parent when you are six years old and then losing one when you are past thirty," Celeste said. "I didn't know my mother. Her boyfriend called Granny when she died. They were living in Northern California. He said that she died with a high fever and that he had followed her wishes and cremated her. Her ashes had been scattered at their favorite spot in a stream at the base of a mountain. Granny was upset, and I cried with her. But my tears weren't so much for Roxy, since I never knew her, as they were to share in Granny's grief."

I came to a halt at the top of the stairs. I expected Celeste to plow ahead, right on down the long hallway and into my father's room, but she stood still and waited beside me. "Even though I didn't know my mother and I was just a little kid when we got the news that she was gone, I can relate to how you must be feeling."

"Do you feel abandoned? I mean, your mama was dead, and you didn't even know who your father was." I slapped my hand over my mouth. "I'm sorry. That was insensitive," I whispered after a moment. "Crazy as it sounds, other than you and Mandy and Luis, I feel like I've been left behind my whole life. But this is not a new emotion. What is giving me problems right now is that I feel guilty because . . ."

"Because he was like a stranger, and you can't find any emotion in your heart for him? I can understand that. It must be tough, knowing your father and yet not having a father, either, but living in the same house with him," Celeste said. "I'm talking in circles."

"Yes, but you nailed it right on the head," I agreed.

Celeste sat down on the top step and patted the place beside her. I sat next to her and took a few deep breaths.

"We are kindred spirits. Roxy lived far away, and she was just as much a stranger to me as Harrison was to you." Celeste laced her fingers through mine and gently squeezed my hand. "We were very young, but you helped me get through my mother's death. I wasn't here for you to lean on when Sophia died, but I'm here now."

"I wasn't even in school yet when we got the news about Roxy. How could I have helped you?" I tried to remember that day, but nothing came to light.

"We were going up to your bedroom to get your shoes for church, and I told you that my mama was dead. We sat right here on this step, and you took my hand. Remember what you said?" Celeste asked me.

I shook my head.

"You asked me if I wanted to cry, and then you said if I did, you would cry with me," Celeste went on. "So today, I'm asking you the same thing. If you want to cry, I'll cry with you."

"I should shed a few tears, and I feel so guilty that I can't," I admitted.

"Maybe you should do what I've done through the years," Celeste said. "Grieve for what could have been."

"I'm not even sure what that is, but I'm really glad you're here to help." I untangled my hand from hers and nudged her on the shoulder.

"Me too," Celeste said with a smile. "Now, let's go take care of this job. We'll both feel better when it is done."

My father's room was the last one on the left at the very end of the hallway, and my mother's bedroom was right across the hall from his. I was a teenager before I knew that some parents actually shared a bedroom.

"When my father married my mother, my grandparents, Clifford and Inez, were still living, and the downstairs bedroom was theirs. That was the one I insisted that Mandy have when I moved her into the house," I said.

Celeste grinned. "You *are* nervous. I know because you have always blurted out whatever surfaces when you are nervous."

"Do not!" I argued.

"Oh, yeah, you do. But that's okay. I'm glad that you gave Granny a room where she didn't have to climb the stairs. I imagine Harrison was an old bear about that." Celeste stopped in front of my father's closed bedroom door.

Several times through the years, I'd heard sermons about the day that Jesus died on the cross and the veil of the temple was rent in two. Since I had always been guilty of letting my mind roam instead of listening to the sermon, the opening words were all I'd heard. The memory had come back to me a few years ago, so I had researched it. According to the scripture, only the high priest could go into the inner sanctum, but when Christ died, all that was taken away, and a new way was established. Harrison Duncan was not Jesus Christ, and he had certainly not died on a cross—but death was death, no matter who the person involved was.

"I'm not sure I can go in there," I whispered. "You want to take care of all that for me?"

"No, ma'am, this will bring you closure," she answered.

I told her my thoughts on the inner sanctum, and she patted me on the shoulder. "Granny would tell you that was a little bit sacrilegious."

"Probably so, but it's the way I feel." I reached for the doorknob but couldn't make myself turn it.

Celeste grabbed the knob and threw open the door. "There—that much is done for you. It's open now. And look! It's just a bedroom, not a place of atonement for sins."

I was frozen in place for what seemed like more than one eternity, but in all reality, it was probably just a minute. A king-size four-poster bed barely filled half the room. The dresser, chest of drawers, and night-stands all matched the rich mahogany wood of the bed. A sofa sat over to the left, and a huge rolltop desk to the right. No matter how hard I tried, I couldn't imagine my parents ever sleeping together in that bed, but I was proof that they must have had sex at least once. The most vivid pictures that came to my mind were of my mother in the downstairs office and my father reading the morning paper while he had his coffee. No matter how hard I tried, I couldn't bring up a memory of them kissing each other—or even flirting, for that matter.

I took a step inside the room only to get a faint whiff of his cologne, which still lingered in the air. "Take a deep breath," I whispered.

"I don't have to," Celeste said. "His cologne or shaving lotion, whichever one he used, is everywhere. It must be on his pillows. But wouldn't the cleaning ladies have taken care of this room since he passed away?"

"They quit a few weeks ago," I answered and noticed all the pictures collecting dust on his dresser.

Curiosity, they say, killed the cat, but satisfaction brought him back. I crossed the room and picked up a photograph of my mother and father on their wedding day. They had gotten married in front of the fireplace in the living room. My father was wearing his signature white shirt, a bolo tie with a gold clasp, and a black Western-cut suit. Mother's long white dress was covered with lace and had fitted sleeves and a little stand-up collar. Their wedding must have been during the Christmas holidays, because the fireplace was decorated with boughs of cedar, and the very edge of the Christmas tree was in the right side of the picture—right where it still was that day, even though the holidays had come and gone.

"Neither of them is smiling." Celeste startled me when she spoke. "I've dusted these pictures many, many times, but I'm just noticing that bit of a Christmas tree in the corner of the wedding photo." She touched the photograph. "It reminds me again that we need to take down the tree in the living room and put it away this week."

"Yes, we do," I agreed, but I kept staring at the picture. Mother was beautiful, with her dark hair and brown eyes. They both looked serious—as if they were attending a funeral rather than their wedding.

"They don't look very happy, do they?" I asked, and I waved at all the other pictures on the dresser. "What do you make of these?"

"I often wondered why Harrison kept pictures of the two of us, but I figured that since we were together all the time, it would be difficult to get one of you by yourself—unless he followed you and Luis out to the barns," she answered.

"You never mentioned that they were even here," I said.

"You never told me you had never been in this room," she said with a shrug.

Lined up right there in front of us were nineteen—I counted them—framed pictures of me and Celeste together. The one right next to the wedding photo had been taken when Celeste was a year old and I was a newborn. The next one had been taken on my first day of school. Celeste was holding my hand on the way out to the bus stop at the end of the lane. Mandy had told us that we were both pretty that day—I in my gingham sundress and white shoes, and Celeste in a floral dress and black patent leather shoes. Even though she was only a year older than me, she was already a head taller, and I never did catch up to her.

"I figured he didn't even know I was alive, and now this," I muttered.

"Me too," Celeste whispered.

My mother had had a few pictures taken of me through the years, but none had Celeste in them. Most of the photos she'd had were in an album that I found in the drawer of her nightstand after she passed. There was one of me in a fancy dress, sitting on Santa's lap with her off to the side, and one of her beside me in front of the church on Easter Sunday, but there wasn't a single one of me with both my parents.

I picked up the last one on my father's dresser and tried to brush away the tears that were streaming down my face. Someone had taken a picture as I hugged Celeste goodbye the morning she left home. Just thinking about the ache that I'd had in my heart—not only that day but for weeks after—caused another round of tears. "Why would he have these, and who took them? I don't remember him or my mother ever taking pictures of the two of us."

"Granny took lots of pictures, but not these." Celeste pulled a tissue from the box on the nightstand and then handed it to me. "I never could let you cry alone. Granny has got several albums full of her family—Emma, Roxy, you, and me—but I've never seen these photos in any of them. Evidently, Harrison took them. Go ahead and cry." She took a fistful of tissues out of the box and wiped my cheeks. "According to Granny, it's all a part of the grieving process."

"I'm not crying because my father is dead," I told her. "It's because I'm reliving that horrible day when you left me behind. We had been together my whole life, and I felt like half my heart had been ripped out."

"I'm so, so sorry," she said. "I thought that I had to get away from here. Now look at me—I'm right back in the same place."

I willed myself not to cry anymore and picked up a picture of me and Celeste in our fancy dresses on prom night, when she was a senior and I was a junior. "Do you think he had them on the dresser when my mother shared this room with him?"

"Nope," Celeste answered.

"How can you be so sure?"

"Like I said, this isn't my first time to be in this room."

I was surprised that jealousy swept over me. It wasn't Celeste's fault that she had gotten to come into the inner sanctum and I was forbidden. She didn't ask to have to dust all those pictures on his dresser.

Oh, stop it. Enough of playing the poor little rich girl who nobody loved, Mandy's voice scolded. *We were little more than hired help, and I swore Celeste to secrecy. And besides all that, I loved you enough for ten people.*

"Granny didn't trust anyone to come in this room," Celeste said. "She didn't want anyone else in here, because the cleaning crew might have snooped in his things, and there could have been talk about how the mighty Harrison Duncan lived. Granny said there was always as much gossip about your mama and daddy as there is about the royals in England."

The little green monster that had been sitting on my shoulder disappeared in an instant. I couldn't hold on to bad feelings of any kind for Celeste. She'd been my playmate, my friend, and the one I had always turned to my whole life. Having her back with no deadline for when she had to leave again was a blessing.

"And all these pictures were here then?" I asked again.

"No, but they appeared through the years," she replied. "Your mother's room was cluttered with perfumes, jewelry boxes, and a fancy hairbrush set—I can even close my eyes and still see where each one was placed. When I was just a little girl, I pretended that I was a princess and the pretty things were mine." Celeste went to the closet and opened the double doors. "Do you want to put all this in boxes or just take it down to my vehicle on the hangers?"

"Hangers is fine," I answered. "That way, you can just carry them from the SUV to the racks in the church clothes closet."

"I'll take down an armload at a time while you go through the dresser drawers," she said as she gathered up several shirts and laid them on the bed. "I figured he had a few shirts that weren't white, but I'm not finding them."

"I never saw him wear anything but white ones," I said. "There should be a couple of robes in his closet. I gave him a red one for Christmas a few years ago, but he never wore it. The gray one is frayed around the collar and faded. He wore that one to breakfast almost every morning."

Celeste pulled the gray one out of the closet and tossed it on the bed with his shirts. "This thing is hardly good enough for the rag bag. I wonder what made it so special."

I shrugged. "Maybe Mandy knows. We'll have to ask her. Would you please bring back a garbage bag? I'll need one for all the stuff in the dresser drawers."

"Will do," Celeste called and disappeared out the door laden down with an armload of clothes.

I opened the top-right dresser drawer to find it filled with his underwear. The second one held socks, and a dozen white T-shirts were folded neatly in the third one. I laid them on the bed and had started to close the drawer when I noticed two pieces of paper. I picked them up and turned them over; they were two photographs that were beginning to fade, as old Polaroid pictures did after several years.

I'd seen enough pictures of Emma and Roxy out in Mandy's old house to recognize the first photograph in my hand was of Roxy. Someone had written *1987* at the bottom in black ink. She wore a denim miniskirt and a shirt unbuttoned far enough down to reveal a lot of cleavage and a butterfly tattoo between her breasts.

"Oh my!" I gasped, and then something like those light bulbs you see in cartoons flashed above my head. Could it be that my father had had a fling with Roxy? The picture would have been taken right before he married my mother. Could Celeste belong to him?

"No," I whispered, but I couldn't take my eyes off that one picture.

Did Mandy know that her granddaughter was dressing like this? And where and how had she gotten a tattoo in the late eighties? My mind swirled with questions, but there were no answers. I looked at the picture more closely and realized that the background was the old willow tree down by the creek. From the green leaves, I would guess it had been taken in the spring. Roxy had a sly smile on her face, and she posed provocatively with one hand on her hip and the other behind her head.

The other picture was almost identical to the first one except the woman was different. The setting by the willow tree and the pose were the same, but when I looked closer, I realized the photo of the second woman had been taken in the fall. The leaves on the willow tree were beginning to turn colors, and quite a few lay on the ground at the woman's feet. Her hair was parted in the middle and hung down to her shoulders, just like Roxy's was in her picture. The other woman wore a denim skirt, and her shirt had enough buttons undone at the top to reveal a hummingbird tattoo. The date at the bottom of the picture was 1982. In the little space at the bottom, someone had written, To my darling Harrison. Summer Rain.

Who in the hell was this woman? My eyes went back to Roxy's photo. Those two women were enough alike to have been related.

I should have torn it up, but I just couldn't. The resemblance between Roxy and the other woman was uncanny. Could it have been a friend of Roxy's from high school? And what was my father doing with the pictures, anyway? Had he found them and tucked them away so that Mandy would never get her hands on them? Or had he taken them? I heard Celeste coming up the stairs, so I slipped the photos into the pocket of my skirt.

"Here you go," Celeste said and tossed a box of garbage bags on the bed. "Looks like I can get the rest of the clothes down to my vehicle in two more loads. Somehow, I always figured Harrison would have more stuff in his closet than this."

"He's just full of surprises, isn't he?" I muttered and eyed Celeste closer than I ever had before.

"Just goes to prove that we really never know someone, doesn't it?" Celeste draped more shirts and jeans over her arm and headed out of the room again.

"Amen," I agreed with a nod and took one more look at the two pictures before I tucked them back into my pocket. If my father had been protecting Mandy, he would have burned those pictures. I figured there was more to that story than met the eye. I would have given away the title to the farm—all of Meadow Falls—to know why my father would hide the pictures or even keep them. Had my mother known about them? Was that why they'd had separate rooms? I slipped the pictures out of my pocket and studied them harder. Was Celeste my father's daughter? Could she be my half-sister?

❖   ❖   ❖

In the winter, the sun disappears beyond the far horizon pretty early, and it was barely giving off any light at all when Celeste left the farm to take Polly home and deliver my father's things to the church clothes closet. As I watched the white SUV disappear down the lane, I thought of how many times I'd seen my father's truck kick up dust as he left the farm on what seemed like a daily basis. Then, when he returned, a hired hand was always there to take the keys from him and drive his vehicle out to a barn to clean it up. My father had definitely been born with the ability to delegate—one of the many things that had never been easy for me.

"I guess I'll have to learn or else wear myself out trying to oversee everything. At least Celeste is willing to take some of the load," I said with a long sigh.

"Learn what?" Mandy asked from her chair over beside the Christmas tree.

"To delegate more," I answered.

"That's why you hire a really good foreman," she told me.

As if on cue, a truck drove up in front of the house, and Devon got out. "Looks like the man you hired is here." I watched him walk across the yard and up onto the porch.

"I didn't hire anyone," Mandy declared. "I'm not the boss around here. Harrison is, and he didn't mention hiring anyone."

That she had forgotten what happened within the last week wasn't any big surprise. She had endured the shock of my father's sudden death, then another shock when Celeste came home so unexpectedly, and then a third one when Celeste told us she and Trevor had split up.

The first thing I'd learned when we found that Mandy had symptoms of memory loss was that she needed a good support team. I wasn't a team back then, but I had help now that Celeste was home. The second thing I learned was that I shouldn't argue with her when she was having a problem. That would just frustrate her and make things worse.

Mandy narrowed her eyes at me and asked, "Has the cat got your tongue? What man are you talking about?"

"Remember when Celeste's friend Devon came by, and we asked him if he would work for us?" I asked.

Mandy frowned. "Did he say yes?"

"He did, and he's already here."

Her brow furrowed as she tried to get things straight in her mind. "I remember him being here. I like that boy. I'm glad we've got some help. You work too hard, and Celeste is good at cooking and bookwork, but she doesn't know a hammer from a pitchfork when it comes to farming, so she's not worth much to you outside of the house."

"She can drive a tractor," I argued.

"She could eighteen years ago," Mandy said with a nod. "But I bet she hasn't had to shift gears on any vehicle in all that time. Let's just hope she doesn't strip the gears, if it comes down to her going out into the fields."

"It's like riding a bicycle, Mandy. She'll do fine, but I'm hoping to have enough help not to need her outside of the house." I didn't take my eyes off Devon. From his walk, anyone could tell that he had military training. His back was straight, and his shoulders squared off, but he had a swagger that spoke of confidence.

"Is it all right if he stays out in your old house?" I asked, hoping that she would remember offering it to him and wouldn't get angry about another person staying out there.

"Of course it is." She eyed me carefully. "I told you when Thomas quit working for us to hire someone as foreman and give him that house to live in. I'm going to watch some reruns of *The Golden Girls* while you go show him his new home. The key to the house is hanging on the rack by the back door, right where I put it when I moved into this place."

Too bad Mandy was staring at being a hundred years old. The way she barked out orders, she would make a wonderful foreman, and I would hire her without a moment's hesitation. I left the living room window and opened the door before Devon even knocked.

"Come on in," I said and motioned him inside.

"I'd rather get my stuff unloaded," he said. "I've been lucky so far, but the weatherman says it's going to rain this evening, and I'd like to at least get everything inside before that starts."

"Okay, then. Drive around back and follow the path to the house I pointed out when you were here before. I'll get the key and meet you there." I grabbed my heavy work coat and shoved my feet down into a pair of boots.

By the time I had walked a couple of hundred yards through the pasture on the other side of the yard's fence, Devon had already parked his bright red pickup truck and had a duffel bag thrown over his shoulder and another one in his hand. I unlocked the door and held it open for him. He tossed the bags onto the living room floor. They landed with a thud, but the old place was still so sturdy that the impact didn't even rattle the sugar bowl on the kitchen table. He turned around and headed back out the door.

"Need some help?" I asked.

"Nope, just got a couple more boxes and the groceries," he answered.

The idea of someone other than Mandy living in the house bothered me more than I had thought it would. This was more my home than the big house had been. I hadn't been back inside since I'd moved Mandy out, but nothing had changed. Mandy hadn't been too keen on leaving—but that morning, she had set a dish towel on fire when she forgot what she was doing.

She had argued with me and declared that she couldn't leave her house, but after thinking about it that day and night, she finally said she would move into the big house under one condition: it was only for a one-week trial period. We shook on it, and I'd helped her pack an old metal suitcase.

At the end of a week, she'd said she would give it another week, and I started moving more and more of her personal things from one place to the other. In a month, she had settled in and was bossing me around like always.

I stood in the middle of the living room and took a long look at everything Mandy had left behind and tried to fix a permanent picture in my mind. Devon would probably rearrange things to suit himself, and I wanted to remember exactly how it all looked when I was growing up. I slipped my phone from my pocket and snapped several pictures, then closed my eyes and took a mental snapshot that involved more than a flat photograph. I took in the aroma of freshly baked cookies and hot coffee that was always brewing—even though neither was there that evening. Then I took a deep breath and sucked in the peace I'd always felt in the small place, hoping that it would forever come back to me when I looked at the pictures I had taken.

Her words from when I'd said I wanted her to move in with us drifted through my mind once more: "What did Harrison say about the hired help living in the house with him?"

"He didn't like it, but his opinion doesn't matter when it comes to you," I'd answered.

"So, you finally stood up to him?"

"I did."

"Good for you. That took a lot of nerve, and I'm proud of you—but it's just for one week," she had told me. "This forgetfulness I'm having affects what happened yesterday or five minutes ago, not so much my memories of things that happened in the past. I'm hoping the good Lord won't take them away from me."

Mandy still came out to her old house occasionally—especially in the springtime—and sat on the porch, but to my knowledge, she had never gone back inside. She said she liked to remember the wonderful days when she and Edward had first moved into the house.

Celeste had come out the day before and adjusted the thermostat, so the place was warm and cozy for Devon's arrival. I wondered how she felt about a stranger living in her house, then remembered that she and Devon had been friends, so he wasn't a stranger to her. She had said there was no physical attraction between them—but how was that even possible when just being around the guy made my hormones whine?

Devon brought the last of his things into the house, shed his coat, and then smiled when he saw the coatrack in the corner. "This reminds me so much of my grandparents' home on their little farm down in Post. Nice and cozy. I'm really going to like it here."

The temperature in the room seemed to rise a few degrees. I wanted to take my coat off, but that would indicate that I was staying for a while. He needed time to unpack and settle in, not have to entertain or even talk to me.

"I'm glad you aren't disappointed." I held out the key, which was attached to a "World's Greatest Nanny" fob I had given Mandy for Christmas more than thirty years before. "That's the only key we have, so if you lose it, you'll have to change out the whole knob assembly."

"I won't lose it," he said as he took it from me. "But if I do, I'm a locksmith in addition to being a mechanic, so I can make another one."

I took a couple of steps toward the door. "A jack-of-all-trades, huh?"

His brilliant grin lit up the whole room despite the dreary sight outside the windows. "And master of few," he admitted.

"I hope you are master of the machinery, at least." I nodded toward all the paper bags of food sitting on the coffee table. "I don't know why you bought so much food. We told you that room and board came with the job."

"Yes, but I like to snack at night, and I always need something for break times," he said. "What time should I come over for supper?"

"We should have it ready in half an hour. Celeste has taken Mandy's friend Polly home, but she'll be back soon," I answered as I opened the door, but the cold air that rushed in did little to cool me down.

"Front door or back?"

"The key fits both front and back doors."

"No, which door do I use when I come for supper? And do I knock or just walk in?" he asked. "This is my first day. I don't want to start out on the wrong foot."

"You don't have to knock—but what's the difference in which door you use to come into the house?"

First rule of me being the boss, I thought, *is that we want the hired hands to be comfortable in the house.*

"Back door is less formal," he answered.

"Then by all means, make it that one. We aren't going to follow proper rules anymore," I told him.

"Anymore?" he asked.

"It's a long story for another day," I told him.

He took the paper bags back into the kitchen and began to unload the groceries. "I'll look forward to hearing it."

I headed back to the house but stopped at the big pecan tree at the edge of the yard to collect not only my thoughts but my emotions. I fanned myself with my hand. I could not allow my hormones to get ahead of my common sense. My hormones screamed that I'd never been so attracted to a man; common sense said a fling wouldn't work now that Devon had moved onto the farm. If a relationship developed and then flopped, working with him would be awkward.

My thoughts kept running around and around in my head like young squirrels chasing each other around and around the tree. The wind had died down to a gentle breeze, but it was still chilly, and my insides seemed to be cooling down somewhat. Come July, when we were working the fields—watering, plowing, praying for a good crop—we would welcome a cool wind. By then, we wouldn't be able to beg, borrow, or steal the slightest hint of a breeze. Whenever I'd complained about the heat, Luis told me that the wind blew constantly in the Texas Panhandle until the last day of June, and that was a good thing. When I'd asked him why, he'd said because it got so hot after that day that if the wind blew, it would cook the skin right off our bones.

I was so engrossed in my roller-coaster emotions and thoughts that I didn't even realize I was walking again until I'd reached the porch. I could hear voices inside, which meant that Celeste had come home. It wasn't the first time I'd stood outside the house in the semidarkness and heard people talking. From when I was a little girl, I had been pretty good at eavesdropping, but back then, it had been either my mother telling Mandy that she could go home as soon as all the dishes were done or else Luis and my father discussing the schedule for the next week.

"I want a home, not a house, and I don't want to be a boss. I want to—at the very least—be friends with whoever becomes the foreman here on Meadow Falls," I muttered.

The scent of rain off in the distance filled the air, and the wind picked up as if it agreed with me. Shivers went down my spine at the sound of wind blowing through the bare limbs of the redbud tree at the edge of the yard. Could it be telling me that things needed to be settled where those two pictures still in my pocket were concerned?

Although the noise didn't send an answer to me, it brought to mind a memory that I had completely forgotten. But now that it was in my head, I couldn't shake it.

I was on my way back to the house after spending time with Mandy and Celeste. I must have been about seventeen, because my mother was still alive but had already been diagnosed with cancer. In the middle of the yard, a ray of light shining from the supply-room window in the workshop caught my eye. The tightness I'd had in my chest that night hit me again, and I whipped around to check things even though what had happened back then was years ago. I took several breaths and reminded myself that this was a memory. It was not happening in real time.

The memory played on like a movie in my mind. As I had jogged across the grass, I'd kept telling myself that Luis could be in the supply room, taking stock of what we had in the way of oil, transmission fluids, and all the other things we'd need when we started servicing the machinery during planting time.

A shadow off to my left had registered in my peripheral vision, but I had figured it was just one of the hired hands out for an evening walk. The crew had arrived the week before, and planting would start the next day. The odor of whiskey mixed with something I couldn't identify hit me when I entered the barn. The supply room door was wide open, and the window was up, but the place was still scorching hot.

My father was sitting on an old worn sofa with a bottle of Jim Beam on the table and an empty glass in his hands. I had never seen him so disheveled before or after that night. His shirt was wrinkled, unbuttoned, and pulled free of his jeans. The hair on his chest was flat from sweating. His boots had been tossed over across the small room, and there was the distinct scent of something floral in the air. The light night breeze had picked up the smell of the red roses from the backyard.

"Your mother is restless," he said. "You should sleep on the sofa in her room tonight."

"Yes, sir," I said.

"She just wasn't my type, Angela Marie," he had whispered, "but she was good for the farm."

There had to be an underlying story there, but I was just glad that I wasn't in trouble, and shocked to see my father in that condition. Who was not his type? He didn't drink very often—mostly just socially—and even back then, he usually had a whiskey sour. I had never seen him drunk, and it could have been the whiskey talking.

"Who wasn't your type?" I had asked.

"Go on back to the house and leave me alone," he'd snapped.

I didn't ask any more questions, and I never mentioned that night—not ever.

"Why would I remember that?" I asked myself as the memory faded. I pulled the pictures from my pocket and looked at them again. Why did that memory spark something about these pictures? Again, I didn't get a single answer from the universe, so I tucked them away and went inside to find Celeste stirring stew and Mandy sitting at the table.

"How did Devon like the house?" Celeste asked.

"He loved it," I answered, and got plates and bowls out of the cabinet. "He said it reminded him of his grandparents' house when they lived out on the farm. I told him supper would be ready in half an hour."

"Is he eating with us or . . ." Mandy asked.

"*We* promised him room and board if he would take the job," I answered. "But as boss, I've decided that things are going to be different around here from now on. No more separation between the master of the farm and the hired hands, so Devon will be eating his meals right here with us. And at the end of the day, if he wants to prop up his feet and watch a movie with us or play a game of gin rummy, then he can."

"That's a good thing—and, honey, there's no *we* involved here. *I* offered him room and board, not you or Celeste." Mandy chuckled. "But I wouldn't advise you to start offering to feed the whole harvest crew every evening."

"Never!" I declared, glad that her mind had switched gears and she remembered what had happened.

"Thank God," Celeste declared. "I love to cook, but I wouldn't want to have to put out enough food for a whole crew every day."

"We will keep taking sandwiches to the barn for their lunches, won't we? I always enjoy visiting with all the folks when they take their noon break," Mandy said. "Speaking of that, we could have popped one of those funeral casseroles into the microwave for supper tonight."

"Stew made from the leftover Sunday roast is better than a casserole." Celeste took an apron from off a hook and slipped it over her head. "I boiled a couple of potatoes and threw in a couple of handfuls of baby carrots. We have plenty of rolls left to go with it."

"Yes, ma'am, Captain Murphy." I saluted her.

She returned a sharp salute. "Right back at you. Thank you for being the first one to call me that since I was eighteen—I took my maiden name back when Trevor divorced me, so I'm legally a Murphy again," Celeste said.

Mandy giggled and shuffled toward the pantry. "I'm going to get out an apple pie that got brought in here last week. If we put it in a warm oven, it'll be ready for dessert. There's still half a gallon of ice cream in the freezer, too."

"Granny, we can get that," Celeste scolded.

"I'm old," Mandy said, "but I'm not dead yet, and I'm the one who offered room and board to Devon, so I can and will help. Did you add a couple of beef bouillon cubes and a little onion powder to the potato water to flavor up the stew?"

"Who's really in charge now?" Celeste whispered.

"'What your mother says is important,'" I said, quoting Mandy from years ago, "'but what I say is the law.'"

"And there were consequences when you broke it, right?" Mandy reminded us as she brought out an apple pie, put it in the oven, and then set the temperature on low.

"Yes, ma'am." I raised my eyebrows.

I wanted to ask what had happened to Roxy when she broke the rules, but I held my tongue, even though those two pictures were burning holes in my pocket.

"I've always loved stew that is made from pot roast as much as I love the original meal," Mandy said. "Harrison wouldn't eat leftovers of any kind, and your mother seldom ate any kind of meat, Angela Marie. So rather than throw them out, I took them home with me at the end of the day. Inez gave me permission to do that when Harrison was a little boy, and I just kept right on doing it after she was gone. Back when I first started cooking for the folks here in the house, I often took enough home in the evening to help feed the hired hands their supper because those folks didn't eat leftovers either."

"Did my mother like to cook?" I had never seen her do anything in the kitchen other than give Mandy orders about what to fix each day for that week.

"Sophia couldn't boil water," Mandy answered. "Her job wasn't to cook, clean, or do anything other than be beautiful."

She was good for the farm. My father's words from that night all those years ago came back to me again.

"So, she was a trophy wife?" I asked.

"I guess that's what folks would call her these days." Mandy sat down at the table. "Harrison needed someone like her. She had a real good business head on her shoulders until she got sick—but, honey, she got you trained before she passed away. And the angels in heaven couldn't have done a better job of singing than she did. Inez used to say that her brother wanted her to live with him and his family. With that singing voice, she would draw a crowd into the church."

"I never heard her sing," Celeste said.

"Some birds never sing again when you put them in a cage," Mandy said with a sad smile. "She sang in church a couple of times, but after you were born, she never sang again."

"What took her song away?" I asked.

"Hello, the house," Devon greeted us as he came through the back door.

"Dammit!" I swore under my breath.

"Angela Marie!" Mandy scolded, but then her expression changed when Devon came into the kitchen. "Come right in. Pour yourself a glass of tea. Supper will be ready in a few minutes." She motioned toward the pitcher and the glasses on the counter.

"What can I do to help?" Devon asked.

"Not a thing tonight," Celeste answered. "But maybe another night, you can make us one of your famous lasagnas."

"Anytime. Just name the day, and I'll get one ready," Devon said.

He was sexy, he knew about peanut farming, *and* he cooked? And the most important thing was that so far, I hadn't seen him in a white shirt.

Chapter Seven

I must have looked at those pictures twenty times over the next couple of days. I was beginning to understand what I had heard about never really knowing another person. The man who'd hidden the two pictures in his dresser drawer could not be my father—a man who was just as staid as my mother had been. Had she driven him to drink? Or were the two photographs his own personal demons? The memory of him disheveled out in the barn must have stuck in my mind because it was so unusual for him.

I tried to chase the vision from my head and focus on the work Devon and I were doing. We were still working on getting the tractors ready for planting season, and it was taking longer than I had thought it might. Space in the maintenance barn was tight, with a big piece of machinery in it, so every time I crossed paths with Devon, either my shoulder or my arm brushed against his. He must not have feel the heat that I did, or else he would make a really good poker player since his expression never changed.

"What's on your mind?" Devon asked as we were changing the transmission oil in the third tractor he'd driven into the maintenance barn that day. Mandy and Celeste had been right about him being the right person for the job. With each tractor, we changed out all the fluids, I wrote down dates and hours used, and then either Celeste or I would transfer the data to the computer that evening. I fussed at myself to keep my mind on my job and stop acting like a teenage girl with her first crush.

"Are you ever surprised by the actions of someone that you thought you knew—maybe not well, but at least a little bit?" I asked, wondering if I was talking about Trevor or my father.

"All the time." He stopped what he was doing and leaned on the front of the tractor. "I thought Celeste and Trevor were the perfect married couple. I was blown away when I found out that he had been cheating on her all that time."

"Me too," I said. "I still see red when I think about how he duped all of us."

"I read once that seeing red is what happens when the emotional state supersedes the rational one, and the shock or anger makes it hard to process things," he said. "Just another bit of useless information that's stored away in my mind."

"Very seldom has my emotional state been allowed to get ahead of my rational one, but it did when she told us what he had done." Had that reaction happened because my father was gone and there would be no blowback from him if I pitched a fit?

"I'm here anytime you want to talk about anything," he said.

"Thank you, but not yet," I answered.

He went back to work. "Well, the offer doesn't have an expiration date."

"I'll remember that." I wanted to talk about the pictures in the bib pocket of my overalls and the memory of my father out in the work-shop, but I just couldn't—not until I figured out a few things. I told myself that I kept the pictures on my person because I couldn't leave them behind for fear Mandy or Celeste might find them. But what I wanted most was to talk about this attraction I felt toward Devon. Celeste and I had always shared everything, but how could I admit that I felt something for a man I'd only known a few days?

"So, you are a muller." Devon checked the transmission-suction screen and then did the same with the front-axle oil level.

"What's a muller? Is there a cure for it, or is it terminal?" I was shocked that I could tease about anything.

Devon must be good for the farm. When the same words my father had said about my mother came back to my mind, the idea brought me up short.

He wiped his hands on a red shop rag. "It's not terminal, but it's not healthy. You analyze everything for days—maybe weeks or months—before you decide to talk about it. That's not really a good thing. Anger or frustration can lay down there in your gut and fester, you know."

"I thought stuff like that laid in the heart, not the gut," I argued, even though I not only knew but also felt what he was talking about. For years, so many things had festered, and only since my father's death had anything begun to make a bit of sense.

He closed the hood on the tractor and patted it. "All done with this one, Angela Marie. But remember that whatever can make you see red stays inside you until you get it out."

I stared at him so long that he shrugged and said, "I'm just speaking from experience, but . . . I'll change the subject. *You* surprise me more than the situation with Trevor and Celeste."

"How's that?" I picked up all the tools we'd been using and carried them to the worktable, not sure if I wanted to hear how I had surprised him.

"You own this place, and yet you are out here working right along beside me," he answered.

"Working is the only thing I've ever known. It's been my escape as well as my . . ." I couldn't find the right word.

"As well as your salvation?" he asked.

"Pretty much." Working with Luis and Mandy had saved me, so that was no lie.

"What's your very first memory?" he asked.

I was almost offended for him to ask such a personal thing—but then, the conversation had edged around the idea of escapes and salvation.

"That would be when Celeste and I used to beg Mandy to tell us a story. We loved the one about where Meadow Falls got its name."

"And?" Devon raised a dark eyebrow. "What was that story . . . if that's not too personal? I don't mean to pry."

I thought of that old saying about being hung for a sheep as well as a lamb. I knew it was a silly thing to come to mind, but if he was going to stick around Meadow Falls, maybe he should know a little of the history.

"Mandy's stories always started with, 'Once upon a time,'" I said with a smile. "So, once upon a time, there was a prince who married a princess. She loved the prince so much that she followed him to a faraway land that was so flat that dirt and sky met out there where the sun came up and where it went down every day. But she was sad because she missed her beloved waterfall at her parents' castle, in a county where there were lots of hills and green trees and flowers grew in abundance. So the prince dammed up the stream on this property and made her a waterfall. They named their new farm Meadow Falls because of that little place," I told him, giving him the short form. "Mandy had made the story go on a lot longer, but that's the core of it."

"That's pretty," Devon said. "My Granny didn't tell me fairy tales, but when we all got together at family reunions, I loved listening to the stories that the old folks told. I didn't care if I heard them the year before; they still entertained me."

A family reunion—the idea made me downright jealous. "I would love to have enough family to have a reunion."

"They are so much fun, and my favorite part is hearing all the stories," he said. "My first memory was when I was about four years old, and my Uncle Chester told a story about his time in the military during World War II. I played soldier for a whole year after that, and it's probably the reason that I decided to go into the air force. What's your second memory?"

"My second one is sitting on this stool right here." I sat down on it, picked up a shop rag, and began wiping down a box-end wrench. "I must have been about four years old, because I hadn't started school yet. I didn't want to spend the day cleaning tools in the hot workshop. I wanted to stay in the house with Mandy and play with Celeste, but my father said it was time for me to start learning the business from the ground up. At that age, I had no idea what he was talking about, and I cried when my mother dressed me in a new pair of bibbed overalls and sent me outside with our foreman, Luis, who told me that, someday, I would be glad for the lessons because I would own the whole farm and that nobody wants to start off a day with nasty tools. By the time I started school"—I pointed to the pegboard, where all the tools hung in their right places—"I knew the names of everything hanging on that wall over there, and I could fetch them for him without a problem."

"And they were always spotless," he said with a grin as he slid onto the stool across the table from me and used the shop rag that he'd wiped his hands on to start cleaning tools himself. "Sounds like you got some of the same lessons I did. My grandpa didn't use those exact words, but the meaning was the same. Did you get paid to do your first jobs?"

"My father said my pay was a roof over my head, clothes on my back, and food on the table to eat," I answered. "But sometimes Luis would give me a dollar at the end of a day."

"Did Celeste work with you?" Devon asked.

"Nope, and I was so jealous of her." I had to use a little extra elbow grease to get the crescent wrench shiny again. "She got to stay in the house with Mandy, and I imagined that I was missing all kinds of stories. The first week that my father made me tag along with Luis, I cried every day."

"And after that?" Devon asked.

"Mandy sat me down and gave me a talking-to. She said that crying was not going to change anything and if I would just do what I was told, she and Celeste would bring snacks out to us for our fifteen-minute break in the middle of the morning and afternoon. And she promised that she would save the stories until bedtime." I'd never thought about how she had finagled things in the house to be able to take that time to bring a thermos of milk and pastries or cookies to the workshop twice a day.

"Then were you okay?" He lined up the tools on the right side as he cleaned them.

"No, but I learned that crying didn't work with my father and that my mother wasn't going to step in and save me from having to wear bibbed overalls and getting dirt under my fingernails." I heard a bit of bitterness in my tone. "I guess the lessons were a good thing, though, because now I know every step of the peanut-farming process from cleaning a crescent wrench to taking the crop to market."

"That's a silver lining in a really black cloud," Devon said.

"I guess it is," I agreed with a nod as I finished the last tool, slid off the stool, and put them all away in their proper places.

"I'm wondering if Luis and my grandfather were related," Devon said. "Grandpa said that when he needed a hammer, he didn't want to reach for it only to find he had a pair of gardening shears in his hand."

"Luis was originally from Mexico. Was your grandpa?" I asked.

"Not quite, but almost," Devon answered. "My grandpa was from Baja, California. I visited with relatives out there when I was stationed in that state, and they still hold with some of the customs, like Day of the Dead. They made me feel right at home and told me stories about my grandfather."

I snuck little peeks at him as he worked. He must have inherited his black hair from his grandfather's side of the family, but those clear blue eyes had to have come from his maternal side.

As if he could read my mind, he said, "My mother is Irish to the bone. Red hair and blue eyes, and her maiden name was O'Malley. I'm a good mix of both my parents, with a little of my grandparents thrown in for good luck."

"Me too," I said. "My great-grandmother, Victoria, had red hair, but I got my eyes from my father. Looks like we're done for the day. Are you ready for supper?" That earlier little thought nagged at my mind—Celeste's eyes were the same color as mine.

"Yes, ma'am. I'm really hungry," he said with a nod. "Three tractors down, seven to go. We should have them all ready by the end of next week."

I picked up my work coat and shoved my arms down into the sleeves. "Then during that first week of harvest, they'll all run smoothly from eight to ten hours a day. On Saturday morning, we bring them into the shop and do this all over again."

"How do you do that?"

"We work weekends," I answered. "We have to keep good records on each tractor. If we didn't, things could get very confusing. After fifty hours, we have to redo everything we're doing right now. We'll run them hard from daylight to dark that first week, then we'll put about three of our top hands—the ones that know about machinery the best—to work and get the tractors ready to go back out on Monday morning."

Devon followed me outside. "Won't they complain about not having any time off?"

"The guys who work on the machinery will get time-and-a-half pay, and then they get Monday and Tuesday off with regular pay to rest up," I explained. "It's a process, but Luis and I made it work."

Devon frowned. "It's doable, but it'll be a rough couple of days."

"Yep, it is, but it's only for two or three weekends. Just until we get the crops in and ready to take to market," I agreed and got a whiff of something that smelled like chili wafting out across the yard. I sent up a silent prayer of gratitude: *Thank you, Jesus, for sending Celeste back to us. And for dropping Devon to us.*

❖　❖　❖

Winter had never been my favorite season. The cold didn't bother me like it did Mandy, with her aging joints, but the evenings were very long. To pass the time, Mandy and I binge-watched seasons of her favorite shows on television. She had watched *The Golden Girls* and *Justified* so many times that she knew the dialogue.

That evening, after Devon had helped clean up the kitchen after supper, he disappeared out into the darkness, leaving us three women alone for another long night. Mandy left her cane in the kitchen and shuffled into the living room, where she claimed one of the two chairs that had a matching hassock.

Celeste sat down in the other one. "We really should take the Christmas tree down or else we need to decorate it for Valentine's Day."

"Let it stay up until the end of the week," Mandy said. "I love the holidays and always hate to see them end."

"It can stay as long as you want," I told her.

The tree was artificial, so it didn't need any maintenance, and it didn't shed like a real one would. If it made Mandy happy, it could sit there until summer. My father had insisted the tree be taken down and put away before New Year's Eve. That's when he and my mother always had a big dinner party at the house. After she died, he'd continued to have the parties for all his cronies, and I was forced to attend, though he'd never speak to me. I'd hated those affairs so much that I usually stayed in the kitchen with Mandy most of the evening. I pushed aside the feelings that caused the visuals of him hobnobbing with his friends to surface. I needed to let go of the past and hug the future, but somehow memories kept coming back to haunt me.

I pulled off my work boots and set them at the end of the sofa and then tossed a throw pillow to the other side. In the process of stretching out, one of the pictures I had hidden away in my shirt pocket fell out on the floor.

"What's that?" Mandy asked.

At least it isn't the one of Roxy, I told myself as I held my breath so long that my chest hurt. "I found it among my father's things. Do you know who Summer Rain was? She signed her name on the picture."

"Yes, I do," Mandy said in a flat voice that I hardly recognized. "Summer Rain was your father's first wife—or maybe I should say Harrison's *fake* wife."

"I hear a good story coming," Celeste said.

I gasped. "My father was married before my mother?"

Had I heard her right? Why had no one ever mentioned that before?

"Summer Rain? Was that really her name, or was it a nickname?" Celeste asked with half a giggle.

"Did she and my father have children? Do I have a brother or sister out there somewhere?" I asked. "And why on earth would anyone name a child Summer Rain?"

I should have said something about Roxy looking so much like her, but I couldn't bring myself to show the picture to Mandy. Not until I figured out why my father had hidden the picture. I glanced over at Celeste.

"One question at a time, please," Mandy replied with a long sigh. "To start with, that is or was her real name, the one on her birth certificate—or so she declared when Inez asked her about it. She'd been born to a couple of hippie-type people who seldom stayed in one place for very long. When she was sixteen, her folks moved from somewhere in the Tennessee mountains over to Levelland and tried to start one of those commune things, but it never got off the ground. Harrison met her when he was in college. I never knew where, but he was . . ."

"Was what?" I pressured.

Mandy seemed to struggle with words. "He was different back when he was a young man than when you were growing up. I think folks today would say that he felt like he was entitled to all the benefits of being a rich kid and didn't want any of the responsibilities. Back then, I just said he was wild as a March hare. Inez insisted that he be given a new truck for his sixteenth birthday and that he be put on the payroll when he was fourteen. Clifford didn't like it, but she had lost all those babies and couldn't have any more after Harrison was born, so he let her have her way. He did make the boy work, though—just like your father made you learn the business, Angela Marie."

"Is this going to be a little-prince story?" Celeste asked.

"Depends on what you girls want to hear," Mandy said.

"Tell me the truth, please," I begged. "And don't sugarcoat it with a story of how Summer Rain was a princess."

Celeste finally picked up the picture and handed it to Mandy. "We're adults now. We can handle the real story, Granny."

Mandy stared at the photograph for several minutes. I crossed my fingers and hoped that she didn't sink into one of those black holes where her memory was concerned. It must have worked because she laid the picture to the side, sighed, and started talking.

"Summer was the downfall of your father. I believe he really loved that woman, even with all her back-to-nature ways. One of the biggest arguments he ever had with his mother was over Summer wanting to get rid of Inez's rosebushes and plant an herb garden. That might have been the start of the reason she didn't stick around here very long."

"She left him?" I asked.

"Yes," Mandy answered. "But that's getting to the end of the story, and you need to hear all of it."

"Once upon a time?" I asked.

Mandy gave me one of her best smiles. "That's right. Once upon a time, there was a young man named Harrison who hated the peanut business."

"Okay, Granny," Celeste said. "Now tell us the real story."

Another smile, only this time it was impish. "Okay, starting again: Harrison not only didn't like peanut farming, he didn't like his father for making him learn it. He was a sweet baby and little boy, but he never liked getting his hands dirty. The drinking and carousing started when he was about fifteen and got worse after he got that new truck. Inez thought he would outgrow it—but then, so did I when it came to my daughter, Emma, who had a little bit of a wild streak in her. Nothing compared to Harrison. The difference was that boys didn't—and still don't—get pregnant at seventeen like Emma did. Whether the world wants to admit it or not, boys and girls are judged different."

She paused. The smile vanished. "I need to keep the story straight. I think I already told you that my own Emma was ten years old when Harrison was born. All of us—Inez, me, and Emma—doted on him. Looking back, that was probably the wrong thing to do, because he wanted to do just what he wanted, and mostly we let him do just that. If he wanted to draw or paint for hours, he did just that. He was almost six years old when Emma had Roxy. She didn't have time to help him paint his pictures, read to him anytime he wanted, or take him out to the creek to play in it, or any of the other things that she did anytime he had a whim. About that same time, Harrison started to school. Looking back, he started acting like . . ." She paused and scratched her head. "What is it y'all call it these days—enriched?"

"Entitled?" I asked.

She nodded. "That's it! Things got worse and worse, and then when Emma died, he tormented Roxy about her mama's ghost coming up out of the grave. I wanted to take a switch to him, but Inez would have fired me on the spot for even thinking such a thing."

Patience is not my personal virtue, so I wanted her to tell me more about Summer, not talk forever about my father.

"Harrison was smart and quite the manipulator—always talking someone else into doing his work for him, even here on the farm. When he got to high school, he was suspended several times for cheating, and he just barely had enough credits to graduate. He wanted to go off to a fancy college, but his grades weren't good enough. Clifford used his influence to get him into one that he could commute to, but he insisted on living on campus. Inez confided in me that she hoped Harrison would flunk out and hit rock bottom, but he didn't—probably because he figured out how to cheat his way through." She paused and picked up the picture to stare at it again.

I hoped that she hadn't forgotten where she was in the story, and I held my breath for a minute before she went on.

"Harrison went to college before harvest that fall after he got out of high school," Mandy said. "We didn't see him again until Christmas, and then he announced that he wouldn't be home in the summer because he had to make up the classes that he hadn't passed. According to him, it wasn't his fault, and he used every other excuse in the book—the professors were too hard, the little high school here in Meadow hadn't prepared him for the classes, and so on. Clifford wanted to cut off his support right then, but Inez talked him into giving Harrison another semester and the summer to do better. She kept telling me that he was just getting his wild oats sown, and he would straighten out and realize what his responsibilities were in a year or two."

"Did he?" I asked, hoping that Mandy wouldn't slip into a forgetful moment and go off on a tangent about someone else.

"No, he did not," Mandy said and shook her head. "He got worse instead of better. Finally, after two years, he got caught with whiskey and drugs in his dorm, and they kicked him out. Inez hoped that he had really hit bottom and would be ready to settle down."

She paused and sighed again. "I felt so sorry for her, but by then, I had my own problems. Roxy was almost a teenager, and she was getting hard for me to handle."

"What happened? Was that when he settled down and got to be so strict?"

"Nope," Mandy answered. "He came in that summer with Summer on his arm, saying that they'd gotten married, and she would be living here on the farm with him. Inez went to bed for a week, and I thought for sure we'd have to put her in one of those places that take care of folks with a nervous breakdown."

"And Clifford?" Celeste asked.

"He ignored Harrison and the woman. The tension in this house was so thick that it almost suffocated me. Roxy grumbled about helping me out in the kitchen in those days, but she liked the money she made. We could at least go home at night, but poor Clifford and Inez had no place to get away from it," Mandy said. "I was so angry with Harrison that I cornered him and told him what he was doing to his mother."

"Did it help?" I asked.

"Not one bit. That was back in the days when I was running the staff here at the house. We had a crew of three cleaning ladies that came in every day, plus a cook and two gardeners. And the peanut business was in full swing. He said that he and his wife were on their honeymoon, and after harvest season, they were going to travel to Europe for a year."

"How was he going to do that?" Celeste asked.

"He thought his parents would give him his inheritance and then he'd leave Meadow Falls," Mandy answered. "His big plan was to show Summer Rain the world and then settle down and be an artist, maybe in India or Africa. To get ready for the world tour, he took her shopping every Saturday, and they'd come home with bags full of expensive stuff. Then Inez finally confronted him and took away all his credit cards." Mandy's voice had an edge to it that I hadn't heard very often. "I could have wrung Summer's neck for the hissy fit she threw over that, and Harrison's right along with hers for the way he was acting—like he was the king and his parents worked for him."

"Did they have children?" I asked when Mandy stopped and caught her breath.

"No, thank God," Mandy gasped.

"How long did their marriage last?" Celeste asked.

"About three months. Right in the middle of the busy season, she ran away with one of her old boyfriends. She left Harrison a note saying that she couldn't and wouldn't be tied down to just one man and that he hadn't lived up to the promises he had made her. According to what she wrote, the note would suffice as a bill of divorcement. She had jumped backwards over a broom or some other such nonsense. Clifford and Inez were frantic about what she might ask for in a divorce, but Harrison told us that she and her parents didn't believe in marriage licenses issued by the government," Mandy explained. "I'd never seen Clifford cry, not even when Harrison acted like a jackass, but he and Inez broke down and wept on each other's shoulders in relief that day. Harrison was furious and blamed them for his wife leaving. If they'd been nicer to her, she would have stayed until they could go off to some faraway country for him to be an artist. The tension was even worse after that, but Roxy was a teenager, and . . ." Mandy sighed. The long-winded tale was more than a little bit anticlimactic, especially when Mandy sighed a second time and then covered a yawn with her hand. "I think I'll turn in early. I've got a book in my room, and I want to read a few chapters in before I go to sleep. If I let it go too long, I'll have to start all over."

"What's the title?" Celeste asked.

"I don't remember." Mandy stood up and headed out of the living room. "If it was a book I read years ago, like *Gone With the Wind*, I could tell you, but this forgetting disease is stealing my short-term memory a bit at a time. Don't look at me like that, Angela Marie. I knew long before you did that my brain wasn't working right. I've accepted it, and you girls should, too. Y'all don't stay up too late. Watch some of that *Justified* on the television. Raylan Givens kind of reminds me of Devon."

"How's that?" Celeste asked. "I don't see anything in the two of them that's alike."

"It's in their smiles and that strut they've both got when they walk." Mandy pointed to the picture of Summer Rain. "Good night—and, Angela Marie, you can burn that picture. I'd rather lose my memory about that woman."

"Yes, ma'am." I slipped the picture back into my pocket. "But one more question, please: Did my father straighten up after Summer left him?"

"No, darlin', he just got worse," she answered as she made her way across the floor.

"Are you really going to burn it?" Celeste whispered.

"Nope—not for a while, anyway," I answered. "I wonder where Summer went and if she's even still alive."

Celeste picked up the remote and turned on the television. "Are you disappointed that there's not a sister or brother out there?"

"Not really, but if there was, I'd like to know. Do you think my father left behind a kid or two in his wild times?" I asked.

"Probably not," Celeste replied. "If he did, they would be swarming to Meadow Falls, wanting their share of the farm. But if any come around saying they're your long-lost brothers or sisters, we do have DNA tests these days."

"We should each take one of those," I suggested. That would prove for sure that my father hadn't had a fling with Roxy and having that picture meant nothing.

"Do you want to have a sibling?" Celeste asked.

I moved over to the chair that Mandy had vacated. "I don't know. Maybe."

That could explain why Celeste and I had the same color eyes and had always had a sister bond. But then, it was probably just wishful thinking on my part.

"What are we watching?" I asked as Celeste flipped through the channels until she found what she wanted.

"Since Granny mentioned *Justified*, I'm going to find some reruns. I don't see a resemblance of that character in the show to Devon at all," Celeste said.

The first episode showed the character, Raylan Givens, sitting down to a table with who I supposed would be the villain.

"What do you think? Does he look a thing like Devon?" Celeste asked.

"Devon is better looking than either one of those men," I said. "I hope Devon has got some good running shoes."

"Why?" Celeste asked.

"Because every woman in Terry County is going to be chasing him as soon as they know he's on the farm."

"You are probably right," Celeste said with a giggle. "Are you one of those women?"

"No, I am not!" I felt heat rising in my face and the need to cross my fingers behind my back like I did as a child when I told a little white lie. "I've got a business to run—and besides, I'm not so sure there's a man out there honest enough to earn my trust."

"Crawl in this canoe with me," Celeste said. "We'll paddle it together."

"Hold it steady," I told her. "Together we can conquer the world."

Chapter Eight

Getting the machinery ready for another year was so familiar to me that I could have done it blindfolded. That left me plenty of time to think about all the questions I had about my past, my father's rebellious years, and even Roxy. I didn't know a lot about her, other than she had given birth to Celeste, then left Meadow Falls with a boy who'd come with the harvest crew that year. I hadn't even been born that year, so I never knew her. The picture of her out by the willow tree popped into my mind. I didn't need the two pictures—now stashed away in my dresser drawer—in front of me anymore. Everything from those two women's sexy poses to their tattoos was burned into my memory.

I did the math and figured out that Summer and my father had been young, but they were adults when they had their fake marriage. The same with my father and Roxy—both adults. But I wondered if he had taken that picture of Roxy because she reminded him of his first love.

The question plagued me all day, but at the end of the afternoon, I had no answer—just an empty spot in my heart.

Devon and I had finished the last tractor the day before, and that day we were servicing the old work truck. Long ago, it had started out as a white vehicle, just like all the ones my father had bought, but now it had rust spots and looked like it was ready to be hauled to the scrap-yard. I couldn't send it off to that great junk place in the sky when the engine still purred like a kitten, so we were changing the oil, checking all the other fluids, and putting a new set of tires on it. Devon had proved that he knew his way around anything that ran on four wheels. That he didn't think we had to carry on a constant conversation while we worked was another plus. Like it had been with Luis, it seemed that both of us could predict what the other one needed at just the right time, and that made for smooth sailing.

"That's it for the week." I tightened the last lug bolt on a new tire we'd put on the truck. "Are you anxious to get away and go see your grandparents for the next couple of days?"

"They are on a little day trip with the senior citizens of their church," he said as he carried all the tools to the worktable. "I'll go down there on Sunday and go to church with them and then take them out to dinner. I thought maybe we'd go ahead and get another tractor ready tomorrow, unless you've got other plans? Maybe a hot date?"

"No date, so I'm game to work tomorrow." I picked up a shop rag and went to work on one of the last two crescent wrenches that needed cleaning. I hadn't even had a little summer fling for several years. I was up at the crack of dawn and worked until almost midnight, either on the farm or in the office. That left no time or energy for romance of any kind.

He looked shocked. "A beautiful woman like you doesn't have a boyfriend?"

"Have you got a girlfriend?" I fired back.

He raised an eyebrow. "Show me yours, and I'll show you mine."

"You go first," I told him.

"No girlfriend at the present. I've only been in one serious relationship, but that ended two years ago," he answered. "I'm thirty-eight years old, went into the military right out of high school, but I do *not* have a halo."

His age didn't surprise me. I had figured that out by noting his birthday on the tax forms he had filled out on Monday. The fact that he hadn't been an angel was not a big shocker either. Military guys had a reputation for letting off steam—most of the time in places that involved liquor. But only one serious relationship in twenty years? Were all the women he had met crazy?

"Your turn," he said as he laid a tool over to the side and picked up another one.

"No boyfriend," I replied. "If I had a halo, it would be crooked, and if I had wings, they would smell a little like smoke. I've never trusted anyone enough to be in a serious relationship—and besides, I've got too much on my plate to think about relationships."

"All work and no play . . ."

"Makes a profitable peanut farm," I finished for him.

"But does it make a happy owner of said farm?" he asked.

"According to my father, happiness is a good crop that pays the bills and stashes away a goodly sum in the savings account," I said.

"How about according to Angela Marie? What makes happiness for her?" he asked.

"I wouldn't know," I answered. "I was never given the chance to think about that."

He put the tools he had cleaned back on the pegboard and then came back to hike a hip on the stool on the other side of the worktable. "Why? Didn't you have dreams that made you happy just thinking about them when you were young?"

"I learned early on that my dreams didn't matter," I answered. *Was that the way my father felt?* "I was here to do what I was told."

Had he dreamed of living far away from all this with Summer Rain? Had he simply raised me to have no dreams so that I wouldn't be disappointed in my life?

"What about now?" Devon asked. "If you could be anywhere in the world today, doing anything you wanted to do, what would it be?"

"That's a big question," I whispered. "I'll think about it for a few weeks or months and get back to you. What about you? If you could be anywhere, doing anything, what would you be doing?"

"I'd be right here, working with you. I choose to love where I am and what I'm doing every day. That makes for a happy heart—not my words but my grandfather's. I feel like I'm one lucky man to have a job that I enjoy. And as a bonus, I get to work with a woman who is intelligent as well as beautiful."

"Flattery will get you nothing but fried chicken for supper," I told him.

It had been so long since I'd flirted that I wasn't sure if that's what we were doing.

"My favorite food in the whole world." He led the way to the door and held it open for me.

He's showing you that he's a gentleman. All you need is a kiss good night, and it would be a date. Celeste's teasing voice was in my head.

In your craziest dreams, I argued with her.

Mandy said a quick grace before we started passing food around the small kitchen table that evening. Something was on her mind—or maybe something was lacking in her mind, because she wasn't her usual talkative self. Perhaps she was trying to remember something and couldn't get a hold on it. I was glad that her dementia hadn't gotten worse when my father passed away so suddenly.

"Why aren't we eating at the dining room table?" she finally asked. "Has Harrison decided that since Celeste is home and you insist on Devon eating with us, we have to have our meals in the kitchen?"

"Granny, Harrison died two weeks ago, remember?" Celeste answered.

Mandy frowned, cocked her head to one side, and then teared up. "That's right. He loved his fried chicken. I guess that's what made me think he was still alive. So many are gone . . . Edward, Clifford, Inez, Emma, Roxy, and now Harrison." She dabbed her eyes with a napkin. "I'm sorry that he didn't live to have some with us tonight, but I like sitting here with you kids instead of in the dining room with just me and him and Angela Marie. Did he die of a broken heart because Summer left him for that no-account Billy Grady?"

"No, he had an acute heart attack," I answered. "Who was Billy Grady?"

Mandy's expression reminded me of what Celeste and I had seen on her face when we were being scolded back when we were little girls. "He was the one that Summer ran away with. Harrison's heart was broken and couldn't ever be fixed. That's what killed him. Billy Grady was one of her old boyfriends." She frowned and blinked several times, as if trying to remember him. "I wondered if he might have been your father, Celeste, but Roxy told me there was no way, since she didn't meet him until she was already pregnant with you." She lowered her voice. "I figure that she wasn't sure who you belonged to, since she flirted with so many guys back then. But enough about that, tonight. Let's talk about something else."

That wouldn't have been easy for Celeste to hear, and I noticed that her eyes filled with tears. But she blinked them all way. "Why don't you ever want to talk about my mother, Granny?"

"Talking about her makes me sad," Mandy said.

"Where did Summer go with Billy Grady?" I asked, determined to clear up a few answers connected to Roxy.

Mandy just shrugged. "Summer said where she was going in the note she left for Harrison, but I didn't ask. I figured it was good riddance."

I didn't even think to record what she was telling us, but I repeated the name several times in my head so I wouldn't forget it. Later, I would write every detail in the journal I was keeping.

"That was kind of harsh," Devon said. "A man deserves to be told that kind of thing in person—at least, that's my opinion."

Mandy smiled across the table at him. "*Rude* might as well have been her middle name. Now, after supper we need to get that Christmas tree taken down and all the decorations taken to the attic. I'm surprised that Harrison has let it stay up this long."

"I'll be glad to help," Devon offered.

"See," Mandy said, and cut her eyes to me, "I was right to hire this young man, but I'm glad that Summer is gone. She flirted with all the men on the farm, and Harrison went out to the workshop and drank too much when she did that kind of thing."

Had he been angry at my mother the night I found him drinking and in such a mess so many years after Summer had left? Mother had already been bedfast by that time. What could they have argued about? Was it about Summer or Roxy?

"Didn't Harrison usually hire the cleaning ladies to put the tree up and then take it down?" Celeste asked.

"Yes, but Angela Marie is doing things different now." Mandy's eyes brightened like they did when she finally got a grip on things again. "We're eating at the kitchen table like a family, and we're going to take that tree down tonight. Next year at Christmas, we'll have the fun of putting it up ourselves."

"Yes, we will," I agreed. "But right now, would someone pass the hot rolls? I never did master the art of making good bread like Celeste does."

Celeste passed the basket to me. "Granny taught me."

Mandy shot a dirty look my way and then smiled at Devon. "I taught both of them, and Angela Marie is a good cook. She's just being nice tonight."

"I'm nice all the time," I argued.

"Whoa!" Mandy threw up a palm. "You are certainly not nice all the time. You brood like your mother used to. And like her, you don't let your feelings surface very often, but they are like a volcano ready to erupt at any time, and it's not pretty when it does. I only saw Sophia really mad a couple of times in all the years she was here. Most of the time, she was as cool as a cucumber."

Celeste helped herself to another piece of chicken and then sent the platter around the table for everyone to have seconds. "Granny is right: you do brood—"

"I don't brood," I butted in before she could finish. "I mull things over until I get them all straightened out."

Celeste rolled her eyes. "That's the same thing. And before I was so rudely interrupted, I was going to say that I haven't seen you get really mad very many times, but it's 'Katy, bar the door' when you reach that point."

"What does 'Katy, bar the door' even mean?" I asked.

Mandy took another piece of chicken and set the platter down on her end of the table. "It means that there's a storm coming, and the barn doors better get locked down tight."

Devon slid a sly wink my way. "Well, now, that's good to know since I work with her every day. Does she throw things when she's mad?"

"No, she does much worse than that. She gives you the silent treatment and just shoots daggers at you for a while," Mandy answered. "But then she explodes. And don't let Celeste fool you, either. She mulls everything over just as bad as Angela Marie." She finished off the last of her supper. "It took her two years to show Trevor the door."

"Yep, I'm guilty of analyzing everything, even after it's dead and buried," Celeste replied. "But rest assured, when Angela Marie and I make up our minds about something or someone, we move forward and don't look back."

"Enough of this," Mandy declared. "We don't need to air our laundry in front of Devon. We want him to stay, and all this might scare him away."

I had been happy to have the spotlight shift over to Celeste but was even more glad when Mandy said we should change the subject. Having it shine down on me for most of the meal had begun to make me entirely too warm. I wondered, if we switched the bright light over to Devon, what might show up—or even over to Mandy, for that matter.

She had ninety-seven years of stories in her mind. She had told us some of the Meadow Falls secrets, but I wanted more. I wanted to be on top of that iceberg and know everything about my past.

Devon picked up his plate and Mandy's and carried them over to the sink. "It'll take more than women that mull over things and blow up occasionally to scare me away. I've put up with servicemen who pout and who have short fuses, and servicewomen who do the same. I come from a big family. What we're doing tonight is just normal dinner conversation for the Parker family. Is this cake for dessert?"

"It's gingerbread, and that's lemon sauce beside it," Celeste said. "Help yourself."

He cut a large square of gingerbread out of the pan and covered it with warm lemon sauce. "I'm going to have to start running five miles in the morning if I keep eating like this."

"Just say the word, and I'll be ready to go with you at five o'clock," Celeste told him.

"I'm not ready to get up that early just yet. Can I get anyone else dessert?" he asked.

"I want about half as much as you just fixed for yourself," Mandy answered. "And before I forget—which happens more and more lately, it seems—the Second Saturday Meadow Musical is tomorrow night, and Polly and I want to go. Polly don't see well enough to drive at night, and she's got a heavy foot even in the daytime. She scares the bejesus right out of me sometimes. So who's taking us?"

"But, Granny, would that be the right thing to do? Out of respect, shouldn't we be in mourning for a little while?" Celeste asked.

"It'll come around again next month." The few times I had gone to the event, I had felt out of place and spent the whole evening in the shadows, counting the minutes until I could go back to Meadow Falls. The boys my age didn't ask me for a dance or to buy me a soda. At the time, I figured it was because I was a plain Jane—but looking back, I realized a big percentage of them worked on Meadow Falls during the harvest season. They were probably all afraid Harrison would fire them if they made me cry or broke up with me.

"I could be dead by then," Mandy said. "You"—she pointed at me—"need to come out of that hard shell you live inside, and you"—she whipped that finger around at Celeste—"can't just lock yourself away in this place. Polly and I are going to the musical, with or without y'all. If we have a wreck and die on the side of the road because Polly can't see to driving in the dark, then make sure you bury me by Edward."

"Now, that's a guilt trip, for sure," Celeste scolded.

"Take it any way you want it," Mandy snapped.

"I'll drive you," Devon volunteered. "What is this musical thing?"

"Live music—mostly country—and a dance," Celeste answered. "Locals and even some folks from a distance come to sing."

My father and mother had attended the musical every second Saturday. He'd said that it showed the folks around Meadow that he was supportive. I must have been thirteen when he'd said I could go if Mandy wanted to take me. That first night, I had sat in the corner, had a soda pop, and listened to the music. My father had made the rounds like a politician soliciting votes; I was surprised he didn't kiss the babies and dance with the ladies. My mother had played the wife of the most-important man in the county and looked gorgeous in her long denim skirt and Western-cut lace blouse.

Why had my father's death caused so many memories to surface? I shook the thought out of my mind and carried my dirty plate and utensils to the sink. "I'm going to have to save my gingerbread until after we take the tree down. It will be my night snack."

Devon put a square on a dessert plate, scooped some sauce onto it, and served Mandy. "There you go, ma'am. Will you save a dance for me at the musical?"

"Yes, I will." She grinned. "But I've got to warn you, Mr. Parker, I don't kiss on the first date."

He bent at the waist, took her hand in his, and kissed her knuckles. "I'll be the perfect gentleman."

She smiled up at him. "All three of us will be ready at six o'clock. Don't you stand us up."

"Wouldn't dream of it," he said and then sat down in his chair.

And just like that, the mood in the room changed: Mandy was all smiles and happiness, Celeste giggled, and I realized that I was not the little girl who hid in the shadows anymore. Mandy had been right about going to the musical—it was time for me to let go and start living. I wasn't sure I could change, but with Celeste by my side and Mandy cheering us both on, maybe I could take a baby step or two in that direction.

❖ ❖ ❖

I had never really looked at the house where I'd been born and raised. For some strange reason that I couldn't wrap my mind around, I saw it through different eyes that evening. This was *my* house now. It did not belong to any ancestors who had built it. It did not belong to my father. It belonged to me. That meant I could do whatever I wanted with it. Not that I would sell it or raze it, but if I didn't like the way the two seating areas in the enormous living room—built for entertaining a big crowd—were arranged, I could redo it.

Your father will turn over in his grave if you change a single thing. My mother's voice popped into my head, and suddenly I flashed on one of the times I had seen her temper rise to the top.

I was ten years old and had refined my skills at eavesdropping. That night, I'd hidden by the credenza and listened to my parents argue. My father had insisted, through gritted teeth, that my mother call the furniture store the next day and cancel the order for a new sofa. She came back with the threat that if he didn't let her change a few things, she would take me and leave him.

"You can walk out the door anytime you want, and this farm will go right on without you, but Angela Marie stays here," he'd growled at her. "The prenup you signed before we got married will hold up in court. Any children we have will be raised at Meadow Falls, and if you leave me, you will go with what you brought into the marriage, plus ten thousand dollars. We both read and signed it."

She'd yelled and screamed and even thrown the glass of iced tea she had in her hand at him, but she did not get a new sofa. That very night, I figured out that I was just a pawn in their fight for control. My father had to have his way because he had married a woman who was totally different from his first wife. She had probably figured out by then that my father didn't love her like he did Summer Rain.

Blue velvet sofas with curved backs and matching wingback chairs made up a seating arrangement on either end of the room. In the far corner, a chaise longue covered in tapestry sat between a couple of tall bookcases. With the heavy wood paneling on every wall, the room reminded me of exclusive men's clubs—or maybe old Western brothels—I'd seen photos of in magazines and on television. No wonder my mother had wanted to make some changes. So did I, and I had the power to do it. But should I?

Celeste, Mandy, and Devon came in from the kitchen, and I was surprised when the grandfather clock over in the corner chimed seven times. I'd been ahead of them by less than a couple of minutes, and yet I could have written pages in my journal about the argument I'd overheard when I was just a little girl.

"Celeste, have you ever painted—as in, walls, not on canvas?" I asked.

"A couple of times," she said and then giggled. "Trevor said that I painted three coats at once—the wall, the floor, and myself."

"When I oversaw the shops on bases, I had to do some of that to get ready for inspections. What are you thinking about painting?" Devon asked.

"This room for starters." Had I really said that out loud? "Maybe the whole downstairs if we have time before we start planting peanuts."

In for a penny, in for a dollar, came to my mind. I might as well step off the tip of the iceberg and start climbing. Maybe—just maybe—a face-lift on the house would give me some closure.

"Well, halle-dang-lujah!" Mandy clapped her hands. "I don't think much has been changed in this house since the place was first built. Sophia wanted to do a little updating, but Harrison wouldn't allow it."

I was relieved to know that the memory I'd had wasn't just something I'd fabricated in my mind like I had done when I was a child. I'd loved to pretend that my father and mother had taken me to the beach on a vacation. We'd collected seashells and walked barefoot in the sand. That had never happened, and the shells I had in a box in my bedroom had come from the dime store, but Mandy had just verified that the argument I had overheard between my folks was real.

I drew in a lungful of air and let it out in a whoosh. "Well, we're about to do a major overhaul—or at least, as much as we can get done until the planting season starts. This is not what you hired on to do, Devon, but I would appreciate the help. I've never done anything with paint that required more than a sheet of paper and some cheap brushes. I don't want to paint this paneling; I want it taken out completely."

"I'll help, too," Celeste said.

I could already imagine all the dark paneling gone and the walls painted a soft yellow. The heavy drapes could go to the nearest homeless shelter, right along with the furniture, and I'd replace the curtains with something airy and the furniture with something light, comfortable, and inviting.

"Mandy, do you remember how many years we've had this Christmas tree?" I asked.

"Let's see." She eased down into a chair and propped her feet on a matching hassock. "I fussed at Roxy for peeking around the door to watch the ceremony when your folks got married right here in this room. We were supposed to stay in the kitchen, out of sight, and I didn't want any trouble on Harrison's big day. Roxy cried during the whole service, and while we were washing dishes, she said that as soon as the baby came, she was leaving Meadow Falls, and she was not taking the baby with her. I thought she just had a case of baby blues, but I found out later she was dead serious."

I wasn't sure what that had to do with the age of the Christmas tree, but if this was the same one that had been standing back then—in the corner of their wedding photograph—that would mean it was about my age, because I was born about fourteen months after that.

Mandy frowned and then smiled. "That would make that tree thirty-five years old. It was Inez's first artificial one, and Clifford wasn't too keen on the change. His folks had always had a real one, but she had insisted on getting a new one to have for the wedding."

"I'd say that it's time for a new one." No one could accuse me of mulling over anything now. "We'll take the ornaments off, and then we'll donate the tree to a homeless shelter."

"Why are you keeping the ornaments?" Mandy asked.

"Aren't some of them heirlooms?" I answered with a question.

She frowned. "Not any more than the paneling on the walls or the coffee table that's been here ever since I first arrived—and most likely, for years before."

"Then they can all go to the shelter, right along with the tree and the tables," I said. "It's past time that Meadow Falls became a home instead of a shrine."

"Out with the old"—Celeste waved her hand around to take in the whole room—"and in with the new."

"Amen!" My heart felt lighter than it had in a very long time— maybe ever.

Chapter Nine

*A*whiff of Devon's shaving lotion came through the door before
he did the next evening. The scent of something woodsy with
a hint of vanilla reminded me of springtime out by the creek. I could
visualize the wild forget-me-nots underfoot and a soft breeze swaying
the weeping willow limbs. The blue in his plaid shirt was the same color
as his eyes. His jeans were creased, and his black cowboy boots were so
shiny, I could almost see myself in them.

"All of you ladies look lovely this afternoon," he said as he glanced
around the foyer at the three of us, "but Miz Mandy takes the cake."

"Don't you flatter an old woman like that," she fussed at him, but
beamed at the same time.

"Just statin' the truth, ma'am." He helped her get her coat on. "Do
we have a curfew?"

"Yes, we do," Mandy said, playing along. "We have to be home
thirty minutes after they shut the place down at eleven o'clock. There'll
be no hanky-panky tonight, and I never kiss a man on the first date."

Devon laid a hand on his chest and looked like he might break out
in tears. "My heart is broken."

Mandy tucked her arm through his. "Don't you be teasing me like
that, Mr. Parker."

"That's just Devon," he said. "Mr. Parker is my dad or my grandpa."

"Not on a first date, it's not," she scolded. "I don't use a given name when I go out with a man on a first date. I called my husband by Mr. Murphy until our fourth date, and he called me Miz Nelson."

He slid a sly wink at me and Celeste over the top of her head. "Yes, ma'am, Mrs. Murphy."

Mandy smiled and gave him a curt nod. "Now you are understanding the proper way to court a lady."

January is always cold in the Texas Panhandle, but that night, the moon and stars hid behind low-hanging dark clouds. I wondered if that was an omen that more bad things were about to happen.

No, I admonished myself. *Do not think bad thoughts. Think about spreading your wings and flying tonight.*

Celeste bumped me with her hip and whispered, "Should we go back and get our slickers? If Granny gets wet and chilled, she could come down with pneumonia."

I shivered at the thought of Mandy being sick. Was that the sign in the sky that evening? Was my sweet Mandy going to follow in my father's footsteps and drop suddenly?

"Mandy, are you sure you want to get out tonight? It sure feels like rain. What if . . ."

She shook her gloved finger at me. "I don't live in the world of what-ifs, child—not anymore, anyway. I figure that God gave me this life to use, not waste on what-ifs. You girls get in the back seat, and don't think about what *might* happen. Just enjoy life as it comes to you."

Devon chuckled as he settled her in the passenger seat. "Good advice."

That wasn't the first time Mandy had fussed at me for worrying about the past, the future, and even the present. I had used the what-ifs too many times in my lifetime to count, and that could be the reason I was afraid to fly. As I fastened my seat belt, I remembered some of the thoughts I'd had through the years: What if I'd been born to Roxy instead of my parents? What if I had gotten to go to college? What if I'd gotten married and had two or three children by now?

Mandy had lost her husband and had become an instant single mom back in the early fifties. Like she had said about my ancestors, *things were different back then*, so life couldn't have been easy for her, trying to support a child without a husband in the picture.

"She's a strong old bird," Celeste whispered as if she could read my mind.

"And stubborn," I added.

"What are y'all whispering about back there?" Mandy asked.

"We were saying you sure look pretty tonight," Celeste answered.

"Thank you," Mandy said. "Now, Devon, it's time to snap a whip over the horses and get this wagon train going."

He started the engine and backed out of the driveway. "I'll drive this covered wagon, but you have to navigate and tell me where Polly lives."

"Make a left out of the lane and go all the way to town. Her house is the one right next to the first gas station," Mandy said. "See there, you don't need all that fancy GPT stuff to get from one place to another—not in a town the size of Meadow."

"GPS," Celeste corrected her.

"Don't matter what you call it," Mandy argued. "Nobody needs it."

Polly must have been watching for us, because she came right out of the house, locked the door, and was walking across her yard by the time Devon had parked. He was quick to hop out of the vehicle and help her into the back seat with me and Celeste. She was dressed just like Mandy, in jeans and a red sweatshirt screen-printed with MEADOW MUSICAL on the front. I scooted over to the middle, and she was already talking before he closed the door.

"I've been going to the musical for more'n fifty years," she said.

That meant they had been going back before I was born, when my father was just a little boy. I wondered how old he'd been the first time he went and if he'd flirted with the girls.

"You and Granny are twins tonight," Celeste said.

"Yep, we are," Mandy agreed. "We bought these shirts for each other for Christmas this year. We've got a lot of memories around the musical."

"I met my second husband there," Polly said. "Wilson Matthews asked me to dance with him and sweet-talked me all the way through that Charley Pride song, 'All I Have to Offer You (Is Me).' I fell in love with him right then."

A memory of my father surfaced. He had parked in the driveway on a cool spring day, and the windows of his truck were rolled down. I could hear that old Charley Pride song playing for just a few minutes before he turned off the engine. Could he have been thinking about Summer?

Celeste cocked her head to one side and frowned. "But your last name is Davis."

"Yep, it is now." Polly giggled. "Wilson was my second husband, and like the song says, he offered himself to me. That lasted for about two years, and then he went off and gave himself to a younger woman."

A Bobby Bare song, "Marie Laveau," came to my mind. The lyrics talked about what would happen to a man who did Marie wrong. "So then you took your maiden name back?"

"Oh, no, honey, my maiden name is Scully," she answered. "I married my first husband, Fred, when I was eighteen, and that marriage didn't last until the ink was dry on the license. He was the man of the house, and I don't do too well with that submission stuff. He hit me, and I took an iron skillet to his head. Thought I'd done killed him, but his head was hard enough that he only needed a few stitches."

"Did he file charges against you?" Celeste asked.

"No, but he filed for divorce the next day. If he hadn't, *I* would have," Polly said.

"I learned that lesson from her marriage to Fred as well as she did," Mandy added. "Some men can be deceiving. I just happened onto a good man when I got Edward. Never did see a reason or have the time to give marriage a second try after he was gone." She patted Devon on the shoulder. "Just remember that we've got cast-iron skillets of all sizes in the house if you ever lose all your charm and turn mean."

"Yes, ma'am, but I do not believe in hitting or abusing women," Devon said. "My granny would take a switch to me if I disrespected a lady."

"That's a smart woman," Polly told him. "I didn't trust men for a long time, so I just had a good time for more than a decade. I tried to fix Mandy up with guys, but she wasn't having no part of it. She was with me the night I met Wilson, and she told me not to trust the man, but I wouldn't listen to her. You girls need to pay attention to what she says. She's the smartest woman in the whole great state of Texas."

I patted Polly on the shoulder. "You got that right. Now, what happened after Wilson ditched you for another woman?"

"Wilson was a romantic, and he'd bring me flowers and little presents. I found out later that sometimes he picked the same bouquets for his other women, but at the time—and after Fred—all that romance seemed real nice," Polly explained.

So don't trust a romantic, was the lesson I got from the story Polly told. I thought about Trevor and how he'd been so sweet to Celeste when they were dating—always bringing her a bunch of wildflowers he'd picked and a plate of her favorite brown sugar fudge, which his mother had made, just to name a few. Did some men just like the chase, and when they had bagged their prey, they lost interest in it? I shook my own thoughts from my head and tuned back in to what Polly was saying.

"After Fred, I married Paul Davis. We were together thirty years before he died. The third time was the charm for me. Turn into the parking lot where you see the lights and cars, Devon," she said.

I'd only been to the musical a couple of times, and that was years ago, but the old building still looked like something straight out of a

Western movie. The lights around the top of the stair-stepped false front testified that it was really a modern-day place. The country music that I could hear from the time we turned into the gravel parking lot said that it was somewhere in between the shoot-'em-up cowboy shows and the techno age that we lived in now. Devon snagged a parking place only a few yards from the wide front porch.

"Our wagon train is here," he said. "Are we ready to get this party started?"

"Bring on the drinks and the dancin'," Polly said. "I'll drink the root beer, and the girls can dance with you. My old knees would cuss me for a week if I even tried to waltz around the floor one time."

Devon helped Mandy and Polly out of the truck. The chilly night air draping itself around us like a thick, wet blanket put a desperate feeling in my heart to get Mandy's stories recorded. Maybe something in what she could tell us would shed some more light on my life. If I understood the past, then there was a greater possibility that I could really spread my wings and learn to fly.

I wasn't sure how to do that, but I was almost ready to open the cage I'd lived in for all those years and really taste some freedom.

The inside of the place hadn't changed since I'd first gone there with Mandy as a teenager. The stage was right in front of us, and a family of four was lined up behind the microphones. I recognized the singer as Scotty Randolph's daughter. His son, Tyler, was playing an acoustic guitar, and down on the end, his teenage grandson, Dallas, was making a fiddle whine. Scotty was on the banjo at the far end. He had been playing at the musical for years, and Tyler had been a teenager—just a couple of years older than me—when he first took the stage with his father. They had all worked at Meadow Falls in the past.

I loved music and had often thought about taking piano lessons or learning to play the guitar, but I knew the answer would have been no, so I didn't even ask. I pushed the thoughts out of my head and looked around the room.

An American flag hung to the left of the stage on a knotty pine-paneled wall that reminded me of the wood I was about to have ripped off the walls at Meadow Falls. Burlap-covered baskets filled with daisies and sunflowers sat between the speakers. The bright colors could be a sign of sunny days in the future.

Stop looking for signs in everything, the voice in my head scolded. *Enjoy the evening and forget about the past, or even the future. Concentrate on the here and now. That's where freedom is—it's right now.*

My eyes had barely gotten used to the dim lights when Polly grabbed Mandy's hand and started across the room. "We're in luck tonight, folks. I see an empty table, so we don't have to sit on the benches. All y'all can pull up some extra chairs."

Devon beat us all to the table and seated both Mandy and Polly before Celeste and I could make our way through the crowd. A few folks wanted to shake my hand and give me their condolences. Other than at the funeral, no one had ever paid much attention to me, so that was a big surprise.

"What was that all about?" I asked Celeste.

"They're bowing to the new queen," she answered.

I frowned. "Yeah, right!"

We finally made it to the table, and Devon seated us both. "What can I get you ladies to drink?"

"Root beer in a bottle," Mandy answered and began to sway to the music with her upper body. "I can still dance very well when I'm sitting down."

"So can I," Polly said and pulled a ten-dollar bill from her pocket and tried to give it to him. "I'll have a root beer, too, and I'll buy the first round."

Devon shook his head. "First round is on me. Celeste and Angela Marie?"

"Root beer," Celeste and I both said at the same time.

"Five bottles coming right up," he said and disappeared into the crowd.

The place was pretty well packed that evening—but then, after the holidays, folks were probably ready to simply visit with friends and have a good time. In just a few minutes, Devon returned with our drinks and sat down between me and Mandy. When the band started playing a slow country song, he stood back up, smiled at Mandy, and held out his hand. "May I have this dance, ma'am?"

She put her hand in his and let him lead her out onto the dance floor. "Yes, you can, but I haven't danced in years, so you'll have to be patient with me."

"That right there is a good man," Polly said. "One of you girls should latch on to him before one of these hussies wearing short skirts and tight tops corners him."

Celeste almost choked on a sip of root beer. "I'm barely divorced. I'm not ready to dive into those waters again."

Polly glanced over at me.

"Oh, no," I protested. "I've got to figure out a lot of things before I think about a boyfriend."

"Such as?" Polly asked.

"Who I am, for one thing," I answered. "I've always been told what to do, when to do it, and how to do it."

"That's just on the farm, darlin'," Polly said. "You are thirty-five years old. You should have figured out who you are as a person outside of work long before now."

"But I didn't, so now I have to play catchup," I said, but my eyes kept drifting over to Devon and Mandy while we talked. Trevor had been nice to Mandy all that time, and look where that had led—eighteen years and a lifetime of wasted love down the drain.

No love is ever wasted. Cherish each moment. I'd read that on a plaque in a gift store once, and I still wasn't sure I believed it.

Polly nudged me. "Mandy says you are thinking about redoing the farmhouse."

"I'm starting with the living room." I told Polly my plans. "That might help me find myself."

Polly took a long gulp of her root beer. "I'm too old to paint, but I can still cook. So I'll come over and help in the kitchen while y'all work on the house."

"Thank you, Polly," Celeste said. "That's so sweet of you, but—"

Polly held up a palm. "No buts. I'm bored out of my mind, and I need some company on these cold winter days. Besides, Mandy and I are nearing the end of our time on this earth, and we need to be sure that we've caught up on all our visiting before one of us leaves. So don't give me any sass. I'm coming to help in the kitchen."

"Yes, ma'am—and thank you," I said.

Having Polly at the farm would keep Mandy from insisting that she was able to help with all the remodeling projects. She had always had her fingers in everything on Meadow Falls. If we gave her and Polly the job of baking cookies or muffins for break times, that would make her think she was helping.

Devon brought Mandy back to the table and pulled out her chair. "Thank you for the dance."

"My pleasure, but it'll take a week for my old knees to stop whining, so don't be beggin' me for no more." Mandy shook her finger at him. "I'm just going to sit here for the rest of the evening, drink my soda pop, and enjoy the music." She leaned over toward Polly and lowered her voice. "Look over there at Glenda Johnson flirting with Digger Smith. I wouldn't be surprised if they've got something goin' on."

Polly clucked like an old hen gathering in her baby chicks before a tornado. "And they're both married. I wonder where Glenda's husband and Digger's wife are tonight."

Births, deaths, and everything in between were fodder for gossip, and they seemed to enjoy every minute of it. Tomorrow, Mandy would entertain me and Celeste with stories about everyone at the event—from what they were wearing to who they were flirting with and who they snuck outside with for a little sip of whiskey or beer and some parking lot fun.

Devon finished off his root beer and glanced over at Celeste. "Looks like the folks are getting in position for a line dance. Want to see if we've still got what it takes?"

She shook her head. "Not tonight. I'm just going to sit here and listen to the music like Polly and Granny."

"How about you, Angela Marie?" he asked.

"Maybe later," I answered. "It's been a while since I did any line dancing. I'm not sure if I even remember the steps."

Polly nudged Mandy and nodded toward the door. Digger's wife had arrived with his two teenage boys. She glanced around the room, and then she and the boys went straight to the concession stand. Digger looked like a little boy who had been caught with his father's girlie magazine. He quickly left Glenda's side and joined his family. Celeste had said that she was worried about being a parent because of Roxy and her father. I wondered what kind of parenting genes I had inherited.

Glenda must have been out that night to have a good time, and Digger's wife wasn't going to ruin her evening. She zeroed in on Devon, smiled, and began to weave between the line dancers on her way over to us. Her jeans looked like they had been spray-painted onto her curvy body, and her plaid shirt had been tied in a knot right above her belly button. She flipped her bottle-blonde hair over one shoulder and never took her eyes off Devon.

Glenda and I had gone to high school together, and she had gotten married the next week after graduation. Within the first two years of their marriage, she and her husband, Bennie, had had two boys, who were now teenagers. They had worked at Meadow Falls the last two summers and were on the list to come back again this year.

"She's on her way to ask you to dance," I told Devon.

He nodded. "Looks that way."

She finally made it to our table and leaned down to whisper in Devon's ear. I hated to admit it, but a bit of jealousy boiled up inside me. I didn't care if her marriage had gone sour or if she was regretting getting married so young. She had no right to try to seduce a man when she had a husband at home.

Mandy's mouth pursed up so tight that her lips flat-out disappeared. "Glenda, darlin' . . ." Her smile and voice were both fake and sugary sweet. "How is Bennie doing? Bless his heart—out there working on those dangerous oil rigs to support you and the boys."

Glenda straightened up and shot Mandy a dirty look. "Bennie has been laid off and will be home tomorrow. I'm mad at him right now. The reason why is none of your business."

"Where are your boys? Do they know you're out on the town and flirtin' with men?" Mandy's tone went from sweet to sour in an instant.

Glenda ignored Mandy and held out her hand to Devon. "It's just a dance, darlin', and maybe getting to know each other a little. I'd be glad to show you around town since I heard that you're new in Meadow."

"Sorry, but I don't dance with married women," Devon said. "But thanks for asking me."

"He's with me," I said, and then wondered if I'd really said the words out loud.

Glenda glared at me like I was warm cow manure she'd tracked into her house. "Oh, really? You're not woman enough for a man like this one." She twirled around and headed back across the room.

Devon turned around and wiggled his dark brows. "So, I'm with you?"

"Have you got something you need to confess?" Polly asked.

I took a long drink of my root beer and came close to snorting it out my nose when I burped. "I lied to protect Devon from married women."

"That's a good thing for right now," Celeste said. "There's a difference in the way the single men—and even some of the married ones—are looking at you tonight."

"She's right," Mandy said. "They've got dollar signs in their eyes. So that was a smart move, to pretend to be with Devon. They'll back off and leave you alone."

"Or maybe all bets are still on," Polly said seriously. "There's few men in the state of Texas who wouldn't leave their girlfriends—and some of them, even their wives—for a shot at owning Meadow Falls. Look at Glenda flitting around from one group to another, spreading gossip. There's men with that same attitude right here in this room, and they've got the same hungry look in their eyes."

I scanned the room and located Glenda sitting on a bench with a bunch of women gathered around her. They were all sneaking glances toward my table, and some of them were even handing dollar bills off to Glenda. "I wonder if they are taking bets," I said with a sigh. "And if they are, it doesn't take a rocket scientist to figure out that the wager is whether the plain Jane daughter of Harrison Duncan has what it takes to hold on to Devon Parker."

Good grief! Had I really said that out loud—and if I did, what did Devon think? I wanted to run—not walk—to the door. Maybe even walk all the way back to Meadow Falls.

"If that's really happening, I would imagine that they are betting on how long you and Devon will last," Mandy said. "But, honey, this is a brilliant plan. Devon won't be bombarded with women, and all the men who have their eyes on the farm will back off. Polly, you and I can help keep the story going."

Polly flashed a grin across the table. "You bet we will. This will be so much fun—Celeste can help us. Just to keep it honest, in about a week, we can put it out that Celeste says they're arguing and about to break up. That will make them hussies over there anxious to see who wins the money."

Mandy's old eyes glittered with mischief. "Then, after they get all excited, I'll let it slip that they're back together and she even spent the night with him out in his house."

My cheeks felt like they were on fire. I picked up my cold bottle of root beer and rolled it across my face. That the heat didn't boil the soda pop was a surprise. I set the bottle down and waved to take them all in. "I can't believe you are plotting to spread lies."

"There's a difference between lies and rumors—and if those mean girls are betting on you, they deserve to be made fools of." Celeste held up her root beer. "Here's to our new mission."

Mandy and Polly clinked their bottles with hers.

"Quite frankly . . ." Devon scooted a little closer to me and draped his arm over the back of my chair. "I like the idea of being with you tonight. And since we're together, you owe me the last dance of the evening."

"Why's that?" I asked.

Celeste nudged me with her shoulder. "Don't you know the rule? Whoever you dance the last one with is who you go home with."

Another blush started at the back of my neck and crept around to my face. "Well, I guess that's the truth because after we drop Polly off at her house, we'll all be going home together anyway."

"I hope we can keep the gossip going until harvest," Mandy said.

Devon leaned over, tucked my hair behind my ear, and whispered, "And for the record—and this is gospel truth, according to Devon Parker—you are not a plain Jane. Besides being pretty on the outside, you have a big, kind heart. Don't ever let anyone convince you of anything else."

His words made me blush—yet again.

"What was that all about?" Celeste asked.

"Just playin' my part so everyone knows that I'm with Angela Marie. I may sneak over there and put down a few dollars in the wager pot that we last until Christmas," Devon said as he stood up and held out his hand toward me. "Let's make it even more official. Dance with me."

What could I say? He had agreed to save me from any vultures who might be wanting to get their hands on the farm, the money in the bank accounts, and what my father had invested in other things—and for that matter, what I had accumulated in my own personal accounts. I'd been on the payroll for years now, and I'd used very little of the money.

I put my hand in his and let him lead me out onto the dance floor. A new lady had taken the stage and was singing "Hey, Dear Miss Loretta." The lyrics were a song to Loretta Lynn about being an inspiration for the songwriter's life. I could agree with the chorus that said she knew why Loretta sang that way. I'd never lived near a coal mine, but I was a peanut farmer's daughter, and I could so relate to the words, which seemed to cover a lifetime of pain in a three-minute song.

I was aware of other people dancing around us, but they were just shadows. Right then, there was no one else in the whole state but me and Devon. The song ended, and the band started to play the intro to another song. The singer who sang "How Do I Live" had an amazing voice and hit all the high notes just like LeAnn Rimes had done in her rendition. Devon pulled me closer to him and looped his arms around my waist. My arms snaked up around his neck, and I let myself be swept away by the words. There wasn't room for air between us, and the sparks that danced around reminded me of falling stars.

"We would make really good actors," he said.

"I was just thinking the same thing," I whispered and wished that we weren't pretending.

That was crazy thinking. My life had been financially comfortable rather than full of love, and I could easily be the poster child for dysfunctional families everywhere, but I wasn't naive.

"Ready to call it quits?" I asked when the song ended.

He kissed me on the forehead. "One more, just to prove that we're really together."

"And now, a request," the woman on the stage said, "from one of the folks here tonight." The guitarist strummed a few chords, and I immediately knew the song.

As Devon waltzed me around the floor to "Love Can Build a Bridge," I wondered if there was enough love in the whole world to build a bridge between me and my family. Even though my mother and father were gone, I still held on to the idea that someday I could find the ability to forgive them for being lousy parents.

When the song ended, Devon led me back to the table, pulled out my chair for me. "I'm going to the concession stand. Root beers for everyone?"

We all nodded, and he disappeared into the crowd of people two-stepping to "Walkaway Joe."

I was glad we had left the dance floor, because even in a fake relationship, I didn't want Devon to be a walkaway Joe, like Emma's boyfriend had been. Mandy had told us once that he'd said he wasn't ready to be a father, so he'd simply left her at the end of harvest; at seventeen, she had given birth to Roxy a few months later. Two weeks after the baby's birth, they got word that the baby's father had been killed while out riding his motorcycle.

Poor Mandy had endured so much tragedy that I wondered how she could smile and go on with life. First, she'd lost her husband. Then Emma had died before Roxy was school-age. And *then* Roxy had had Celeste and left her with Mandy to raise.

"Wow!" Celeste poked me in the arm. "I had no idea you were such an actor. You should have run away from home and come to live with me in California. You would have made a fortune in the movies."

Polly cocked her head to one side and studied me long enough that I felt a little uncomfortable. "She does look a little like a young Nicole Kidman."

"Oh, hush! Y'all are being silly." I didn't have the heart to tell them I wasn't acting.

"Angela Marie *had* to learn to act," Mandy said. "If she hadn't, Meadow Falls would have destroyed her."

"That's the truth," Polly agreed with a nod. "I'm glad that you survived and that you're going to make some changes out on the farm."

Devon came back with a tray bearing fresh drinks for us all and a couple of paper containers of nachos for everyone to share. "I haven't been to a dance in years. Forgot that it could wear a guy out, but it was worth it."

He set the tray down in the middle of the table and eased down into his chair. Then he picked up a nacho and fed it to me. "Just keeping up our story," he whispered.

"You are doing a fantastic job," I told him and wished again that, for just one evening, we were telling a real story instead of a fictional one.

Chapter Ten

*M*andy shuffled into the kitchen for breakfast on Sunday morning and sat down at the end of the table. "I'm not going to church this morning. It's cold and rainy. I'm tired, and Jesus knows I love Him."

Celeste poured a mugful of coffee and set it in front of her. "I was dreading having to go scrape the ice off the windshield."

Mandy took a sip and closed her eyes. "That's the best part of the morning. Thank you, sweetie. But don't let me keep you girls from going. After last night, the two of you might need to go get a dose of Jesus in you this morning."

"I didn't sow any wild oats," I protested. "All I did was say that Devon was with me, and it wasn't a real lie. He did drive me there and back to the house—and besides, I believe that Jesus would understand that, so I'm staying home."

"I'm not going, either," Celeste declared. "I'd rather cuddle up on the sofa and be lazy. Going to church every time the doors open isn't our ticket through the Pearly Gates."

"Why did you say that about wild oats?" Mandy's weary tone testified that we had kept her out too late the night before.

"Years ago, you told us that most people go out and sow wild oats on Saturday night, then go to church on Sunday and pray for a crop failure," I reminded her as I set a plate of pancakes in the middle of the table and took my seat.

She frowned. "Did I say that?"

"More than once," Celeste answered.

I realized just how tired Mandy was when she didn't say grace before she forked three pancakes over onto her plate and got busy adding melted butter and maple syrup to them. She had cut off a forkful and was on her way to her mouth when she laid it down and bowed her head. "Sorry about that, God. I guess I'm more worn out than I realized. I didn't mean to forget You, so thanks for another day that I'm aboveground, thanks for my girls, and for this food. Amen."

Celeste brought the coffeepot to the table and took her place. "If we're not leaving the house, then I'm going to save the roast for tomorrow and get out one of those frozen casseroles from the funeral to thaw for lunch today."

"Why don't we just have sandwiches?" I suggested.

"Or hot chocolate and popcorn?" Mandy asked.

"We'll have whatever you want, Granny, if you'll tell us a story after breakfast," Celeste told her.

"What do you want to hear?" she asked.

"Will you tell us more about my father and mother's life after they were married?" I asked.

"And maybe tell me more about my mother," Celeste said.

"Some things are best left unsaid," Mandy whispered.

"You told me once that to make it through the present and to be able to enjoy the future, a person needed to understand the past," I reminded her.

"You are right." Mandy sighed. "I have trouble remembering what I told you girls when you were growing up. So I might repeat myself."

"You told us fairy tales, but we're old enough now for the real stories," I said, and hoped that she didn't get a foggy brain before she even got started.

"I guess so. I wouldn't have told the real story while Harrison and Sophia were alive out of respect for them," Mandy said. "But, Celeste, you'll have to wait for your story about your mother. I'll tell that one another day. Two stories in one day will spoil you girls."

"Granny, you've spoiled us our whole lives," Celeste said. "Matter of fact, you were the *only* one that spoiled me."

"And me too," I added.

"From the way Devon was acting last night, he might be spoiling Angela Marie in this fake-relationship thing y'all have got going. He might even be trying to steal my spoiling crown," Mandy said with half a giggle.

"But he only has a rhinestone crown," I countered. "Yours is the real-diamond deal, and no one will ever take you off the throne."

"If they try, I'll fight 'em like a mama bear protectin' her cubs, and that goes for both of you," she said. "Now, you have to eat all your breakfast and drink every bit of your milk if you want a story."

"I can do that," I said.

She frowned again. "Why am I so tired this morning? What did we do last night? Did I tell you stories until midnight? My memory disease is acting up really bad today. Maybe I'd better drink an extra cup or two of coffee. I hear that helps to jump-start the mind in the mornings."

Celeste laid her hand on Mandy's arm. "We went to the Meadow Musical, and you danced with Devon. We haven't heard a story since you told us about Summer."

Mandy touched her forehead with her finger. "That's right. I remember now. Seems that when I get tired, I forget what happened an hour ago, or yesterday. Getting old and having a foggy brain takes willpower and strength. It's not for the weakhearted. Sometimes I wish I could forget the past and remember what's happening around me today."

I patted her on the shoulder. "God lets you remember the important stuff so that you can tell us how things really were. You are a walking history book when it comes to Meadow Falls."

"Polly is the one who knows all the gossip in Terry County." She giggled. "How much fun we all had last night is coming back to me. Glenda was flirting with Digger, and then his wife came in." She was still spilling the tea about what all she and Polly had seen when we finished eating and made our way to the living room. She finally stopped talking and looked around the living room. "Let's push this settee and a chair up close to the fireplace and start a blaze. A fire will warm my old bones and maybe even thaw out my memories."

"I'll do it," Celeste offered.

Not once in all my years had I ever started a fire. I wouldn't even have known where to begin, so I was glad when Celeste gathered sticks of wood from the rack at the end of the fireplace and in minutes had a blaze going.

"I hope you don't do away with the fireplace when you remodel. Remember when we were little girls, and Granny would let us throw a blanket on the floor and then read to us until we went to sleep?" Celeste asked.

"Those were the good times—and besides, if we lose electricity, we need it for heat." The two of us worked together to move the furniture closer to the fire. "I wonder why there was never a grouping of furniture here."

"Inez said that Victoria arranged the furniture, and Clifford refused to let anyone mess with anything his mother had done." Mandy groaned as she eased down into the chair and then popped up the footrest. "I really am tired, even more than I realized. If I'm going to talk through this story, I'll need a bottle of water," she said. "My throat gets awful dry when I talk too much, and this is a long story."

"I'll get one for each of us." Celeste headed toward the kitchen.

I sat down on the floor and used the settee for a back rest.

"Why aren't you sitting on the sofa?" Mandy asked. "You took the trouble to move it over here."

"That thing is more uncomfortable than the floor." I pulled my cell phone from the pocket of my robe and laid it on the floor beside me. "But it is a pretty good back rest, and it's not too bad to stretch out on for a nap if I'm really tired. When I buy new furniture, I want something that's soft and comfortable."

Celeste returned with a bottle of water for each of us and a plateful of cookies, which she put on the floor beside me. Then she sat down next to me and gave me a very brief nod when she noticed the phone.

"I hardly know where to begin this story." Mandy twisted the cap off her bottle, took a drink, and set it down beside her.

"Why don't you start at the beginning?" I pushed the record button and hoped that the battery wouldn't go dead before she finished.

"Then we'll have to go back a little to Summer. I never did like that girl, but looking back, I can see why Harrison loved her. She represented freedom from Meadow Falls, with her big ideas about them making a living by painting pretty pictures. The biggest reason I didn't like her, though, was that Roxy was in a rebellious state, and she idolized Summer. She spent every minute that she could with the woman, and you'd have thought Roxy lost a sister when Summer left without even leaving my baby a goodbye note." Mandy pursed her lips and frowned.

So that's why Roxy was dressed like Summer, I thought. But she had to be older than thirteen or fourteen in the picture I'd found—maybe more like sixteen or seventeen.

"I told y'all about Harrison bringing her to the farm," Mandy said. "I always knew that he wasn't happy here. From the time he was a little boy, he hated to get his hands dirty. Who knows? He might have done well as an artist."

I remembered scrubbing my nails every evening to remove all the grease and dirt from under them, so that much I understood and agreed with.

"I can relate to that," Celeste said. "I'm not an outside person, either. I'd far rather be in front of a computer than digging in a flower bed."

"Was that why, when he got older, he wore white shirts and left the actual workload to the foreman?" I asked.

"Most likely," Mandy answered. "He was happiest when he could take his sketch pads and go to the creek to draw and paint. He told me more than once that it wasn't fair that Emma wasn't told what she had to be when she grew up."

"Are there any of his works anywhere in the house?"

"Oh, no, honey!" Mandy answered. "Clifford would never have allowed that. Harrison was supposed to be a man's man, one that got dirty and knew how to fix tractors and drive pickers and work from dawn to dark during harvest. He was born to be the boss of Meadow Falls, not to draw and paint. You might wonder what this part of the story has to do with Harrison and Sophia. To understand him, you have got to know him as a child. He was a sweet little boy and loved Emma like a big sister, until . . ."

She paused so long that I reached over to turn the recorder off, but then, after a long sigh, she went on. "When Emma was pregnant with Roxy, Harrison overheard Clifford fussing at her for breaking a dish, and while he was yelling at her, he called her *the hired help*. I don't know for sure, but I figure that other things were said about us *just being the help*. Little by little, Harrison started treating us different. See, I told you—my mouth gets dry when I talk very long." She stopped long enough to take a deep drink, then put the cap back on the bottle and set it aside. "I've often wondered if Clifford and Inez would have given him his inheritance and let him go off to some other county and be an artist. I don't know jack squat about art, but his pictures were pretty."

"But you said that wasn't an option," Celeste reminded her.

"Yes, I did," Mandy answered. "His mama told him that his inheritance was the farm, and he didn't get that until she and Clifford were both dead. If he didn't want to live on Meadow Falls, he didn't have to, but he wasn't getting a dime to go gallivanting around the world while she and his father worked their fingers to the bones, preserving a life for him to take over someday."

For the first time, I felt sorry for my father. He'd deserved to be happy, to paint his pictures and be with the woman he loved. I almost got lost in my own thoughts again, but I didn't want to miss a word of what Mandy said.

"His happiness faded and then disappeared completely when Summer left him. It was like she took all his hopes and dreams with her, and he was just trying to find something to replace that time in his life when he was going to run away from here and be an artist. Inez told him repeatedly that the woman had been a gold digger, and he needed to realize that he didn't have a lick of sense when it came to choosing a wife. He worked on the farm from then on, but he hated it, and he partied so hard on weekends that most Monday mornings, he was an old bear. I tried to talk sense to him, but he wouldn't listen to me. I had raised that boy, and he even told *me* I was just the hired help and didn't have any business butting into his life." She swiped a tear from her eye.

Celeste stood up, walked across the room, and came back with a box of tissues. She set it in Mandy's lap and then returned to sit beside me.

Mandy pulled one out and dried her wet cheek. "Sometimes when I look back, I regret not leaving Meadow Falls after the peanuts were harvested that first fall when we came here. Edward and I had arrived with the harvest crew and planned to go on back to where our folks lived when the season was over."

"Why did you stay?" Celeste asked. "Did you keep in touch with your family?"

"We had written letters back and forth, but I was the youngest child in the family. My brother, Ralph—he was the youngest boy—and I wrote to each other once a month, faithfully, until he died a long time ago. He was the last one alive, other than me, and after that . . . well . . ." She shrugged. "None of this generation would even know me."

"They might see your name on a family tree if they did the DNA testing," Celeste said.

"I've heard and read about that, but I'm not sure I believe it," Mandy said. "But to get back to the story, Inez didn't want me to leave, so Clifford offered me a job as a cook and overseer of what went on in the house in the way of cleaning ladies and gardeners. Edward was such a good handyman that Clifford said he would put him on the payroll permanently, too. Edward really knew his way around the equipment. We'd been living in a makeshift thing that Edward built on the back of our pickup truck and using the bathroom that's out in the machinery barn, so when Clifford offered us the house as a bonus, we jumped on the deal. Emma was three months old that fall, and that meant she would have a good house to grow up in," Mandy explained.

"*You* were shaking peanuts when you were pregnant?" I asked.

"No, not here on Meadow Falls while I was pregnant with Emma— but I did in the southern part of the state. By the time we got here, I'd given birth to Emma, and Inez took a liking to me right away and put me to work in the house. Then Edward was killed when he fell from a barn roof right around Christmastime. I had a good job, and I could bring my daughter with me every day. Inez loved that baby girl, and she seemed to be the happiest when she could spend time with Emma. Then Harrison was born, and Emma kind of got pushed to the side. Not so easy for a ten-year-old little girl, but I tried to make up for it by loving her even more."

She had gotten off topic about my parents, but I didn't stop the recording. I turned to Celeste and asked, "Did you know that about Emma? She would be your grandmother, right?"

She shook her head. "That's right, but Granny never talked much about her."

"That's because it hurt too bad to even say her name," Mandy said. "I wouldn't be telling y'all about her now, but . . ." She raised one shoulder and sighed. "I shouldn't withhold the past from you. Emma was my only child, and too many times, I had to make her take a back seat to Harrison. It was my job to take care of him. If I didn't have a paycheck, I couldn't have raised Emma on my own. I blame myself for the way things happened, and I regret not just packing up and leaving Meadow Falls after Harrison was born. She begged me to take her away from here, and she might still be alive today if I'd done just that. I could have moved into town, gotten us a little rent house, and worked in the cafeteria at the school like Polly did, and maybe even picked up some ironing or seamstress work on the side."

"Why didn't you?" Celeste asked.

"I couldn't have made as much working at both those jobs as I did here on the farm once I paid rent, and I wanted to save up enough money so Emma could go to college," Mandy answered.

"Why did Emma want to leave here?" I asked. Had my father been mean to her, too?

"She was Cinderella, only not the pretty one in the fancy dress." Mandy wiped another tear from her eyes. "She was the one in the ugly outfit. Not in a real sense, but that's the way Harrison made her feel. Inez pushed her to the back, and then in so many ways, I did, too. Inez liked me, but I really was the hired help, and Clifford made sure I knew my place. Emma saw all that and wanted out of here."

I wasn't sure I wanted to hear any more depressing stories that day—not even if Mandy had a good one to tell us about my parents. Something that would bring some virtual sunshine into the cold room. I turned off my phone and shoved it back into my pocket.

"But back to the story of Harrison and Sophia," she said. "I told you this would take a spell, so you might as well start recording again, Angela Marie."

I gasped. "How did you know?"

"I might be old, but these eyes see as well as they did when I was a kid."

"Yes, ma'am." This time I laid the phone on the arm of her chair.

"Now, where was I?" Mandy asked.

I sent up a silent prayer that she wouldn't look around the room and ask where Harrison was or tell us that if we didn't hurry, we were going to miss church service. Finally, she took another long drink of her water and went on.

"After Summer had gone, Harrison and his mother argued all the time." She frowned. "But we already went over all that. Inez finally told him that if he wasn't married in a year, she and Clifford were cutting him out of their will. I never knew why she did that, but I suspect that it had to do with the bad reputation he had gotten all over this part of the state. She told me more than once that if she could see him settled and if he would have a son to inherit Meadow Falls, then Jesus could come get her and take her on to heaven."

"She really said that?" Celeste asked, shocked.

"Yes, she did," Mandy said. "I told her it was the wrong thing to say and pressuring him into getting married wasn't right—but she turned on me and said that I wasn't one to give her advice and that she hadn't raised a daughter like Emma, who left me with an illegitimate kid to take care of, and now Roxy was pregnant and following in her mother's footsteps. I tried to chalk it up to her being angry, but our friendship was never the same after that."

"Did my mother hear her say those mean things?" Celeste asked.

Mandy nodded and wiped at her eyes again. "That night, Roxy told me that she would stay here until the baby was born, but as soon as it came, she would be leaving—with or without me. I asked her if she would be taking the baby with her, and she told me she couldn't raise a child on her own, so if I didn't go, the baby would stay with me. That all went down near the end of harvest season that year. The next week, there was another big row in the house, and it ended with Clifford storming outside and with Inez telling Harrison that he had a deadline: be married by the first of the next year to a woman she approved of or find another place to live."

Mandy popped the footrest down and stood up. "Three cups of coffee and a bottle of water has hit bottom. You can turn off the recording until I get back from the bathroom."

"Whew!" Celeste wiped her brow with the back of her hand. "That's some heavy stuff. I would sooner hear the princess-and-prince stories."

"Me too, but I'm getting to know my father a lot better and dislike him a little less. Still, I wonder why he made me learn the business and refused to let me . . ." I stopped and slapped a hand over my mouth. "He didn't want me to ever know happiness like he'd known and then have to give it up for the farm."

"That might have been the reason—or it could have been that he was so angry that he couldn't love anyone, not even you," Celeste said.

"You could be right—and don't lay all the blame on Roxy. She knew Mandy would take good care of you and love you," I answered. "Remember, she was only eighteen, and who knows where she went. Did Mandy ever even know what state she moved to at first? Did you ever think that maybe she intended to come back and get you?"

Her chin quivered as she picked up a peanut butter cookie. "I never thought of my mother coming back. Back then, California was as far away as the moon. Looks like we both got the short end of the stick."

"Or did we?" I asked. "We had Mandy to look after us, and that was a blessing."

Mandy shuffled across the room and settled into the chair. "Turn on the recorder now. Where was I?"

"You were telling us about the argument when Inez gave Harrison the ultimatum," Celeste reminded her.

"That's right." Mandy nodded. "Harrison's temper shot right up worse than it ever had. He accused her of just seeing him as an heir to a peanut farm and not a son. But if Meadow Falls was all that important to her, he told her, he would get married and produce an heir, and he would be sure her precious farm was taken care of even better than his grandpa and his daddy had done. According to him, his happiness wasn't important to anyone, so he would just be an unhappy peanut farmer his whole life. His voice had gone all cold and quiet—something I'd never heard from him before—and it chilled me to the bone. Usually, when he was angry, he raised his voice. He threatened to groom his child—boy or girl—to take over the place, and he told her that he would never let his child have a say-so in anything else about their life. 'That's the proper way to raise an heir to this precious piece of Texas dirt.' Those were his exact words."

"And you witnessed the whole thing?" Celeste asked.

"I was washing dishes, and they were standing between me and this very table," Mandy answered. "Inez got up in his face and told him that wasn't fair to a child. His next words would have cut through steel when he said that he hoped he had a daughter and that she hated the farm as much as he did."

"Holy smoke!" The words came out of my mouth in a hoarse whisper.

"Yep," Mandy said. "And the next week, Harrison didn't go out on Saturday night. On Sunday morning, he was ready for church when it was time to go. A new preacher had moved to town—not at our church but a little community place that's not even here anymore. One of those that sprung up in an old, abandoned grocery store and only lasted about a year. Seems like the name of it was Church of Grace."

"What did Clifford say when my father and grandmother argued?" I asked.

"After the Summer incident, Clifford more or less washed his hands of Harrison and told Inez that she'd been the one to spoil him, so she could have the job of straightening him out," Mandy answered. "But back to the church—the preacher's sister had come for a visit, and from what I could understand, Harrison had met her in the grocery store a few days after the big fight."

"And that was my mother?" I asked.

"Yes," Mandy answered. "He courted her for six weeks, proposed to her, and they were married right here in front of this fireplace on New Year's Eve. I already told you that Roxy and I watched the short ceremony from the doorway. Her brother married them, and then there was a big reception right here at the house for all Clifford and Inez's friends. It was like they were showing the whole county that Harrison had settled down."

She stopped talking and motioned for Celeste to hand her a cookie.

"Is that the end of the story? Do I have cousins or relatives somewhere on my mother's side?" I was in shock that no one had told me that before now.

"To my knowledge, you do not," Mandy said. "Sophia and her brother, Luke, were the only children in the family. That spring after the wedding, he took a missionary position in some foreign country. I found her weeping on the front porch in the middle of harvest that year, and she told me that her brother and his wife had died over there. It might have been complications from some bad stomach illness. She said that she wished she had never married Harrison and had gone with them instead. She declared that she would rather be dead than living in a house with Harrison, but she had no place to go.

"I tried to comfort her and say that she didn't have to stay on Meadow Falls if she was that unhappy." Mandy took a few bites of her cookie and asked Celeste to get her a glass of milk. "Got to have something to wash them down."

She finished her cookie and then drank half the milk before she continued. "I tried to console Sophia, but it didn't work. In between sobs, she said that her faith didn't allow for divorces and that she had to stay married to Harrison because she had just found out she was pregnant. But . . ."

"But what?" I crossed my fingers like a little girl in hopes that she would go on to tell us more.

"But she knew that he didn't love her, and she'd figured that out too late, and she didn't love him, either," Mandy answered. "She gave birth to you in the bedroom where she died—where all the babies on Meadow Falls have been born—and she never went back to his bedroom again. She was a good actress—when they were in public, she was a perfect wife, but in reality, she was miserable and never bonded with you like a mother should. In that respect, she was like Roxy. And that is the end. Now, I'm going to my room to take a long nap. Wake me up when dinner is on the table."

I held up a finger. "Just one more question: Why didn't my parents try again for a son?"

"Like I said, she had her own bedroom after you were born. She might have had a chance at having more children, but Inez refused to let her have you in the hospital. Duncan women have always had their babies in this house. That led to complications, and she had to go to the hospital and have a hysterectomy soon after your birth. Inez's health was failing at that time, so they just handed you off to me."

I turned off the recorder and felt as if someone or something had sucked all the oxygen out of the house. Mandy and Celeste were a blur as they left the room. I heard Celeste thank her for telling us the story and say something about Roxy, but her voice was coming from a distance—seemed like maybe she was all the way at the far horizon. Then a vision of the willow tree by the creek flashed through my mind, and suddenly all I wanted to do was go there to think.

Chapter Eleven

reathe, Angela Marie," Celeste kept saying over and over. I tried to gasp several times before I could finally put air down into my lungs.

The room looked strange from where I was curled up in a fetal position. Everything was either sideways or upside down, or it was spinning so fast that it nauseated me. I closed my eyes to make the weirdness go away, but that didn't help.

"You have to take a breath. You have to open your eyes," Celeste demanded.

She had never talked to me in that tone. She didn't understand that the movement was making me sick. My chest hurt. My brain told me that sucking in more air would be painful. My eyes couldn't focus on anything. Even the floral pattern on the sofa was blurry. Had I died of a heart attack like my father? If so, why wasn't there a bright light to guide me on into eternity? Finally, when I felt her tears dripping onto my face, I took a long, deep breath.

I tried to sit up, but the room did a couple of more spins, and the walls started closing in on me. "What happened? Is Mandy all right?"

"Easy, go slow," Celeste said. "Do I need to call an ambulance?"

"Is Mandy all right?" My voice was shrill and demanding in my own ears.

"She's fine, but evidently, you just fainted." Celeste pulled a tissue from the box, dried her wet face, and sat down beside me. "She's probably already snoring. You were okay when I left with her. What happened to *you*?"

"That story hit me . . ." Now it was playing through my mind at warp speed. "And suddenly, everything went black."

I'd never realized the importance of air before, or that I was gasping over and over again, until Celeste poured water on a paper napkin she had brought from the kitchen earlier and began to wipe my face with it. The constant movement and nausea finally settled down, and I sat up with my back against the sofa.

She handed me the water and said, "Drink. Your face is the color of fog. It's a good thing that you didn't hit your head on the corner of the coffee table."

I took a few sips—air and water, two things I would never take for granted again.

"Thank you," I muttered.

"Why did it affect you like that? You already knew a lot of the story."

"It was . . ." I couldn't find the words.

"A lot to take in, right?" Celeste said.

"Right," I said with a nod. "I've never fainted before. It was a strange experience."

"I've passed out a couple of times, and you are right," she agreed. "It's like you are there one minute, and then everything goes dark. Want to talk about it?"

I got up slowly and sat on the sofa. "I need to go to the cemetery to talk to my folks."

"Angela Marie," she said softly as she laced her fingers through mine, "they can't hear you, and it's too late to go out there tonight."

"They don't need to hear me or speak to me in any way, but I need to get some things off my chest. Not today but later—maybe next

Sunday, when Polly is here to be with Mandy. They might not care what I've got to say to them, but that's okay. I just need to say it out loud," I told her. "The last thing I heard is when you asked her to tell us more about Roxy. Is she going to do that after we have dinner?"

"Nope," Celeste answered. "She says that we've had enough stories for a few days but that she'll tell us about my mother another time."

"A strong, independent woman wouldn't have fainted," I groaned. "Why would I pass out over that story?"

"Sometimes the body shuts down when it doesn't want to face something," Celeste said. "What were you thinking about just before you passed out?"

"I had a vision of the willow tree beside the creek, and then everything went black."

"Why would you think about that old tree?" she asked.

"When anything bothered me as a child, I would close my eyes and go to my happy place. That old tree is what I would think about, and I would imagine that I could hear the water splashing over the rocks."

"Want to hear something crazy?" she whispered. "That was my happy place, too. I came home to it—in my mind—a lot these last few years."

"I feel sorry for both my parents," I admitted.

"Why?" Celeste handed me a cookie. "Eat this. Your blood sugar levels might have taken a plunge. When have you had blood work done?"

I took the cookie from her. "I've never had any blood work done. What about you?"

"The military doctors checked me out every six months," she answered. "I have low blood sugar, and my blood pressure borders on high."

"I'm not surprised about your blood pressure, after what you've been through. After all of what we're finding out, do you think you'll ever want to have children?"

"That's an abrupt change of the subject—and I love kids, but right now, I don't trust a man enough to have a child with him, anyway. So, if I did have one, it would be with the foreknowledge that I would be a single mother. How about you?" she asked.

"Can I think about that question for a few minutes while I eat another cookie or two?"

"Sure," Celeste agreed. "I need some time to let my heart settle down. I thought you had died for a minute there, and I'm pretty sure I know exactly how Harrison felt when he had his heart attack. My chest went all tight, and I had trouble breathing. I'm sure my blood pressure was out of the ceiling for a few minutes. Lord have mercy, as Granny says. What would happen to her if we both died?"

I had never thought about what would or could happen if I died before Mandy. I knew there was no provision made for her in my father's will; he'd handed me a copy of it after my mother passed away. I didn't understand all the legalese, but basically, it had said that upon his death, everything he owned would be passed down to me. I'd called the lawyer the day my father died, and he said he would have papers for me to sign within thirty days.

"I need to see the company lawyer as soon as I can and have my will made," I said and then frowned. Somehow, my thoughts had taken me in a whole different direction from the conversation we'd been having. I tried to remember what we had been talking about, and then it hit me like a blast of icy wind bringing in freezing rain.

Children!

I broke out in a cold sweat just thinking about the word. The little kids at church always flocked around me, and I often took little treats in my purse to give to them. Had my mother been like that? Her brother, my uncle, was a preacher, so maybe her religious upbringing had made her love to be around kids.

"Why would my father choose a woman who came from a strict religious background?" I wondered out loud.

"How do you know it was a strict one?" Celeste asked.

"Didn't it sound that way to you? Her brother was a minister and then a missionary. She didn't believe in divorce, so she felt like she couldn't leave Meadow Falls—even before she got pregnant with me. Looking back, it seemed like she was only happy when she and I went to church on Sunday morning. I never thought about it until now. That was just my mother—kind of like how my father always wore white shirts, and life was what it was here on the farm."

Celeste shrugged. "I often wonder who *my* father was and if he's still living. I've often thought of doing a DNA test just to see if I could find any relatives, but . . ."

All the questions I'd had about that picture of Roxy came back to my mind. "We've talked about being bombarded with money-hungry relatives, but we should do it anyway. As wild as my father was when he was younger, there could be a whole string of children somewhere out there. But to answer your question about children, I don't know. Like you said, I'd have to trust a guy to even consider a relationship that could produce a baby, and that would take a lot."

The sound of Celeste's giggle lit up the mood of the whole room. "We could each have a child and raise them up together as single moms."

"That's not funny," I scolded. "What if we turned out like our parents? God only knows that Mandy is too old to raise another generation, and neither of us know anything about babies. I pretty much know that there's not a lot of family out there for me to find, but Mandy mentioned coming from a big family, so you might have lots of fourth and fifth cousins."

"It's kind of scary," Celeste said. "What if my father is a serial killer—or if he was just a one-night stand with Roxy and now he's one of those strict preachers like your uncle?"

"We'll never know if we don't look into it." I was eager now for an answer to the question that had been nagging at me: What if Celeste was my half-sister?

"I've lived thirty-six years without knowing, and Roxy wouldn't even tell Granny who she thought I belonged to. We need to think about doing something like that before we dive right into it, Angela Marie. We can't unknow this stuff."

We sat there in silence for a couple of minutes. I'm sure she was just as deep in her thoughts about relatives as I was in my own.

Then she asked, "What would you do different as a parent if you did have kids?"

I thought about that long enough to eat another cookie before I answered. "The first thing I would do is fall in love. I would want to raise my kids in a home that was filled with love and happiness. I would want to be involved with my children's lives, and I'd want a husband who was as devoted to them as I was and as we were to each other. I would have three or four kids instead of one. That way, I might get one that would *love* the peanut business. If one or two didn't like rural life, they could follow their passion and not feel forced to learn everything there is to know about farming because they had to carry on the Meadow Falls tradition."

"You've thought about this for a while," Celeste said.

"Not really, but I know if I can't have it all, then I don't want any of it," I said. "How about you?"

"I would have more than one, too," Celeste answered. "We had each other, but basically, we were raised as only children, and the ideal thing would be that I'd fall in love with a man that comes from a huge family so my kids would have cousins."

I stood up and was surprised when everything was as it should be— no dizziness or feeling like the walls were closing in. "Mandy said that we need to spread our wings and fly. I think we should do the DNA test. If we know who we are, it might help us to know where we are going, and I would love it if, and when, I do have children, they had cousins."

"You know who you are," Celeste said.

"Not so much on my mother's side," I argued. "We both need to know more than Mandy can tell us." I knew that I was pushing Celeste, but now that the question had planted itself firmly in my heart and soul, I wanted answers.

"I'm ready for hot chocolate and popcorn." Mandy interrupted us as she came through the room. "Polly called me, so I didn't get a nap. She says that folks are talking about the new relationship you have with Devon. Since no one in town knows him, the gossip is heating up the phone lines like a Texas wildfire. One rumor that's going around is that you met him on one of them dating sites, and when you told Harrison about it, he dropped with a heart attack. Another has it that you have been seeing him for years."

"Let them talk," Celeste said with a nervous giggle.

"Yeah, right." I finally stood up. "If they're talking about me, they are leaving you alone."

"You got it!" Celeste said.

"Don't you two start arguing," Mandy said. "Let's move the chairs back to where we can watch television. I haven't seen that movie this year about the little boy who got left behind when his family went off to Paris—or was it London? Anyway, I haven't seen it in a long time, and it always makes me laugh."

"Sounds like a good plan for a cold Sunday afternoon," I agreed. "And I haven't seen *Home Alone* in years, either."

Giggling at the antics of a little boy might just be what we all needed that afternoon.

Chapter Twelve

G ood mornin', everyone," Devon said as he came through the kitchen door the next morning. "It's going to be another cold one. The thermometer out on the porch post says that it's twenty-seven degrees." He crossed the room and poured himself a cup of coffee.

I motioned toward the countertop. "Good mornin' to you. Breakfast is being served buffet-style this morning. Help yourself."

Devon picked up a plate and started loading it. "I didn't get home until bedtime last night, and all the lights were out in this place, so I didn't stop."

He said *home*. How could he call the farm his home after only being there a short while? I'd never lived anywhere else, and most of the time, I felt like I was just a hired hand who would move on at the end of harvest.

"Did everyone have a good day yesterday?" he asked. "Were you and Polly worn out from our party on Saturday night, Miz Mandy?"

"Neither of us went to church, and this is my third cup of coffee, which should tell you that I'm *still* worn out," she answered from the end of the table. "I can count on the fingers of one hand the times we've missed church in the last thirty years. We just stayed in and relaxed."

Devon brought his full plate and cup of coffee to the table. "Sunday is a day of rest, so it's okay if you miss going to church—at least in my opinion."

"How did your day with your grandparents go?" Celeste asked.

"Wonderful," he answered as he slathered butter on a couple of biscuits. "I told them all about what we have been doing here. I hope I didn't overstep, but I invited them up to see where I live and to take a look at the farm in a few weeks."

I'd grown up without relatives, so no one ever came to visit Meadow Falls. From the time I started to school, my father had made sure if I wasn't studying, then I was working, so there was no time for sleepovers or friends to come over to visit—other than transient help that came to wrangle the peanut business from May until the end of harvest.

Celeste and Mandy were all I had. I hadn't realized just how sheltered or deprived I'd been until that moment. "Do you have a lot of family?"

He took a few bites and then said, "I've got too many cousins to count, but Jesse—the one I'm closest to—is staying with Granny and Grandpa, so we had a good visit. He's a carpenter and was gone on a job last time I was there. He would love to drive up some Sunday afternoon. Would that be all right?"

"It's your house as long as you are working here, but you might want to ask the boss," Mandy was saying when I tuned back in to the conversation after checking out of my thoughts.

"We'd love to meet them," I said. "If they come during planting time, we might even put them to work."

"That's great, but do y'all have a problem with me having overnight guests, like my cousin Jesse?" Devon asked.

"Not a bit," Mandy answered.

Now I really wanted to get the DNA test done. Even if my suspicion about Celeste was wrong, I might have cousins who could come for visits. Heck, I'd even take great-aunts or great-uncles.

"And when your folks can come, they can stay here," I said and immediately wanted to grab the words and put them back in my mouth.

Devon flashed one of his brilliant grins. "Thank you for that, but they have a travel trailer they take places. I can tell you right now that Grandpa would just love to get back on a tractor anytime they are here. Even though he would never tell Grandma, I can tell that he misses farm life since he retired and moved into town."

"My Edward wouldn't have fared too well with retirement, either," Mandy said. "He loved to work—said it gave him a sense of pride to do a job and finish it well."

"That would be Grandpa," Devon said. "And Grandma, too. She was an elementary school teacher until she retired several years ago. She always said that having so many grandkids helped her understand the children in her classroom. And they thought our fake relationship was a real hoot."

"You should hear the rumors going around town." Celeste told him what Mandy had said earlier.

"And," Mandy said, "the best one is that Angela Marie is pregnant and Devon has asked her to marry him."

"Well," Devon chuckled. "I like the idea of being a father better than having caused someone to have a heart attack." He blew a kiss at me. "When's our baby boy due, darlin'?"

"Who says it's a boy?" I fired back at him, enjoying the flirting—but even more just having him close by.

His eyes twinkled. "Boy, girl . . . Doesn't matter to me. We'll talk about names while we work this morning."

Names? What would I name a child if I had one? My mind went down the short list of relatives, and I didn't like any of them.

Celeste snapped her fingers. "Angela Marie. You are staring off into space like you—"

I butted in before she could finish. "Like I do when I'm woolgathering?" I was afraid that Celeste was going to say, *Like when you fainted*, and I sure didn't want Mandy to know about that.

"She's always been good at that," Mandy fussed. "And yet we don't have a single wool sweater in the house to show for all her going off in her own little world."

Devon finished his food and coffee. "I got to admit, I'm guilty of the same thing. Something will be said in a conversation, and it will kick off a whole string of thoughts that run around in circles from one thing to another, and none of them have anything to do with what the topic is. Thank you for breakfast, but now, it's time for us to start to work on getting new tires on that last picker. See you there, Angela Marie—and, darlin', if we can't agree on a name for our fake baby, we'll let Mandy name him."

As usual, he cleaned off his spot on the table and headed toward the sink with his empty plate and silverware. I followed his lead and picked up my dirty dishes. While we were rinsing our plates, our hands got tangled up together. There was no mistaking the chemistry—at least not for me. Maybe Devon didn't get the jolt like the one that sent a little shot of desire through my body, but I did and it was the same feeling I'd had when we danced together and he whispered in my ear.

We both headed toward the barn at the same time, but he veered off toward the one where we kept all the machinery. He drove the picker into the barn, got down out of the cab, and waited beside the doors until I was inside before he closed them.

"I'll be kind of sad when we finish this last little job," he said. "But then after that, we will be working on a remodeling job."

"Luis used to say that there's always a job to be found on a farm this size," I said, and just remembering the words seemed to lighten the whole shop.

Devon carried the tools we had used every day across the room and lined them up on the floor. "Speaking of work—anytime you are in the market for a carpenter to do some repairs around here, my cousin might be available."

"Your cousin? Jesse, right? Why is he looking for work?"

"He had a small construction business, and then jobs dried up during all the quarantine stuff. On top of that, his wife divorced him and moved all the way to Maine with her new boyfriend," Devon explained as he started to work. "I just saw a good many things that needed fixin' up around here in addition to the remodeling you want to do."

A streak of lightning flashed through the window above the worktable, and somewhere not far away, the crackle told us that it had hit a tree. The clap of thunder that followed made me jump, and then a drop of water hit me on the forehead. The hard rain that started after that sounded like bullets pelting against the metal roof. Soon, the leak in the roof made a wet spot on the floor at my feet; then it became a thin trickle. I grabbed an empty five-gallon bucket and set it in the right place to catch the now-steady stream.

"It looks like we do need some repairs done," I agreed. "Tell me more about Jesse."

"He's the son of my oldest uncle on my dad's side. He's living down in Post right now with my grandparents and picking up odd jobs wherever he can. He's as stable as they come and a man of few words. He's dependable, and he's very good at what he does."

"That's a hard sell. I'd love to talk to him—and from the looks of this leak, the sooner, the better." Another drip began over on the other side of the tractor. I hustled up another bucket. Was it possible that the universe was looking after me by sending Devon and now the possibility of his cousin?

"How about tomorrow? He'd wanted to drive up." Devon looked up at the ceiling. "I think we've got the leaks all taken care of right now."

"Like I said, the sooner, the better," I answered. "You said he had a construction business, right? The more I look at the house, the more I want to give most—if not all—of it a face-lift. That might take quite a while, though. Do you want to commit to having a roommate for several months?"

"Jesse and I get along really well, so I don't see a problem there," he said. "I'll talk to him tonight. Yesterday, he told me that he had just finished the last job on his list, so I imagine he'll be glad to come soon. And thank you, Angela Marie."

"I should be thanking *you*," I said. "Luis usually saw to it that things like these leaks were fixed. His nephew Thomas took his place, but he left at the end of harvest last fall. I've been so busy with other stuff that I didn't even think about maintenance on the barns."

"I don't know how one person has done everything you are responsible for."

I picked up a crescent wrench and put it in his hand before he even asked for it. "You do what you have to do to survive and keep the farm going. I'm changing the subject here: Just how big of a family do you have, anyway?"

Devon talked as he worked. "There's just me in my immediate family. No kids, no ex-wives, none of that. But my grandparents in Post have ten kids—all boys. They're all married and have children of their own. My mother has seven siblings. My maternal grandparents—the ones who live out in Jefferson—have four daughters and four sons, but although they all live in a hundred-mile radius, they aren't close enough to help out with taking my Nana and Poppa to doctors' visits and doing their yard work for them. When my dad retired, my folks moved out there to be closer to them."

"Holy smoke! How many cousins do you have?" I gasped.

"Too many to count. The family reunions have to be held at parks because no one has a house big enough to hold all of us. We have one the Saturday before Mother's Day in Post and then one in Jefferson the Saturday before Father's Day," he answered.

"I'm so jealous," I whispered.

"I have four brothers—all older than me—and two sisters who are younger, and I'm the only one who doesn't have kids. That makes fourteen nieces and nephews," he said. "I could bring them all up here for a Sunday picnic anytime you want a big family around you. I'm real good at sharing, and they all live within a couple of hours of Post."

I did a quick count in my head. That would be about thirty people—more or less. My father and mother's Christmas parties didn't have a guest list that big.

"That would be fun." My mind went into overdrive thinking about a picnic down at the old willow tree in the spring.

"Consider it done." He grinned. "Would you hand me that heavy-duty tire iron? I can't get these nuts off with this one."

I gave him the tool, and as usual, sparks flew when my fingers brushed across his hand. After they had settled down, my mind went back to the possibility of cousins I didn't even know about floating around. Generations had passed, but I might find a cousin who knew a little more about their history than Mandy did. That was just on my father's side. My mother's brother was dead, but she might have had some cousins, too.

"From the way that rain is coming down, we might need to go into town and buy some gopher wood," Devon said.

"Why?" I asked, blinking away the notion of relatives.

"Isn't that what Noah used to build the ark?" He chuckled. "Maybe Jesse can knock a boat together if we get a flood."

"That's not funny," I said, but the smile on my face probably told a different story. "Another bolt of lightning might shoot down through the ceiling and fry you."

"It *is* a little bit." He climbed up into the picker when he finished putting the last new tire on it. "It's lunchtime. If you'll open the barn doors, I'll give you a ride to the house and then take it out to the machinery barn."

"I've got a better idea," I told him as I headed toward the barn doors. "We'll park it as close to the back porch as possible and jog into the house. Maybe the rain will slack off by the time we finish eating, and then we can put it back where it belongs."

"Great plan," he said. "How good are you at running between the raindrops and staying out of the mud puddles?"

"Better than you," I said with a laugh.

"Hey, now! I played football in high school, and I'm pretty good at duckin' and dancing," he protested as he started the engine and backed up to where I was standing.

"You got me there," I said, climbing into the passenger's seat. "I never played any kind of sports. But just in case you've gotten too old to do all that fancy footwork, I'll bring along a couple of rain slickers." I'd often envied the girls who wore those cute little basketball uniforms to school on game day, and I'd wondered what it would be like to be part of a team.

"The rain is coming straight down, so I don't think it will blow in too much. We could leave the barn doors open."

I slipped the slicker on and snapped the front—not such an easy feat when I was sitting down, but this wasn't my first rodeo. "I was thinking the same thing."

When we reached the back gate, Devon parked so that I was closest to the house. "Run like the wind, Angela Marie," he said.

I dodged mud puddles the whole way across the backyard to the back porch. He must have really been a good football player, because he beat me and had already opened the door when I arrived. I was disappointed when no good aromas greeted me—not even a little whiff of vegetable soup or a casserole heating up in the oven. A note on the countertop fluttered when I closed the door behind me and floated down to the floor. I sucked in air so quickly that Devon rushed over to me without even removing his slicker.

I had never—not one time—come in at noon to find no food ready. It might be a sandwich and a bowl of canned soup, but there would be something. My first thought was that something had happened to Mandy or Celeste. I checked my phone, but there were no texts or calls. If one of them hadn't even had time to call me, it had to be really bad.

With shaking hands, I picked up the note and read:

Granny is sleeping. I should be back before you come in for lunch, but in case I'm not, don't make anything. I've gone into town to pick up pizzas and a pasta tray. Granny said she was tired of funeral food. See you soon, Celeste.

The room did a couple of spins, and I felt the color leave my face. I grabbed for the cabinet, but Devon caught me before I could even get a grip on it. He pulled me close to his chest.

"What's going on?" he asked.

"It's just that . . ." I took a deep breath. "T-that . . ." I stammered, hunting for words.

"Is everything all right?" he asked.

"Yes, but nothing cooking, no one right here in the kitchen . . ." I had to stop and breathe in again. "It scared me." I handed him the note.

He quickly read it and then brushed a strand of hair away from my face. "You thought something had happened to one of them, didn't you?"

Other than a simple cold, I was never sick—no allergies, even—and even the sight of blood didn't bother me. What could be wrong with me that I fainted dead away earlier and now I almost passed out? And yet I couldn't blame all my breathlessness on the dizziness, because I had the urge to drag Devon's face down to mine and kiss him in the same moment.

"Yes," I whispered. "They are the only family I have."

"Well, honey, I'm your fake boyfriend. And as such, I'm willing to share all of my family with you," he said with a grin and then kissed me on the forehead.

"Thank you for that," I said and took a step back.

"Hello!" The noise of a slamming door filled the house ahead of her voice. The smell of hot pizza followed that, and then Celeste was in the kitchen with two flat boxes in one hand and a bag in the other.

Mandy had come out of her bedroom and shuffled along behind her. "This smells so good. Celeste, you are an angel to go out in this weather and get this stuff."

"I remember when you would work all day in this house, then come home at night and make cookies because I wanted them," Celeste told her as she set the pizza box on the countertop. "This doesn't begin to pay back those times. Let's get out paper plates and have a picnic."

Devon reached up into the cabinet beside me and took down four glasses. "I'll pour us up some sweet tea."

"We may be needing five glasses by the end of the week," I said, then headed toward the pantry for the plates.

"Oh, really?" Celeste opened both boxes.

"We have a leaky barn roof, and Devon has a cousin who is a good carpenter, so he could take care of that and our remodeling work." I tend to talk too fast when I'm nervous, and being so close to Devon that I could actually feel his heartbeat just a few minutes earlier had sent my emotions into a spiral.

"His name is Jesse," Devon said.

"That's wonderful," Mandy said with a quick nod. "When is he arriving?"

"Maybe tomorrow," Devon answered.

I nudged Celeste on the shoulder and said, "We *have got* to do that DNA thing. I want to know if I have relatives. I want a big family like Devon has, and we both need closure."

"What are you two whispering about?" Mandy eased down into a chair.

I told her that I thought Celeste and I should get our DNA tested. "I might find some family, and Celeste could find her father."

"Family is sure nice to have around," Devon said. "Granny says they halve the sorrows and double the joys."

"I'm not sure I want to open Pandora's box."

"You didn't have any trouble opening up those pizza boxes," Mandy said with a giggle. "Just do it. I'm not going to be here forever, and right now, I'm all you've got."

"Don't say that," I fussed at her.

"Life is like a roll of toilet paper," Mandy said, her tone dead serious. "The closer it gets to the end, the faster it goes. That's on a plaque in Polly's house, and it's the gospel truth."

"We won't talk about that today," Celeste said. "Let's hear more about this new carpenter that you might hire. What's your cousin's name again, Devon?"

"Jesse Parker, and he is the one I mentioned. I didn't even ask if room and board would come with Jesse's job . . . if things work out."

"Yes, it does," Mandy said before I could say a word. "He can stay with you, Devon, and we'll feed him. Wouldn't be right for him to have to cook for one when Celeste always fixes too much of everything anyway."

Mandy had said that I was now the boss, but I had my doubts.

Chapter Thirteen

Devon entered the house by the back door and hung his coat on a hook. "Hey, everyone, I'd like to introduce you to my cousin Jesse."

"I didn't know what time to be here, so I just drove on up last night," Jesse said. "Devon has talked so much about y'all that I really don't need introductions. The pretty blonde is his good friend from the military, Celeste. Angela Marie is his fake girlfriend. And you"—he flashed a brilliant smile at Mandy—"are the queen bee of this place, Miz Mandy."

I could believe that Celeste and I were related a lot more than I could that Devon and Jesse had a drop of shared DNA. Jesse was well over six feet tall, built like a weight lifter, and had thick blond hair that he had pulled back into a short ponytail. The only thing the two cousins shared was their clear blue eyes.

"On that note . . ." Mandy motioned toward the counter with her hand. "Help yourself to breakfast, and we'll all talk while we eat."

"Thank you, ma'am," Jesse said. "This all looks mighty good."

Jesse wasn't a bit shy when it came to eating a healthy breakfast. Just like Devon, he loaded up his plate with biscuits and gravy and a big square of the oven omelet. When he sat down, he looked me right in the eye and said, "I know you've got questions, so ask away."

"How long have you been in the carpentry business?"

"Since I was about twelve, but before that, my dad paid me to pick up nails and do other odd jobs around the construction sites where he worked. I was tall enough at twelve to learn to bed and tape dry wall, and it just went from there," he answered. "I've got references if you need them, but they might be biased since a lot of them will be from family."

"Come on now, Jesse," Devon said. "This is not the time to be humble. You have a whole list from clients."

"Yes, I do. I'll be glad to email them to you, along with my résumé," he said. "I would come to work for you just for the food if every meal is this good. I have a proposition for you: I'll work until the end of this month for just room and board. If you like my work after that, you can pay me. If you don't, then I'll be on my way with no hard feelings."

Mandy shot a look straight at me. "That sounds like a more-than-fair deal to me."

Jesse smiled across the table at me. "Any more questions?"

"You should look at the farm and let me tell you about the remodeling job I have for this house before you make up your mind. It could take months," I answered.

"If you had to decide this minute whether you would stay on the job at Meadow Falls, what would your answer be?" Celeste asked.

"Yes, I would take the job and move up here as soon as I could," Jesse shot back without hesitation.

"How do you know all that after just one night?" Celeste asked.

"Devon doesn't snore. Granny and Grandpa can put a hibernating grizzly bear to shame at their house. Last night was the first time I've got a good night's sleep in months," he said and went back to his food.

If there were a prize for snoring, Mandy would win it. Thank goodness the distance between her room on the first floor and mine on the second muffled the sound of a freight train coming through the house.

"And"—he took a sip of coffee—"I like that this place is out in the country. I've never really liked living in town."

I stood up and stretched my hand out across the table. "You've got a deal. Two weeks on the job, and then we'll both decide what to do on the first day of February."

Jesse pushed back his chair, got to his feet, and shook my hand. "Thank you, Angela Marie. I appreciate you taking a chance on me. Devon says the maintenance barn is leaking, so I'll get started on that today. Then I'll go through the other buildings and get them in good repair before we start remodeling your house."

"That sounds wonderful," Mandy said. "Do you know anything about peanut farming? Come summer, we might need you to do some of that, if you stick around."

"Yes, ma'am. Grandpa said all us kids needed to learn farming, that it would make us respect the land. Every one of us grandkids can drive a tractor and a harvester." He glanced over at me and Celeste. "Girls included."

"What's good for boys is good for girls," Mandy agreed with a nod.

"My granny made us boys learn the basics of cooking and cleaning house at the same time Grandpa was teaching us about peanut farming. And the same went for the girls," Devon said.

"Smart grandparents," Mandy said.

Mandy had often told Celeste and me the same thing, only she usually added that we needed to learn to be self-sufficient in all paths of life. Celeste had helped with the planting and harvest, just like I had. She had always been tall for her age, so she never had to sit on a pillow to see over the top of the tractor's steering wheel like I had. She got to spend more time in the kitchen than I did, but Mandy made sure I got trained in that area, too.

"Now, I'm going to go to my room and read some more of my book," Mandy said. "I'm reading the last one in a historical series about a wagon train of mail-order brides on the way to the gold mines in California. Sometimes I wish that me and Edward would have lived back then."

"But, Granny, just think about all the treasures you've seen in your lifetime," Celeste said. "You've seen the first televisions, and a man walk on the moon, and too many wars to count."

"Yep, but of all that, my best memories are of my four girls—Emma, Roxy, you, and Angela Marie." Mandy stood up and shuffled out of the kitchen.

Tears welled up in my eyes. Mandy had done so much for me that bringing her even an inkling of joy could very well be my greatest accomplishment in life.

I swallowed past the lump still in my throat. "Devon, do you reckon that you might help Jesse check out the barns this morning and make a list of what all he needs for repairs? Then you can hitch the flatbed trailer to the work truck and drive up to Lubbock to get the supplies. I really should help Celeste in the office for half a day before I turn the whole thing over to her."

"No problem, boss," he answered.

"I can't be your fake girlfriend and your boss both, so you need to choose which one I am," I said.

"Then no problem, darlin'," he said with a broad grin.

Jesse's chuckle was every bit as deep as his voice. "This is going to be a fun place to live."

I'd never heard anyone say that living at Meadow Falls was fun, so that struck me as strange enough that I couldn't think of a thing to say and filed it away to ponder over later.

"I'm glad you think so, Jesse," Celeste said. "We do have some good times here."

"Yes, we do," Devon said. "Why are we going to Lubbock for supplies instead of using the lumberyard here in town?"

"It closed up years ago," I explained. "We use the one up in Lubbock, on the north side. I'll text you the name and address of the place. Before you arrive, I'll call and make arrangements for you to charge to our account."

His eyes twinkled. "Sounds good."

Stranger than thinking about this being a fun place to live was the realization that in the past couple of weeks, that had been a true statement. With all the tension gone from the house, I hadn't been waking up every morning with a cloud of dread hanging over my head.

❖   ❖   ❖

"So, what do you think of Jesse?" Celeste asked when we were alone in the office.

I started to answer. "If he works as hard as—"

She threw up a palm to stop me and butted in before I could finish. "I'm not talking about his work ethic. I want to know what you think of him as a person."

I booted up the computer and sighed when I realized that there was at least a month's paperwork piled up beside it. This would take longer than half a day—but then, with Devon's help, we were far ahead of the schedule for meeting my January goals.

"Does that sigh mean you think he's handsome, or are you about to tell me that he's blah?" Celeste began sorting through all the mail.

"It means that we've got tons of mail and work to do—and why does it matter what I think of Jesse?" I asked.

She laid what were obviously sympathy cards we'd received since my father's death in one pile, invoices in another, and anything with an IRS return address in one all to itself. "It matters because if he's going to eat with us, live with Devon, and work for you, he needs to fit in with all of us."

"There won't be a problem there. He seems to be a nice guy, and Mandy likes him. I can always trust her judgment." I tore into the first IRS envelope. "Now the ball is in your court. What do you think?"

The first-quarter taxes were four days overdue. I dragged out the business checkbook and wrote a check for the estimated amount, put it in the envelope the government had provided, and set it to the side. "I'll get Devon to drop this in the mail on the way out. I suppose we should get busy doing thank-you cards for the flowers and food that was sent, too. Mandy kept track of all that and put it all in the book the funeral home provided. That should be . . ." I dug around in another stack of newspapers and magazines and found the thing. "Right here. The cards that the funeral home gave us are on the credenza in the foyer."

Celeste started that way but turned before she reached the door. "I think Jesse is a good man who has had some disappointments in life, just like we all have."

"Yep," I replied, but I was already looking over a notice about employment taxes.

A couple of hours later, Devon came through the house with a list and handed it over to me. "I want you to see this before we go to Lubbock. It's a lot, and the price of lumber and corrugated sheet iron isn't cheap. Don't want you to be shocked and fire me and Jesse when you get the invoice."

I glanced through it and raised a shoulder in half a shrug. "Looks good to me. If we don't do maintenance, the buildings will fall down around us. And I don't imagine that this will even be a drop in the bucket compared to the bill I'll get when we start remodeling."

"All right, then," Devon said. "If you think of anything else that you want us to pick up in Lubbock, just text or call."

I handed him the two envelopes for the IRS. "If you could drop these in the mail on your way through town, I would appreciate it."

"Yes, darlin'." He wiggled his eyebrows.

Jesse poked his head in the doorway. "Hey, is it all right if I just take a peek at the living room? You want me to start sometime next week, right?"

"Yep, go ahead," I answered. "And, Devon, you don't have to keep up the fake relationship when we are home."

"Then yes, boss." He snapped to attention and saluted me.

My forefinger shot up so fast that it was nothing more than a blur even to my eyes. "You are testing me, Mr. Parker."

He grabbed my finger and kissed it. "Yes, I am. But it made you smile, so even if I failed the test, it was worth it just to see your eyes sparkle."

As soon as he and Jesse cleared the room, Celeste leaned over from her side of the desk and whispered, "He was flirting with you."

"He was playing at the fake relationship," I protested. "How are you coming along on the notes?"

"Got maybe half of them done," she answered.

"Your handwriting is so much prettier than mine, so if you don't mind, you can keep working on those while I input all these bills into the computer." I didn't want to talk about Devon or the fact that I was really flirting with him, too.

Mandy's bedroom door opened and closed, and then the tapping of her cane against the hardwood floor heralded her approach long before she entered the office. "My eyes got tired of reading. I hated to leave the lady in my story in a bad place, but I had to lay the book aside for a while. I called Polly to see if she'd heard any gossip about you and Devon, and she filled me in." She dropped her cane on the floor beside the second chair and eased down into it. "These chairs are about the most uncomfortable things in the house."

"Rumors are still going on, then?" Celeste asked.

"It's a wonder the news isn't on one of them fake newspapers that you see at the grocery store counter," Mandy said. "Headlines would say, 'Meadow Falls Marriage in the Works' and then go on to report that Harrison had forbid Angela Marie to marry Devon Parker, but now that he was dead, she had brought him to the farm. They might even speculate as to when the wedding was and show some possible dresses."

"Are you serious?" My eyes popped open so wide that they ached.

"That's what is being spread around, even if it's not on the front page of the newspapers," Mandy answered. "Are y'all writing thank-you notes?"

"How can you drop a bomb like that and then just ask about notes?" I gasped.

"Honey, what did you think would come of the idea of you having a boyfriend?" Mandy asked.

Celeste laid down her pen and sat back in her chair. "I bet the whole town about burned down when Harrison brought Summer home."

"Not as much as when he married Sophia six weeks after he met her," Mandy replied. "Things have been pretty quiet for all these years, so folks have been hungry for something to talk about, and you gave them a jewel when you said you were with Devon, Angela Marie. Now, hand over some of those notes, and give me a pen. I'll help write them. I've filled out plenty of thank-you cards in my day. I used to do all of Inez's for her and then Sophia's. After she passed away, Harrison put that job over onto you, Angela Marie."

How on earth did Mandy ever have a moment to herself? I wondered. She had taken care of kids from the time she arrived on Meadow Falls, plus did the cooking and was overseer of the cleaning crew and gardeners. Now I learned that she'd helped with thank-you notes as well.

She picked up the first card. "I don't regret anything now that I'm older. I'm really glad for all the memories, both joyful and painful, because they've brought me to this day."

Celeste pushed the list over so that it was between the two of them and set a box of cards on the other side of it. "How long will it be before I feel like that, Granny?"

"That's up to you," she answered. "The way I figure it, when we learn to love the memories of the past because they are what makes us who we are, we begin to live for today and not let the past interfere with our joy, and we start to look forward to a bright future . . ." She stopped and took a long breath. "That's when we have peace in our hearts."

Peace.

That's what I wanted more than anything now that I had tasted a measure of it with no tension in the house. But to love all the memories of the past seemed like a high price to pay.

"Forgiveness is the secret," Mandy went on as if she could read my thoughts. "That changes us and takes away all the bitterness. It won't happen in the blink of an eye or even overnight, and we might have to go through the process more than once. For instance, Angela Marie needs to forgive Harrison for his attitude toward her. You, Celeste—you need to forgive your mother for leaving you behind and Trevor for being so cruel. You don't forgive to make the other person feel better. You do it to get that hard spot out of your heart. Hate and love cannot abide together. Hate is darkness, and love is light. Love produces peace. Hate eats away at you until there's nothing left but a dark hole inside your chest that nothing will cure."

"Forgiving my mother and Trevor *will* take a long time," Celeste whispered. "She could have at least told you who my father was or maybe left a letter for me to have when I was grown."

"I wish it could come just like that," I said, snapping my fingers.

"Sorry, but it takes effort and determination," Mandy told us.

If I was guaranteed closure and the peace that came with it, I was willing to give it my best.

Chapter Fourteen

I glanced at the free calendar that my father had gotten at the feedstore and hung up on the day that he'd had the heart attack. How could it be that he'd been gone going on three weeks? In some ways, it seemed like the funeral had been a year ago. But then again, walking back from the cemetery seemed like only yesterday.

"Does anyone need anything from town?" I asked when we finished breakfast that Thursday morning. "I'm taking soil samples up to Lubbock this morning. Anyone want to go with me?"

"I'm going to help Jesse with some repairs on the equipment barn," Devon answered. "He's fixed that leaky roof, and now he's moving on to some rotted boards up near the roof in the implement building. We need a couple more boxes of three-inch screws, so it would be great if you could pick those up for us. Jesse didn't realize it would take so many."

I was glad that he and Jesse could work together, but I would miss servicing the last couple of tractors with Devon that morning. After we finished those, we would move on to making sure the diggers and planters were in good working order.

Are you jealous, Angela Marie? my mother's soft voice asked.

Yes, I am, but not that I can't work with Devon. I'm jealous that he's got a big family and a cousin that's more like a brother, and you didn't have another baby or two to share some of this responsibility that's been laid on me.

"I'll put the screws on my list," Celeste said. "I'd planned on going to the grocery store in town, but there's a bigger selection in Lubbock. Granny, do you want to go with us?"

"Nope, but you can drop me off at Polly's," she answered. "I'll spend the day with her, and one of you can come get me after supper."

There you go, Mother whispered in my head. *You can have a day with Celeste. She's always been just like an older sister to you. Now you don't have to be jealous.*

Mandy had put on her coat and was shoving a red stocking hat down over her gray hair before Celeste and I had made it to the foyer. She grabbed her signature black purse from the ladder-back chair, where she put it every time she came into the house, and picked up her cane. "I haven't had a whole day to spend at Polly's house since before the last peanut harvest."

"Well, you've got one today." I took my gloves from the pocket of my coat after I'd put it on. "And anytime you and Polly want to get together, we'll be glad to take you to her house or bring her here."

"Does that mean I'm retired or that you're trying to get rid of me?" Mandy opened the door, and a rush of cold wind blasted into the house.

"Granny, we would never want to get rid of you." Celeste looped Mandy's arm through hers. "Hang on tight. As tiny as you are, this wind could blow you all the way to Canada."

"We need to feed you extra snacks so you will gain some weight," I told her.

"I could just put some rocks in my pockets," Mandy shot back. "And I never had a desire to see Canada. I'm not going anywhere at my age, so y'all just keep me from flying away to anywhere but heaven."

"You never told me that," I said as I helped her into the passenger seat of Celeste's SUV. "I was thinking that we would all take a vacation. Are you sure about not going anywhere, Mandy?"

Celeste slid in behind the steering wheel while I got in the back seat. "Let's save our pennies and make it a real vacation. Let's go to Alaska or Hawaii, or maybe even Paris."

"We don't have to save anything," I said. "There's enough money in my piggy bank to take us anywhere we want to go for a couple of weeks with no problem. Maybe instead of flying all the way, we should catch a plane to a port and do one of those cruises."

"Darlin' girls, I told you, I'm not going anywhere, but thank you for offering. What if I died—don't give me those looks—and y'all had trouble getting me home to be buried by Edward? No, sir, I'm staying right close to Meadow Falls. If y'all want to go gallivantin' off on a vacation, you go right on. I'll stay with Polly or else she can come stay with me while you are gone."

"But, Mandy, other than to drive across the border into Oklahoma a few times, neither one of us have been outside the state of Texas. We could take you to see where—"

She held up a palm. "What does it mean when I say no?"

"It means no," I answered.

"And?" Mandy cut her eyes to Celeste.

"It means that what you say is the law," Celeste said.

"That's right." Mandy nodded. "Get this wagon train moving. Polly already has the coffee brewing."

"Yes, ma'am!" Celeste and I said at the same time.

❖ ❖ ❖

If I had been paying attention to where I was going instead of trying to decide if I wanted to add a bag of oranges to the cart or just buy half a dozen loose ones, I wouldn't have had a head-on cart collision with Glenda. I started to just go around her without even speaking, but Glenda smiled sheepishly. "Shall we exchange insurance information?"

"I don't think any of our apples are bruised." Celeste's voice was cold enough that I seriously wondered if her breath had frozen the fresh broccoli. It sure enough chilled my bones.

Glenda's grin faded. "I'm glad I ran into y'all. I owe you an apology for the way I acted and for the things I said at the musical. I was angry, and I took it out on y'all, and I'm sorry. It's been laying heavy on my heart ever since I got home that evening. Please forgive me."

"Why *were* you so mean?" Celeste asked.

"It's personal," she answered. "But since you asked, I was mad at Bennie because he admitted that he'd had an affair, and like a coward, he told me over the phone. He said he had ended it, that he would never do something like that again and that he would do whatever it took to make our marriage work. I've been faithful to him, but I was so mad that I went to the musical and flirted with Digger and then with your boyfriend, Angela Marie."

"Did it make you feel better?" Celeste asked.

I wondered if Celeste had done the same thing when Trevor told her about his other woman. I thought of the old saying about there not being any fury that could top that of a woman scorned.

"It did not," Glenda answered.

"Why were you exchanging money with all your friends?" I asked. "That looked like you were all taking bets about whether or not someone like Devon Parker would even date me."

"I don't blame you for thinking that about me, after the way I acted." Glenda's chin quivered. "But the truth is, I've started a little side business selling homemade Christmas ornaments and greeting cards. I'm also doing some housecleaning to make ends meet. I was getting paid for the cards that those women had bought last month, and a couple of the girls were paying me for cleaning their houses last month. Bennie's work hasn't been so good lately, and finances are about to get tighter now that he's been laid off."

I remembered what Mandy had told us about forgiveness. "Apology accepted."

"Thank you," Glenda said. "And if y'all hear of any part-time work, Bennie is available."

"Does he know anything about remodeling a house?" Celeste asked.

Glenda nodded. "When we bought our house, it was in bad repair, and through the years, he's redone the kitchen and the bathroom. We've still got work to do, and now he has the time but not the money."

"So, you've been cleaning houses?" I asked.

"Yes, I have, but most folks in this area are too strapped for cash to pay me on a regular basis. I picked up a couple of jobs when ladies were getting ready for Christmas parties," she answered.

"We have been looking for a cleaning crew," Celeste said. "Interested?"

"I don't have a crew—but yes, I'm interested," Glenda said without a second's hesitation. "I'd be glad to work full or part-time."

"Then why don't you and Bennie both show up at Meadow Falls on Monday morning. We're about to do a major overhaul on the old place, and we could use the help. The job should last until planting season, and then, if the oil rig business hasn't picked up, Bennie can help with that," I said.

Glenda's eyes widened. "Are you serious?"

"Yep, I am," I replied.

"After the way I treated you . . ." she whispered.

"Look, just stop. I've been in your shoes, and it sucks," Celeste said. "I'm back here to live because Trevor and I divorced for the same reason you were so angry. And the house hasn't had a thorough cleaning in a month. If you're the only one working, you could work six hours a day and be home when your boys get out of school."

"Thank you." She wiped away a tear that had traveled down her cheek. "What time?"

"Eight o'clock would be good," I answered.

"We'll be there—and thank you again," Glenda said and disappeared around the corner.

"Why did you do that?" Celeste whispered.

"Why did you?" I fired right back at her.

"You said I was in charge of hiring a cleaning crew, and the dust in the dining room is so thick we could write one of Mandy's stories in it," she answered.

I settled on a bag of oranges and added them to the cart. "I did it because I need to learn to forgive like Mandy told us. It wasn't so hard to forgive Glenda. I'm not sure I'm ready to take that step with my folks."

"Did you think about the fact that we might actually help their marriage?"

The way she could read my mind, we should have been blood sisters, and I wished for the billionth time that we really were. "And that since her husband is there, she won't be flirting with Devon or Jesse?"

"Didn't think of that." Celeste picked up a bag of rice and put it in the cart.

"Since we know now that there is no betting going on, Devon doesn't have to be my fake boyfriend anymore," I said, more than a little disappointed at the idea of giving up the flirting.

Celeste took over pushing the cart while I gathered up potatoes, tomatoes, and yellow squash. "How does that make you feel?"

"You sound like a therapist."

"Maybe so, but you are avoiding the question." Celeste rolled the cart on ahead to the dairy products.

"For my part, I don't know how I feel, but maybe Devon will want to keep up the charade. Glenda, bless her heart, can run Polly some competition for being a gossip. If she finds out that Devon is on the market, she'll spread it all over the county," I answered. "Then women will be coming out of the woodwork with excuses to see Devon and Jesse both."

"You've got a point there. But, honey, things have already changed. Can't you feel it?" she asked.

"Yes, I can feel something in the air, and the feeling is so strange that I don't know what to do with it most days," I answered.

Celeste gave me a sideways hug right there in the cheese aisle. "Ditto," she said.

❖   ❖   ❖

Devon and Jesse shucked out of their coats, hung them on the hooks beside the door, and kicked off their boots at the back door. Devon's face was flushed, and his eyes looked tired, but he managed a smile when he looked across the room and saw me.

"Do I smell chicken and dumplings?" Jesse asked.

"You do," Celeste answered. "I just finished making them. Y'all go on and sit down, and I'll bring the pot to the table."

"Are you okay?" I asked Devon when he had eased down into a chair.

"I'm fine," he answered.

"No, he's not," Jesse said. "He started feeling bad a couple of hours ago. I think he's got the flu, and I tried to get him to go to the house and rest. He said he couldn't do that because—"

I laid my hand on Devon's forehead. "Good Lord! You are burning up. Whatever you've got, we don't want it, and we can't take care of you out in your house. So you're going to bed in one of the upstairs rooms right now. I'll bring your dinner up to you, along with some medicine to bring that fever down. We can't have Mandy getting whatever you have at her age."

"I can keep working—"

"Don't you have enough sense to know that you don't argue with the boss?" Jesse fussed at him.

"Okay, okay! I'm too tired to fight with y'all right now. Show me the way, Angela Marie," Devon said. "It's probably just a twenty-four-hour bug. I'll be back at work tomorrow morning."

"Follow me." I motioned with my hand and led the way through the dining room, the foyer, and up the stairs.

"Holy smoke!" he whispered when we reached the top of the steps. "How many bedrooms does this place have?"

"One downstairs and eight up here on the second floor. Mandy has the one downstairs, and six are empty up here. Celeste and I have the two occupied ones. You have a preference?" I asked.

"Long as it has a bed, I'm not picky."

Four bedrooms were on each side of the hallway, and an oversize bathroom occupied the end. I threw open the door to the one closest to the bathroom. He followed me inside and watched while I turned down the covers on the bed. "You crawl in here, and I'll bring your dinner up to you."

"You don't have to do that," he said.

"I don't *have* to do anything but die and pay taxes." I fluffed up a pillow and headed for the door. "I'm not ready to die, and the taxes are paid. I expect you to be under the covers when I get back."

He nodded. "Yes, ma'am—and thank you."

"You get sick days in your benefit package, Devon," I reminded him. "You haven't signed the contract yet, but it allows for vacation days and time off when you're sick."

"Does it get me a private nurse to put me to bed and bring me food?"

"No, that comes with the fake-girlfriend package," I threw back at him and eased the door shut behind me.

I could hear him chuckling and coughing both as I made my way to the end of the hall. Jesse and Celeste were deep in conversation when I made it back to the kitchen. I heard a few words about her time in the military. I dragged out the old tray I had used for my mother when she was sick and put two bowls of chicken and dumplings on it. I added a few buttered biscuits, two bottles of water, and two portions of peach crisp—the last of the desserts that had been brought in after my father passed away.

"Do you want me to carry that up for you?" Jesse asked.

"No, I've got it, but thanks for the offer."

"Remember, kissing spreads germs, and we sure don't need you to be sick," Celeste joked.

"I'm a fake girlfriend, so all he gets from me is fake kisses," I threw over my shoulder.

When I reached the bedroom, I set the tray on the floor, opened the door, and picked it back up—just like I'd always done when I was taking care of my mother. The only time I'd ever entered her room without permission was on the morning we found she had passed away in her sleep sometime in the night. When she didn't answer that day, I had eased the door open, left the tray on the floor, and sat beside the bed with her hand in mine. Eventually, my father had come to check on us, and *he* called the coroner and the funeral home.

Mandy had joined me while he was making the calls and wept for me since I couldn't find a single tear to shed. My mother had looked so peaceful lying there. Her thick, dark lashes spread out on her thin cheeks, and even though her hair was all gone, she was still beautiful.

My father had stood in the doorway, and the expression on his face was somewhere between relief and bewilderment. I could understand the latter, but relief? Surely, at one time, he had loved her enough to marry her. Maybe I understood him a little better now.

I'd held her hand even when they put her on the gurney, and I'd continued to hold it all the way to the hearse. Mandy had held my free hand, and that was a great comfort. My father had walked along behind me but didn't say anything.

I shook the memory from my head, set the tray on the dresser, and headed to the bathroom to get a couple of pills to bring down his fever.

When I returned, he held out his palm. I handed them to him and gave him a bottle of water.

"Take these and then sit up and try to eat a little bit. You need to keep your strength up to fight whatever is making you sick."

"I haven't run a fever in more than ten years," he said after he'd swallowed the pills. "The last time, it lasted a day and then I felt fine. I'm hoping that's the case this time."

When he was propped up with the tray over his lap, I sat down in the rocking chair at the end of the dresser. "Aren't you even going to ask me what the pills are?"

"Honey, I don't care if they are arsenic, as long as they make me feel better and I don't die from them." He took the first bite of food. "These are really good. I don't think I've ever had lunch in bed in my whole life. I keep thinking this is a dream and I'll wake up layin' out in the equipment barn."

"It's real," I told him. "I used to bring my mother's food up here all the time on that very tray. She was sick for a year."

His blue eyes looked downright bleary—as Mandy often said when someone was sick—but even with what looked like a permanent blush, he was still the sexiest man I'd ever laid eyes on. Not that I would ever admit that to Celeste—or anyone else. I reached for my bowl of dumplings, and his hand brushed against mine. Tiny sparks danced around the room like fireflies on a perfect spring night.

"Well, darlin', you would have to just shoot me if I was sick more than a day or two," Devon said. "I'm having trouble staying in here right now when I know Jesse is probably fixin' to go back out to the barn to work. I hate to be still."

"I'm a busy person, too," I admitted as I tried to figure out how to tell him that the fake relationship could be over. "You'll feel better after some rest. I want you to stay up here for twenty-four hours after your fever breaks."

He ate a few more bites of his food and then pushed it aside and drank some water. "I appreciate you totin' all this up here, but I can't eat anymore."

I set my half-empty bowl on the dresser and removed the tray. "I should tell you that we saw Glenda at the grocery store."

His brow wrinkled. "Who?"

"Remember the woman who flirted with you, and I said that we were together?"

"Did you shove onions down her throat until she turned blue?" Devon snuggled back down under the covers.

"No. She apologized, and I not only forgave her, but I also gave her and her husband a job here on Meadow Falls. So now you can end the fake relationship if you want to."

"No, thank you," he said. "I like having a fake girlfriend. She makes me go to bed when I'm sick and even brings me food and talks to me. I'm not going to break up with her. Now, how about you? Are you going to break my heart while I'm sick with the plague?"

He was teasing, but I had never felt so alive, so beautiful, or maybe—most of all—even needed. The feeling was heady, and I loved it.

"You might have the flu, at the most. You do not have the plague."

"If I do and you get it, I promise I will bring you food and spend time with you," he said, continuing to flirt. Could there be a mutual attraction between us?

He didn't realize how much it touched my heart. Only Mandy had done that for me the few times I'd absolutely had to go to bed for a day.

"If you give me your bug, I will make you stand good on your promise." I picked up a bowl of cobbler. "You sure you can't eat a few bites of your dessert?"

"No, thank you. I just need water—and maybe a shower and some clean clothes when this fever breaks," he answered.

"I'll have Jesse pack a bag for you. You'll find everything you need for a shower in the bathroom at the end of the hall," I told him.

"Thank you," he said with a nod. "Tell me again, what jobs did you hire Glenda and her husband for? And when are they starting to work?"

"They start on Monday. Glenda is going to be our new house-keeper. Bennie is a carpenter, so he'll actually be working for Jesse. Now, you get some rest. I'll check on you in a few hours," I said. "Or if you get to feeling worse and need to go to the doctor or just want something, send me a text. Fake girlfriends are real good at taking care of their imaginary boyfriends."

"Thank you again," Devon said. "I could so fall into fake love with you, Angela Marie."

"I'm not ready to take that step, darlin'." I blew him a kiss and closed the door behind me. I sat down on the top step and savored every flirty moment and every nuance. I held on to the vibes between us like I would a Fourth of July sparkler and loved every minute.

Chapter Fifteen

When I made it to the kitchen the next morning, Devon was sitting at the table with a cup of coffee in his hands. He was fully dressed in jeans and a chambray work shirt, and there was no sign of redness in his face. "My fever broke last night, and I'm not one hundred percent well, but I'm close. Thank you for taking care of me. Coffee is made. Anything I can do to help with breakfast?"

I filled a mug of coffee and turned on the oven. "I'm on breakfast duty this morning, and everything is organized. You just sit there and talk to me. You sure you don't need another day of rest?"

"I may not be ready to climb up on a roof and help Jesse, but I can work on a tractor or two," Devon answered.

I had planned to spend the day taking care of Devon, but that idea had been shot out of the sky like it was one of the skeet pigeons my father had liked to shoot with his buddies. I had to confess, I was a little disappointed, but I really didn't think Devon should be doing all that much, so I thought quickly. "We need to get out the pencil and paper and start making lists for the remodeling job that starts on Monday. We'll begin in the living room, figure out what is needed for the entire downstairs, and then go up to the bedrooms."

"I was under the impression that you were only tearing up the living room," Devon said.

I removed a pound of bacon from the refrigerator and laid it out, piece by piece, on a sheet pan. "I'd thought that in the beginning, but then I looked at the bedrooms and changed my mind. I want to have the entire house remodeled—and then, when it's warm enough, I want the outside repainted. It's been white ever since it was built, but I'm thinking a warm shade of yellow might be nice."

"I thought the inside walls were going to be yellow," Devon said.

"I like that color. Maybe the outside will be a shade darker, with white shutters and porch posts."

"Is it your favorite color?" he asked.

"I suppose it is. I love it because it's so bright, and like the sun, it brings light into the world," I answered.

"You think it can all be done by plantin' time?" Devon asked.

I worked as I answered. "I've hired extra help, and if we need more, I bet Bennie has some friends who would be glad to have winter jobs. Work around these parts is scarce until plantin' season comes around."

"Good mornin'," Mandy said and sniffed the air on the way to her chair. "Is that cinnamon?"

"Cinnamon rolls and bacon are in the oven. We're having scrambled eggs and toast made out of that homemade bread that Celeste whipped up yesterday." I poured a cup of coffee for her and carried it to the table.

"We should make one of those caramel bread puddings with the leftover bread and cinnamon rolls," Mandy suggested. "Celeste can use my recipe for that and for the butter sauce that goes on top."

"I've gained five pounds just listening to y'all talk," Devon said.

"Well, look at you!" Mandy turned to face him. "I walked right past you and didn't even realize you were in the room. How are you feeling?"

Devon returned her bright smile. "I'm good. It was just one of those twenty-four-hour things, and I'm over it now. Did you have a good time at Polly's yesterday?"

"Oh, honey," she said with a long sigh, "it was better than good. It was *awesome*, as you kids say these days. We looked through her old picture albums and took a walk through the past. One where we didn't even need to lean on our canes or feel like our knees were going to break afterwards. It was amazing."

Both Celeste and Jesse arrived at the same time. Celeste covered a yawn with her hand, and Jesse did the same thing when he came through the back door.

"Mornin,'" they said in unison.

Jesse glanced across the room toward Devon and said, "I see that you have risen from the dead."

"A good woman's care will cure me every time," Devon joked.

"I don't remember Trevor ever telling me that I was a *good woman*. What makes one?" Celeste asked.

"A good woman is one whose heart is bigger than her ego," Mandy answered.

I had never heard Mandy say that before, and I thought I'd heard all her sayings.

"I agree," Devon said.

"I'm surprised you didn't fake sickness a few more days." Jesse poured himself a cup of coffee and sniffed the air. "I smell cinnamon."

"Yep, you do," Mandy said. "Celeste made cinnamon rolls, and they're about ready to come out of the oven."

Jesse laid his hand on his heart. "I've flat-out died and gone to heaven."

I pulled the pan of bacon from the oven and set it on the stove, then removed the cinnamon rolls and quickly added buttercream icing to them while they were still hot. Celeste grabbed a roll of paper towels and shifted the slices of bacon over onto several sheets to drain.

"Y'all sure work together well," Devon said.

Celeste gave him a curt nod. "Granny trained us to work as a team."

"Yes, I did, and it paid off," Mandy said and bowed her head for a quick grace. When she finished, she said, "Amen. Now let's eat so you kids can get to work on time. What's on the agenda for today?"

"Today we're going to take a trip through the house and decide what we want to do about the remodel," I answered. "Bennie will be here Monday, and Jesse will oversee the job."

"Will Jesse tell Devon what to do, too?" Celeste asked.

"He's going to be the boss when it comes to remodeling. Devon can be the boss when it comes to everything dealing with machinery." Just saying those words out loud took a burden off my shoulders.

"And Glenda is coming to clean for us, right?" Mandy asked as she put food on her plate and then passed the platter around. "We'll have to be careful what we say in front of her. She spreads gossip."

Celeste giggled out loud. "Granny, your best friend is—"

"I know"—Mandy held up a veined hand—"but what Polly tells is the truth." She frowned for a full thirty seconds and then smiled when she thought of the word. "She *researches* what she hears before she spreads it. If it's not pure gospel, it don't go into the rumor mill. Glenda tells things that might not be true."

"One more thing that we forgot to tell you about last evening." I put eggs on my plate and handed the bowl across the table to Devon. I wasn't even surprised at the chemistry between us when our fingertips touched. Could the rumors have a thread of truth in them?

"What's that?" Mandy asked. "You've always been the worst kid in the world to start to tell something and then get lost in the world between your ears. Spit it out, girl."

"Devon and I are still in a fake relationship—for his sake," I answered.

"Then you better make it seem like a real one," Mandy said. "Glenda can sniff out a lie in thirty seconds. You remember how she was in high school? Well, she's had more than a decade now to hone that gossiping skill to a fine edge."

Mandy was so right. My wandering thoughts probably came from living in my own world most of my life—at least from the moment the kitchen was cleaned up after supper until bedtime. But now that I had all these people around me, I thought I should really try to control them a little better.

❖　❖　❖

By evening, I was tired of words. Tired of trying to figure everything out. Tired of answering all Jesse's questions and agreeing or disagreeing with the dozens of suggestions everyone made. We'd written everything in a notebook and decided that the first thing we'd do was pile all the living room furniture in the middle of the floor and strip the wood paneling from the walls. That gave me a while to decide if I wanted to change anything we had talked—and talked and talked—about in the rest of the house.

I just wanted to get away from everyone for a little while and dive back into my own thoughts. Lord have mercy! Why had I ever thought I wanted a big family around me?

When supper was finished, Jesse and Devon headed out to their house. Celeste said that she and Mandy were going to drive into town and take Polly to the ice-cream store for a milkshake. I declined the invitation to go with them so that I could have some time alone. As soon as Celeste's car cleared the driveway, I slung on my coat, stomped my feet down into my boots, and headed out the back door. Another reason I hated winter was that it got dark so early in the evenings, and it always seemed to be colder when the sun went down.

That night was no different. As always, a cold wind blew down from the north, rattling tree limbs, stirring up dead leaves, and making dust tornadoes here and there. A yellow stream of light from Devon's windows flowed out across the still-frozen ground. My thoughts immediately went to the idea that all the darkness in the world couldn't put out a single light. Devon had brought brightness into my life, and to Meadow Falls, and I was so glad for that. Then Jesse had added to it. The way he looked at Celeste made me wonder if, after she had been divorced for a couple of years, there might be a relationship between them.

"Maybe she's been burned so badly that she'll be content to stay away from that flame called *marriage* for the rest of her life. Like Mandy," I whispered.

A million stars danced around the waxing moon that evening. No dark clouds in sight, and the weatherman had said we would have sunshine for the weekend. We would have wind but no rain or snow until the next week, and then we could look forward to a big snowstorm rolling in on Monday. I was glad we would be working inside for the next while and wouldn't have to wade through snow up to our knees to get out to the barns.

My plan was to walk down to the creek, but when I reached the cemetery, I stopped. I was alone so I could get some things off my chest, even if my father and mother couldn't hear me. The gate groaned when I pushed it open, and the frozen grass crunched under my feet. I walked past the big chunk of marble engraved with "Duncan." I paid particular attention to all my ancestors and the babies who would have been my uncles and aunts.

When I came to the section where my parents were buried, I was suddenly speechless. I had never been allowed, or had the courage, to lash out at them. Mandy reminded me often that I should always respect them because—good or bad—they were my parents, and the Good Book said that I should honor them.

"I did what Mandy told me about honoring you two," I finally whispered, "but it was out of fear, not love. I wanted both of you—or even either one of you—to be proud of me, and I was always terrified that I would disappoint you. So I just settled into life like you wanted me to, but I really need to talk or yell or even cuss to get all these feelings out of my chest." I looked down at my father's grave. "Why were you keeping pictures of Summer and Roxy in your dresser drawer?"

Do the math, the pesky voice in my head said.

The math for what? I frowned at the wilted flowers lying on his grave.

Think about it, the voice said.

I clamped a hand over my mouth when I figured out what the math was telling me. Roxy would have been close to the same age as Summer had been when my father brought her to Meadow Falls. Roxy had to have reminded him of his first real love.

That was the reason behind it. "Oh. My. God!" I gasped.

I glared at the tombstone. "If you are Celeste's father, why didn't you acknowledge her?"

Of course, he didn't rise up out of the grave and answer me, but I was more determined than ever to have that DNA test done. I tried to imagine what his mother would have done if he'd told her that he was in love with Roxy.

If all that was true, then it wasn't any wonder that Roxy had shed tears at his wedding to my mother. And if it was, her ultimate punishment to him was leaving her baby on the farm for him to have to look at every day for the next eighteen years. Oh yes, I would definitely be insisting on a DNA test for both of us.

The wind picked up and rattled the bare limbs on the tree not far from their headstones. I looked up and saw a cat sitting in the fork of the tree. I had always, always wanted a kitten, but my mother said she wasn't having cat hair on the furniture, and my father had just said no, and when he said no, I knew better than to even ask again—ever.

"It's my house and my farm now," I said, then called, "Kitty, kitty, kitty," to the cat. "Come on down out of that tree. It's too cold for people or animals to be out in this weather. If you'll let me, I will gladly take you to the house and give you a nice warm home."

As if it understood me, the cat shimmied down from the tree and let me pick it up. "You are a chubby little kitty, and now you are mine." Then I realized that the cat's backbone was sticking up and that the only thing that seemed fat was its stomach.

"Well, well, well." I smiled at the irony of getting not one cat but a whole litter. "There will be a bunch of you to shed on the furniture, and there's no one to tell me I can't keep every one of your babies."

I took my cell phone from the hip pocket of my jeans and called Celeste.

"Did you think of something you need? Maybe a chocolate milk-shake?" she asked.

"Nope, but I do want you to pick up some things for me. We are adopting a pregnant cat, so please get a bag of litter, a box to use for that, a bag of dry cat food, and some of those cans of wet food," I answered.

"Are you serious?" she asked.

I walked out of the cemetery and didn't even try to close the gate. If ghosts of the past came into the almighty Duncan graveyard to pester my father, I didn't really care. And if his ghost floated out to fuss at me over taking a cat into the house, then I would ignore it. He quite possibly really had fathered Celeste, and that was why he'd had all those pictures on his dresser.

My mother popped into my head. *Damn, daughter, you are slow.*

Mother never, ever said a swear word, so I stopped in my tracks. "You don't cuss."

I could almost hear her saying, *Not where you could hear me. Now, go prove what I figured out long ago, and keep those cats off the furniture.*

"Are you there?" Celeste yelled into the phone so loud that I held it out from my ear.

"What?"

"I asked if you are serious," Celeste answered.

"I'm every bit as serious as a sober judge. I'm going to name her Caramel. She's a light-orange kitty with darker stripes, and she was in the tree close to my father's tombstone—so it kind of seems like karma or an omen that she turned up when I wasn't even planning to go to the cemetery."

Celeste laughed. "Kind of does. Do you think Harrison sent her to you?"

"Yeah, right," I answered. "He's probably having a fit right now because I'm changing things so much."

"You're right," Mandy said. "Celeste has the phone on speaker, and that cat and I are going to be good friends. I always wanted pets, but the rule on the farm was no animals. Miz Caramel might enjoy a few bites of that leftover baked chicken that's in the refrigerator before we get home with some proper food for her."

"Thank you, and when the babies are born, y'all can help me name them," I said.

"Are you planning to keep the whole litter?" Polly asked.

"Every single one," I answered.

"You really are making some radical changes," Celeste said.

"Oh, yeah, I am. See you soon." I ended the call and kissed the cat on the top of her head.

Chapter Sixteen

*C*aramel made herself right at home from the moment I set her down in the utility room. She scarfed down a saucerful of chicken, drank some water, and then went to the living room and curled up on the sofa. When Mandy and Celeste came home, she hopped down and purred the whole time that she twined around Mandy's legs.

I already loved the cat, but now I wondered if my impulsiveness in bringing her into the house had been a big mistake. She could trip Mandy and cause her to fall and break a hip. "Oh, no, Caramel." I picked her up. "You have to learn to—"

"Leave that sweet kitty alone," Mandy scolded. "I walk so slow that she's not going to cause me to fall. I can't wait to see her kittens. If one of them is black, it's mine, and I'm going to name it Pepper. I had kittens when I was a kid, but when we moved here, Clifford stuck to *his* father's rules about no animals on the farm." She sat down in a nearby chair and held out her arms. "Give her to me so we can get acquainted."

Celeste stopped to pet her and then started back outside. "Poor thing is just a bag of bones."

"Want me to help bring in stuff?" I asked.

"No, I can get it. Do we want to set up the litter pan in the utility room?" Celeste asked.

"That would be the best place," Mandy said with a nod. "And it will need to be scooped a couple of times a day. I bet the thought of having a litter pan in the house is causing Inez and Victoria to turn over in their graves."

Celeste returned with the last armload of cat stuff and carried it to the kitchen. "I'll get this taken care of, and then maybe you can tell us a story about my mother."

"This would be a good night for that story," Mandy agreed. "She always wanted a kitten, but the rules . . ." She shrugged. "Petting a cat is good for the soul, and they keep the mice at bay. Mama liked to have a few around just for that reason. Sometimes I miss my mother, but I still remember her as if I was standing in the kitchen, helping her make supper. I wonder if Roxy ever missed me," she said with a long sigh.

"Of course she did. I can't even imagine—and don't want to—how much I would miss you if I ever moved away from here," I said.

Celeste entered the living room. "Who's moving?"

"Mandy was wondering if Roxy ever missed her," I answered.

Celeste settled down on the end of the sofa and patted the place next to her for me. "Granny, she probably cried herself to sleep more than one night. I know that she missed you because I did."

Mandy continued to pet Caramel even though the cat seemed to be sound asleep. "Thank you, girls, for that. Angela Marie, bring out your phone and get ready to record, but don't lay it on the arm of the chair this time. If you do, mostly what you'll get is Missy Caramel's loud purrs. I believe she's telling us how much she appreciates the food and a warm place to live."

I slipped my phone from the pocket of my chambray shirt, laid it on the end table, and hit the record button. "Okay, we're ready."

"Roxy had it a little easier in some ways than Emma did. Folks these days don't think anything about babies being born to unwed mothers, but they weren't quite as forgiving in the late sixties, when Emma got pregnant. With all that free-love movement, times were changing, but in small towns like Meadow, gossip . . ." She paused. "Well, you see how things are when it comes to rumors in a small town."

"What kind of rumors?" Celeste asked.

I thought of the picture hidden away in my bedroom. In that day, lots of girls wore miniskirts, but very few—if any—would have sported a tattoo like Roxy had had on her chest. Had she shown off that butterfly at school and gotten a bad reputation because of it? Had Harrison paid for it so that she would be more like the love of his life?

"We knew who Roxy's daddy was," Mandy went on without really answering the question. "Emma even finished high school just before she gave birth to Roxy, and she was a good mother until she got killed in that car wreck when Roxy was almost five. She worked at the grocery store in town and helped here on the farm on weekends. I offered to send her to college, but she wouldn't have any part of it. She told me she had a child to think of, and she wanted to be a part of her daughter's life."

"Then she wasn't as wild as my mother?" Celeste asked.

"Roxy was getting pretty sassy before Harrison showed up with a wife, but after that, she got a hundred times worse. She talked about running away and being an actress or an artist. She hated this place, and the friends she had at school didn't like her anymore. This went on until she graduated. I expected to get up every morning and find her gone, but she seemed to settle down. I thought she'd outgrown her rebellion, and then she told me she was pregnant. I begged her to tell me who your father was, Celeste, but she would not."

That picture of Roxy flashed into my mind again. My father was still running wild in those days, and Roxy was an image of his first real love. There were only about six years between them, so they'd both been adults. I glanced over at Celeste. Right now, she was pinching her nose between her finger and thumb. I'd seen my father do that dozens of times when he was thinking.

"Who did you suspect?" I asked.

"She never said, and I didn't pressure her. I figured she would tell me when she was ready," Mandy replied. "When Emma got pregnant, she told me that the baby belonged to her boyfriend she'd been dating for more than a year. Not Roxy, though. That girl clammed up so tight that I don't think the offer of a million dollars could have gotten the name out of her. Things changed at Christmas. That's when she told me she was leaving as soon as she could travel after you were born. One of the guys who had worked on the farm during harvest was going to California, and she was going with him."

"Do you think he was my father?" Celeste asked.

"There's one way to find out," I told her. "We can do a DNA test and see if any relatives pop up."

"I agree," Mandy said. "We've talked about it before, but you should get serious about it. You might have brothers and sisters somewhere out there in the big wide world."

Celeste rolled her eyes toward the ceiling. "Okay! Okay! I'll do it—but what happens if a bunch of hippies come around, wanting to live in tents on Meadow Falls?"

"The crew we've hired to help with harvest for the past two years brings their RVs and live out behind the barn," I told her. "We don't ask if they're from a commune, but they might be. We might have been working with your brothers and sisters all this time."

Celeste shook her finger at me and frowned so hard that the crow's-feet wrinkles around her eyes deepened. "Don't tease me like that. I'll do the test, but if relatives start emailing me, I'm going to ignore them. Is that understood?"

"Yes, ma'am," I agreed.

"Did my mother ever bond with me?" Celeste asked. "Emma loved Roxy, but . . ."

"She had made up her mind," Mandy answered after a sigh, "that she was not going to raise you. She had you on Valentine's Day, after a fairly easy labor and delivery. I thought that she might learn to love you, but she wouldn't even hold you or give you a bottle."

I reached over and took Celeste's hand in mine. That had to be hard to hear.

"Just like Sophia," Mandy said.

Celeste squeezed my hand. "How's that?"

"Sophia had a very hard labor and delivery. She should have been in the hospital, but Duncan babies are born here," Mandy said. "She was too weak to hold you for days, so I took care of you, Angela Marie."

"Who named me?" I asked.

"That was one thing Sophia was adamant about. You were to be named Angela after her mother and Marie after her sister-in-law and best friend who had died," Mandy answered.

"I never knew that. But the news that my mother wasn't close to me from the beginning doesn't surprise me," I said with a shrug.

"And me? Who named me?" Celeste asked.

"Roxy insisted that you be named Celeste Star," Mandy almost whispered. "I thought if she chose a name for you that she might change her mind about leaving you behind. She told me just before she drove away with that boy that you are named after the stars that she and your father used to watch at night. Celestial beings, she called them. I really didn't want to ever have to admit that to you, but I guess you deserve to know."

Celeste let go of my hand, stood up, and began to pace around the floor. "Thank you, Granny. In your opinion, why didn't she take me with her? If I belonged to that guy . . ."

Mandy breathed in deeply and let the air out slowly. "I don't believe that he was your father. On the morning they left, she told me that she wanted you to be raised on Meadow Falls."

Of course she did. That would be the ultimate punishment for my father, to have to watch his daughter grow up right under his nose. If he admitted that Celeste was his, all hell would break loose, both with Inez and my mother. He'd had a choice to make, and he chose the farm.

Mandy set the cat on the floor and stood up. "And that is enough of the storytelling for tonight. I'm going to bed now. I'll leave the door cracked so Caramel can come into my room and sleep with me if she wants to."

And I'd thought the cat was going to belong to me. Looked like Caramel was going to be a community kitty.

Chapter Seventeen

*M*andy fussed about missing church two Sundays in a row, but she felt better about not going out in a blinding blizzard when Polly called and told her that services had been canceled that morning. Devon sent a text saying that he and Jesse were staying at their house for breakfast, and Mandy declared that she wanted oatmeal and toast, so that was an easy fix.

"I'm going to my room with Caramel. She likes to lay beside me while I read," Mandy said when we'd finished eating. "We need to make her a bed to have her babies in soon. Maybe an old laundry basket with a towel in the bottom."

"Where are we going to put her bed?" Celeste asked.

"In my bedroom, right beside my rocking chair," Mandy answered as she left the kitchen.

"What's on your agenda for today?" I asked Celeste as we started the cleanup.

"I'm going to read awhile, watch it snow awhile, have a snack, and then repeat," she replied. "What about you?"

"I'm going to get files ready to send to the CPA," I answered.

"Why?"

"I like to get all the documents to her early. I don't know what will happen with my father dying right at the end of the year," I explained. "Enjoy your read, watch, snack, and repeat."

She followed me out into the foyer and went up the stairs. I went into the office and found Caramel curled up in one of the upholstered chairs on the other side of my desk. I stopped and rubbed her fur for a few seconds. She didn't look nearly as scraggly as she had when she was soaking wet and half-starved. "So you do belong to me—at least part of the time," I said with a soft giggle. "I bet Mandy fell asleep, didn't she?"

Caramel purred an answer and then closed her eyes and tucked her nose under her paw. I tiptoed around the chair and turned on the computer. While it booted up, I stared at the four oak file cabinets lined up on the north wall. I'd always done everything on the computer, but I kept receipts filed away in the last cabinet—just in case cyberspace failed us.

"Victoria's and Inez's paperwork is probably still stored away in those," I muttered as I crossed the room. Since I'd always worked on a computer and backed up everything on an external hard drive, I'd never been interested in old business receipts. But the ones from eighty years ago probably should be tossed after all these years. I opened the first drawer in the cabinet at the end of the row to find files in alphabetical order, starting with Wyatt Personal and going on to Victoria Personal. I flipped through them until I found my name. I pulled out the folder and carried it over to the desk. I sat down in my chair and opened the folder to find my birth certificate, copies of the paperwork for my social security card, and other important documents. But tucked inside together with all that was an envelope with my name on the outside.

I recognized my mother's beautiful handwriting and wondered when, where, and why she had filed that away. Rather than tearing into it, I carefully cut the end open, and with trembling hands, I slid the letter out.

For a long couple of minutes, I just stared at it, but then I gently unfolded it. I couldn't take my eyes off the date or the first line:

May 15, 2005. To my dearest daughter, Angela Marie.

The letter had to have been written just weeks before she died, and she had called me *dearest* and recognized me as her daughter. Tears flooded my eyes and dripped off my jaw. I quickly grabbed a tissue and wiped them away so they wouldn't blur the ink on the paper.

More tears flowed as I read the first line:

Angela Marie, first let me say that I'm very proud of the good woman you are becoming in spite of this farm.

"A good woman . . ." I thought of the discussion we'd had earlier. "Why couldn't you tell me that while you were alive?" I whispered and then went on to read:

> *I don't even know how to begin this letter, and to explain everything would take more ink than there is in this pen, but I will try. The relationship, or lack of one, I had with your father isn't a nice story, but it is the truth. He was in love with another woman, and according to him, I could never take her place. By the time you were born, I had figured out I didn't love him, either, and that this place was toxic. I couldn't go, and I would be miserable if I stayed—almost as unhappy as he was. I would have left and taken you with me, but when I was packing to leave, he reminded me of the prenup I had signed. If I left, I would receive only ten*

thousand dollars, and I could not take you with me.

That night, I had found two pictures in the drawer of his dresser. One woman was his first wife. The other was Roxy. They had both left Meadow Falls before that time, but I recognized Roxy, and my temper went through the roof. I asked him if her baby belonged to him, and he refused to answer. We were both angry and said mean things to each other. He had never yelled at me before, but he did that night. He said that he'd just had a child with me so that a Duncan would always live on Meadow Falls like his mother wanted. If she would have let him, he would have taken his inheritance, moved far away, and had children with his first wife.

I couldn't leave you behind, so we settled into our roles and pretended that we had a happy marriage. Now that my time is coming to an end, I realize that we were each married to the security of this farm, not to each other. I didn't realize until it was too late that my decision would determine the course of your life as well as mine. Harrison needed a good woman, one to fit in with his world as boss of Meadow Falls. I was true to him because of my faith—not out of love—and that made me a doubly good woman in his eyes. He was drawn to other women of a wild nature, and I didn't care—not after I figured out that he didn't love me. No, that's not right—he couldn't love me because he couldn't let go of Summer Rain—so he was constantly looking for someone to give him the excitement that she had.

I stayed so that I could, hopefully, have a little influence on your life. But Harrison had other ideas for you. The only time I got to go anywhere alone with you was church, and he drove us both there and brought us back to the farm. I never was a good mother, but I just want you to know that since my journey in this life is coming to an end, I wish I had done things differently. Rather than throwing myself into showing him that if I couldn't have you, then I would stay and make his life miserable, I wish I had stolen you away and gone to a place where he could never have found us.

I hope you find this letter and accept my apologies for being as bad a mother as Harrison was a father. We both married for the wrong reasons—I didn't want to go to a foreign country with my brother, and marrying Harrison was a quick fix. He wanted a wife that his mother could be pleased with, so he courted the religious woman who did not know much about his past.

Neither of us did right by you, but Mandy did a fine job of raising you. For that I will always be grateful to her.
Love,
Mother

I laid the letter to the side and let the words sink into my heart and soul. My mother had apologized—maybe not on her death bed to me directly, and it was years later, but there it was.

When the initial shock wore off, anger washed over me. Why couldn't she have told me all this while I was sitting beside her bed all those days and nights? I paced the floor for what seemed like hours, but when I checked the big clock on the wall above the file cabinets, it had only been five minutes. I couldn't stay in this toxic house another minute, but where could I go? Why had my mother thought she had to choose between going to a foreign country with her brother and marrying my father? The more answers I found, the more questions I had.

I didn't even realize I had put on my coat, gloves, hat, and boots until I was opening the back door. I remembered to grab the keys on my way outside but realized after I was on the porch that I was holding my father's pickup keys. Even if I drove away from the farm in his vehicle, common sense told me that driving a big white truck in blizzard-like conditions would be asking for an accident.

Usually, I could see Mandy's—now Devon's—house and the barns from the backyard, but that morning, they were obliterated by what seemed to be a solid sheet of white snow that the howling wind was blowing every which way. Snow had drifted halfway to the first-floor windows, and what was on the ground came up to the top of my work boots. I braced myself for the cold and headed to the workshop. Luis had told me more than once that hard physical work would get rid of anything on my mind. We didn't have a tractor in the barn, but the supply room where we kept cases of oil, transmission fluid, and even a couple of sets of tires could always use a cleaning.

One step at a time, I followed the path to the barn with my shoulders hunched and my every breath coming out in a fog. My anger was hot enough that I could hardly even feel the bitter cold snow slapping me in the face with every step I took. The barn came up so quickly that I almost ran smack into the side of it before I realized it was there. Snow had drifted up against the door, making it hard to open, but my frustration fueled enough energy that I flung it open without much trouble.

I tried to slam the door, but it wouldn't cooperate.

"Sometimes it's too late to say you are sorry," I muttered as I stomped the snow from my boots and hung my coat on a hook.

A yellow five-gallon bucket got in my way on the way to the supply room, so I kicked it with enough force to send it rattling across the barn. When the thing hit the wall, it flipped over and rolled right back to me. I kicked it again, and this time, it learned its lesson and landed in front of the pegboard that held all the tools.

I stomped all the way over there and picked up a hammer in one hand and a screwdriver in the other. I was on my way to beat and stab out my frustrations on the workbench when a picture of Luis flashed through my head. I could see him sitting on his stool as clearly as if he'd really been there. I could never destroy something that reminded me of Luis. I turned around and put the tools back where they belonged and headed to the supply room.

I switched on the light and glared at the old brown-and-gold sofa that sat against the back wall. I could see my father sitting there with his empty glass. "Oh my God!" I gasped when the picture became firm in my memory. "There were two glasses that night. One in his hand and one sitting beside the half-empty bottle of whiskey."

Everything snapped clear in my mind in less time than it took me to blink. The shadow I'd seen had been someone leaving the barn, not someone who had just been out for a walk. The sweet scent that blended with the whiskey had been cheap perfume. My father had just had sex on that sofa while my mother lay dying in the house.

I picked up a box cutter and attacked the sofa like a woman on a mission. My right arm was aching when I'd finally sliced through my anger. I hurled the box cutter across the room and glared at the completely destroyed sofa. "As soon as this storm is over, I will drag you outside and burn you."

"What did that sofa do to you?" Devon asked.

I whipped around, expecting to find that he, like the visions of Luis and my father, was nothing more than a figment of my imagination. But he was there with a frosting of snow on the rim of his hair that his stocking hat had not covered.

"It brought back a horrible memory," I answered and then burst into tears.

He took a couple of steps and wrapped me in his arms. "Let it all out. Tears wash away grief."

"I'm not grieving," I protested. "I'm mad."

"Then maybe the tears will wash that away, too," he said as he switched off the light and walked me backward out into the shop. He sat down in one of the two lawn chairs and pulled me down into his lap. I rested my cheek against his chest and sobbed until I got the hiccups. Devon took a red bandanna from his pocket and dried my tears. The handkerchief made me think of all the times Luis had wiped sweat from his brow with one just like it, and it set off another bout of weeping.

"What are you even doing out in this kind of weather?" Devon asked.

"I might ask"—the lump in my throat made my voice come out high and squeaky—"you the same thing."

"I got stir-crazy in the house and thought I might take stock of the supply room and make sure we've got what we need when spring gets here," he answered.

"Right now, I don't care how . . ." I couldn't finish the sentence.

"Are Celeste and Mandy all right? Are you angry because something happened to one of them?"

"I wouldn't be out here if something like that happened—and I would be grieving, not going crazy on a rotten sofa," I snapped, then cried harder because he was just being kind and I had been hateful.

"Okay, then." He pulled me closer. "Just let it all out."

I opened my mouth, but nothing would come out. How could I ever explain to him how I felt with mere words when I couldn't wrap my mind around the anger?

"I found a l-letter . . ." I stammered. "My mother . . . wrote it . . . when . . ." I stopped and looked around for a tissue.

Devon reached over and grabbed a roll of paper towels from the worktable. "Your mother wrote you a letter, right?"

I took a deep breath and nodded as I peeled off several of the sheets and wiped my cheeks, then blew my nose. I didn't even try to be ladylike, and Celeste and Mandy probably heard the noise all the way back at the house.

"She wrote it when she was dying and hid it in a file," I answered. "I was probably supposed to find it when I needed my birth certificate for something, but . . ."

"But you haven't needed it?" Devon asked.

"That's right, and . . ." A lump caught in my throat. "She loved me, but she never showed it much, and I can't forgive her."

Devon pushed my hair back behind my ear and said, "She's your mother, darlin'. She is supposed to love you."

I threw the paper towel on the floor. "I wanted to know that before she died, not all these years later."

"Maybe you better start at the beginning of this story," he suggested.

"It's like this . . ." I went on to tell him about my parents' loveless marriage and the circumstances of my birth. "And now, I'm almost convinced that Celeste is my half-sister."

"That's easy enough to prove or disprove. Just send in a familial DNA test. You can get one of those back in a week or less," he said.

"We're going to do that—but do I tell Celeste what I suspect now or wait for proof? How's it going to affect her, knowing that she was raised right here on Meadow Falls with a father who didn't even acknowledge that she was his child?"

"You can cross that bridge when the results come back," he said. "And from what you just told me, you were raised by a father who didn't want you, either."

He tipped my chin up with his free hand and gazed right into my eyes. I barely had time to moisten my lips when his mouth closed over mine, and suddenly, nothing seemed to be so terrible anymore. The temperature seemed to get hotter and hotter with each kiss until, when I finally pulled away, I was panting.

"Did that take your mind off your troubles?" he asked.

"This is not a joking matter—but yes, for a minute, it did." I remembered what Mandy had said about love and hate not living in the same heart. Evidently, neither could anger and a flaming desire for more than kisses, but I wasn't going to admit that to my pretend boyfriend.

"Your lips are all puffy, and your eyes are dreamy now, instead of filled with anger." Devon chuckled.

"I guess that means I should wait awhile before I go back to the house?" I was shocked that my hissy fit had ended with the kisses and was all gone, but even more so that I could flirt with Devon.

But I did not regret slashing the sofa into rags.

Chapter Eighteen

DNA kits were paid for, and extra money added for rush delivery by bedtime that evening. Keeping the news of the letter and of my suspicions from Mandy and Celeste wasn't easy. Not telling them about my memory of my father and how I had destroyed the old sofa was even tougher. Keeping quiet about the make-out session with Devon was no problem at all.

When I awoke the next morning, I got out of bed and pulled back the drapes covering the french doors that opened out onto the balcony. A blanket of white covered the ground, and even my footprints from going out to the workshop and back had been filled in and erased. The sun wasn't even a tiny sliver of orange on the eastern horizon yet, but the quarter moon and stars did what they could to lighten the day. The storm had passed—at least the physical one.

My door squeaked when it opened, and Celeste asked, "Are you awake?"

"Yep, but I can't take my eyes off this sight," I answered. "Come join me."

She crossed the room, and together, we stared out the windows. "It's cliché, but it really is a winter wonderland."

"Until we all stomp through it or until it melts and becomes a muddy mess," I said.

"Kind of like when we were kids and everything was beautiful," she agreed. "Thank goodness for those memories. They are the silver linings in the dark clouds of adulthood."

I draped my arm around her waist and said, "Amen, sister."

"I've been thinking about that DNA thing, Angela Marie. I don't think I want to do it. I don't care anything about knowing my relatives, if there are any out there. You and Mandy are enough family for me," she said.

I dropped my arm and started getting dressed. "Too late. The tests have been ordered and are on the way. We can always ignore anyone that emails us or shows up on our family trees."

"Must be fate, then," she said with a sigh. "But I will not go ancestor diving into the pool of my long-lost relatives. You can do what you want to do with yours, and I won't judge you. At my age, I've come to grips with the past."

"What if you and Trevor are kin to each other? What if his uncle or oldest brother had a fling with Roxy?" I asked. "Maybe that's why you had misgivings about having a family with him."

"Don't even go there! I was just afraid I'd have the same genes as my mother and my father—whoever he is—and would abandon my child. Maybe not physically, but mentally." She whipped around and glared at me, giving me the same look my father had always had when he was upset with me. How had I not seen it before? Maybe unlocking that memory of the supply room was connecting things for me.

I held up both palms defensively. "Okay, okay! Don't murder me with your looks."

Celeste shivered. "I guess we do need to know who we are related to, don't we?"

"Yep, we sure do." I sat down and tied my shoes. "Let's go make breakfast. Devon and Jesse will come in pretty soon, and Glenda and Bennie will be here to start in the living room at eight."

"They're picking Polly up on the way. I don't intend to let her—or Granny—do much in the kitchen, but they need to think they're helping." Celeste led the way out of the room.

I followed her down the staircase, across the foyer, and into the kitchen. She flipped on the light and went straight to the coffee machine. While she put on the first pot of the morning, I turned on the oven and got down a mixing bowl for the biscuits.

We had breakfast ready and set out on the counter when Mandy finally arrived with Caramel at her feet. While I was feeding the cat, Jesse and Devon came inside through the back door, wiped their feet on a throw rug, and hung up their coats and hats. Devon stooped to pet Caramel and slid a sly wink my way.

"Feeling better, or should I hide all the box cutters?" he whispered.

"I keep a knife in my pocket at all times," I answered.

"What are y'all whispering about?" Mandy asked.

"Whether your cat is going to have her babies today." Devon stood up and stepped to the side to let me go ahead of him. "She looks like she's carrying baby elephants rather than kittens."

"I agree," Mandy said with a nod. "And babies, whether human or animal, seem to arrive after a storm or when the moon is full. Celeste was born in February in the middle of an ice storm. My old car slipped and slid all over the road when I drove Roxy to the hospital. I was afraid I'd have to pull over and deliver the baby right there in the car, but we finally made it."

"Was I born in a storm?" I asked.

"Oh, yes, you were," Mandy answered. "The tornado sirens were blowing so loud that they blocked out your first cries when you came into this world."

I'd never known either of those stories, but it was another bit of history to file away and write down in my journal later. If that stood true, then Caramel should have had her kittens the day before. Maybe a basketful of babies would have done a little to ease my own anger after I had read my mother's letter and then realized that my father was probably never faithful to her.

Devon's kisses did a fine job of that, the voice in my head reminded me.

Yes, they did, I agreed as I put food on my plate and joined everyone else at the table.

❖   ❖   ❖

I answered the knock on the door just before eight o'clock to find Bennie holding Polly in his arms like a new bride and Glenda standing beside him with an old metal suitcase in her hands. I motioned for them to come on inside.

"What happened to you, Polly?" I asked as they filed past me.

"Not one thing," she answered with a giggle. "Bennie just scooped me up and carried me from my house to his truck, and then when we got here, he did the same thing."

Bennie set Polly gently down on the floor. "I couldn't let her walk through all that snow. It probably comes up to her knees." He helped her with her coat before he took his off. He was as tall as Jesse and even more muscular. His light brown hair had thinned since high school, but the rest of him still had the look of a professional wrestler.

"Thank you, Bennie. I'll take my suitcase—"

Mandy came out of her bedroom and butted in before Polly could finish. "Take it to my room. She'll be staying with us for a while. I'll lead the way." She and Polly looped their arms together and were already talking when they disappeared into Mandy's room.

Glenda removed her coat and hung it beside mine on the coatrack. "From the expression on your face, I'd say that you didn't know Polly planned to stay."

"No, but that's fine," I said.

Bennie stuck out his hand. "Before we get started, I want to thank you for giving me and Glenda these jobs. I didn't know how we were going to make it, and now, not only do we have an income, but I can be home with my wife and boys more."

I shook hands with him and smiled. "We're glad that y'all can help us, so welcome to Meadow Falls."

Glenda laid a hand on my shoulder. "Thank you, again. Just show me where you want me to start."

"That will be my job," Celeste said as she and Jesse came out of the kitchen. "Jesse is our foreman for this remodeling job, Bennie." She made quick introductions, and Bennie went to the living room with Jesse. "Glenda, we'll get started on the cleaning—but first, it's all-hands-on-deck to move the furniture to the middle of the living room."

Mandy poked her head out of her bedroom. "About that moving furniture—could y'all take my bed upstairs and bring down two twin beds before you get started?"

"Of course." I went into the living room, and in less than half an hour, her bed had been taken upstairs and two twin beds brought down.

"Show me where the linens are, and I'll start by making up those beds," Glenda said.

"They are kept in the closet upstairs," Celeste told her. "First door on the right. The cleaning supplies are on the bottom shelf in the same place."

"Then I'm off to work." Glenda started up the stairs.

Summer Rain's and Roxy's pictures came to my mind. Were they hidden well enough? Glenda would be cleaning my room and could possibly find them if she snooped through drawers.

"I'll go with you and help bring down the linens on the two beds. They haven't been used in . . ." I paused halfway up the stairs. "In probably forever, so they'll need to be washed. Celeste, you want to come help me? I'm sure there'll be more than one armful."

"Do you want me to wash everything in the bedrooms, then?" Glenda asked.

Celeste followed behind me and Glenda. "Yes, please, to freshen things up a bit. Other than that, just a general cleaning done this week. You don't need to wash windows or curtains."

I stopped in the middle of the hallway and raised an eyebrow at Celeste. "Did you know Polly was coming to stay?"

"Nope," she answered, "but it's a blessing. She will keep Granny company while all this is going on."

Glenda opened the linen closet and took out sheets, blankets, and bedspreads. "Do all these doors open into bedrooms?"

"Yes, they do, and right now, it's just me and Celeste up here," I said. "You'll only need to clean the other six once a month, but we'll need ours done weekly."

"When I get the beds made, I'll start with the bathroom up here and then work my way around," Glenda said, and then went back downstairs.

"Is there anything in your room that you really wouldn't want her to see?" I whispered to Celeste.

"No . . ." She frowned. "Maybe?" The frown deepened. "Yes, and thank you, but what do I do with it?"

"Take it to the office and put it in one of the file cabinets. I'll be sure that they are locked and the key is hidden," I told her.

"What about you?" she asked.

"Oh, yeah," I said with a nod.

❖　❖　❖

One of the major things that Luis had taught me was that men and women approach jobs very differently. Men stand back, rub their chins, and study what they are about to do with serious concentration. Women dive right in without so much as a blink of the eye.

By midmorning, Glenda had already made up the twin beds and was cleaning upstairs. Polly and Mandy were in the kitchen, making cookies for break times the next day. Celeste and I were ready to help any way we could, but the three guys were still measuring the planks on the wall—and talking, and talking, and talking some more.

Finally, Jesse turned to me and said, "Devon is going to hitch the flatbed trailer up to his truck, and we'll load these boards on it as we take them down. Do you want us to take them out to the workshop, or what are we supposed to do with them?"

"Burn it, I guess. Or take it to the dump," I answered.

"Would you mind if I take it with me?" Bennie asked. "It's really nice wood, and I could use it for all kinds of remodeling jobs at our house or for building a few pieces of furniture to sell. I'd be willing to pay—"

I shook my head and held up a palm. "I don't want any money for it. You just feel free to take all you can use and maybe haul the rest to the dump for me."

"Thank you," Bennie said. "Now, Jesse, let's get busy taking this off. Was it put up when the house was built?"

"Y'all finally through gee-hawing and ready to go to work?" Mandy peeked into the living room. "I expected to see half the room done by now."

"We had to make some decisions," Devon said as he brushed past me on the way out to hook up the trailer.

"Do you know when this paneling was put up, Miz Mandy?" Jesse asked.

"It looked just like this when I got to Meadow Falls in 1952," Mandy answered.

"Got any idea what's behind it?" Jesse asked.

"None at all," Mandy said as she and Polly started toward the kitchen. "But I wouldn't be surprised if all you find is studs."

So there's a roomful of studs in here, a flirty voice in my head said.

A blush started to creep into my cheeks. "Every room on the second floor has paneling just like this, so get ready to take home a lot of boards."

"I'll be glad to have it all," Bennie said.

"While Devon gets that trailer brought around front," Jesse said, "you and I can scoot what furniture is in our way to the middle of the room, Bennie."

Devon was back in time to help move the last of the furniture. My father would have been livid to see what was going on. As I watched three men carefully removing nails, I wondered why Harrison had refused to make any changes—especially after wanting so badly to leave Meadow Falls. I had always thought that he just kept up the tradition, like his grandfather and father before him. But maybe he'd simply accepted the fact that without Summer Rain, his life was going to be miserable and that changing anything on Meadow Falls wouldn't help.

Devon turned and smiled at me as he slipped the first board away from the wall. "There's fiberglass insulation back there, which means the paneling was put up after 1940—right, Jesse?"

I didn't care when it was put up; I just wanted it gone, and there was proof that something had been changed, even if it was before my father was even born.

"That's right," Jesse agreed. "I've remodeled too many older homes to count, and a lot of them have no drywall or insulation at all behind wood paneling. I was pretty sure that this wood was installed either in the forties or fifties, because the house stays too warm for it not to be insulated. I expect it'll take most of today to take all this—plus what's in the foyer—off the walls. I'll measure and put in an order for sheets of drywall to be delivered tomorrow."

"Angela Marie, I think all this old insulation should be replaced, too. What do you think?" Devon asked.

"Jesse is the foreman on this job," I answered with a shrug. "I want the job done right so it doesn't have to be redone in the next seventy years."

"My vote goes with Devon," Jesse said. "This stuff needs to be torn out and replaced."

"Then tell the lumberyard to bring that along with whatever else you need," I told him. "Now, I think y'all can work without me watching you, so I'm going to go to the kitchen and help Celeste keep Polly and Mandy out of trouble. Holler if you need anything."

Devon had moved over closer to me, and he whispered, "I need an hour or so with you in the workshop."

This time, I could not keep the blush at bay. "In your dreams, soldier."

Chapter Nineteen

ove and hate cannot live in the same heart.
Those words kept running through my mind as I made my way
to the Duncan family cemetery—for the second time in a short while.
Dark had already settled, and the sliver of a moon didn't offer much
in the way of light. But I could have traveled down the path blindfolded. I knew every path, every rut, and everything about Meadow
Falls land just as surely as I knew how to run the place without my
father. Especially now that I had help in Devon, Jesse, and Celeste.

The gate was open, but snowdrifts were almost as high as the fence
in places. Two days of sunshine had helped to melt away some of what
lay on the ground. The cemetery was still pristine; not even a bird or a
stray wild animal had messed up the clean white blanket covering everything. Not caring if the cold came through my jeans, I knelt between
my father's and mother's graves and brushed away what was left of the
snow on their headstones.

"I'm here to talk to both of you," I whispered. "It sounds silly to
talk to the dead, but I need to get things off my chest. You basically
gave me to Mandy to raise, and she told me that I need to forgive—not
for you but for myself. That's not easy, because I'm still mad at y'all,
not only for what you did but for all the memories that keep coming
back to haunt me."

The gate squeaked, and I whipped around to see if Celeste had left the house and followed me. Since no one was there, I figured the hard wind that had picked up had tried in vain to close me inside the cemetery with all my ancestors.

What made me choose a night like this to talk to them? I asked myself.

I ran my finger over my father's name. "I'm here to tell you that all that ugly paneling is off the walls in the living room and foyer. By this time next week, the drywall will be up, and I'll be deciding what shade of yellow to paint the walls. The old is going out the door, and I think it's time I made peace with the past. I'm not sure I know how to even begin to do that, but I'm willing to give it a try."

The eerie yowling sound of a coyote off in the distance made me shiver. When another one answered him in the opposite direction, I wondered if that was some kind of omen or simply just two cold, lonesome animals letting everyone know that they weren't happy about the snow. I smiled at the idea of the two coyotes being my mother and my father—miles away from each other and yet howling at the idea of me redoing the house on Meadow Falls.

"If that's your opinion, then you can just carry on all you want," I said with a smile. "I want a home, not a museum, and since the place is mine now, that's what I'm going to have. Someday in the future, Celeste and I may even fill all those bedrooms with children."

A cardinal flew over my shoulder and rested on the big Duncan tombstone a few feet away. Was that my beautiful mother wishing me good luck or reminding me of the Meadow Falls curse that gave mothers who lived here only one child?

"I want my kids to feel loved and at home. I never want them to sit in the shadows like I had to. And if they don't want to inherit the farm, then I'll give it to one of Celeste's kids. She's just recently divorced and not interested in marriage right now, but I'm hoping she finds someone who will be good to her."

The cardinal cocked its head and then flew away.

"Seems like signs are all around me tonight," I said. "One more thing before I go: I want y'all to know about Devon." I went on to tell them the story of how he and Jesse came to live on the farm. "I feel something for Devon that I've never known before, and if I'm going to pursue the relationship, I have to get rid of all this ugliness I'm harboring," I whispered and then glanced over my shoulder to be sure no one was listening to me. "He's a good man, and I think we might have a chance at a relationship in the future. He's a hard worker, and he loves this place. I'm not sure if I'm right, but it seems like God delivered him and Jesse to us on a silver platter, and I do not want to ruin anything by wallowing in the past."

The gate creaked again, but I didn't even turn around. Evidently, leaving that thing open allowed all kinds of memories to roam free and haunt me. "I'll be sure to close it when I leave, because when one of those bad memories come to my mind again, I will cover it up with happy thoughts of Devon and Celeste and Mandy—and even Jesse. You will not ever have control over me again."

I stood up and slowly walked to the gate and kicked away the snow holding it open. As I closed it, I said, "I forgive both of you, and each and every day, I'm going to do my best to forget a little more."

❖   ❖   ❖

A light was on in the workshop, and the memory of my father sitting on the sofa I had ripped apart tried to surface, but I replaced it with one of Devon holding me and kissing away my anger. It seemed strange to see the trailer piled up with the old insulation parked right outside the doors—but then, maybe Devon had decided to add the used tires to the load.

The workshop went dark and then I could see his silhouette as he came outside. He pulled the collar of his coat up around his neck and braced himself against the wind, just like I was doing. When I realized that our paths were going to cross at the same time, something told me it was time for me to choose a direction. The one behind me led to the cemetery—that seemed like going backward into the past, where happiness was just a fleeting thing. The one to my right went to the house—nothing but emptiness there. The one to my left came from the workshop—bad memory of the sofa incident there. The one straight ahead went to Devon's house, a place where I had always been the happiest with Mandy.

"What are you doing out on this cold night?" I asked. "I thought you and Jesse and Celeste were watching a movie."

"I got bored," he said, "and I had one last little thing to load before we haul the insulation to the dump in the morning."

"What was that?" I asked.

He tucked my arm into his and smiled. "There was a pitiful-looking sofa that needed removing from the farm, so I broke it up and loaded it under the insulation. What about you?"

"I had some things to say to my parents so I could get closure, so I spent some time at the cemetery," I answered. "It's cold out here. Let's go back to the house to talk."

"I've got a better idea. Let's go to my house. It's closer and a lot more private. I'll make some hot chocolate to warm us up."

"Yes, please," I said, glad he was on my wavelength. I was amazed at how much lighter my heart felt without all the heaviness that had been weighing it down. "I would love a cup of hot chocolate."

Do you really need something hot to warm you up? Or can just being in Devon's presence do that? The voice sounded a lot like Polly's.

We'll see what the evening holds. I smiled. *But you can go back to the house and talk to Mandy. I don't need you in my head.*

Devon and I had met at the crossroads. I had made peace with the past. He had taken care of the sofa for me. We could leave all that behind and spend time alone in his house. That had to be a sign that something was working for us—at least, that's the way I interpreted it.

"And maybe a kiss or two to warm up your freezing lips?" he flirted.

"Why stop at two?" I shot back.

"Like I said before, I like a woman who speaks her mind." He pulled his arm away and laced his gloved fingers through mine. Even though my gloves were thick, I could still feel the warmth of his hand through them as we made our way to his house.

Once inside, he helped me remove my coat and hung it up on the coatrack. "Make yourself at home while I fix the hot chocolate."

I kicked off my boots at the door and followed him to the kitchen. "I see you still haven't changed much in here."

"No need to," he said as he warmed milk on the stove and added hot chocolate mix. "It all works just like it is, but what you are doing at your place is . . ." He stirred. "Amazing. Taking that wood off the walls and those heavy drapes down really makes the house feel different."

"'Different' good?" I got two mugs down from the cabinet and set them beside the stove.

"'Different' awesome. Are you going to use that new plank flooring or carpeting?" he asked.

"Tonight, I want to talk about us, not work," I told him.

"I've been flirting with you like crazy ever since I arrived and hoping that there might be an *us*," he said. "Are you telling me that you think we might have a chance?"

"Do you want us to have a chance?" I asked.

"Definitely. But why now?" He poured hot chocolate into the two mugs and handed one to me.

"Because I'm ready to live, not just exist," I admitted.

He took a sip before he spoke again. "Did something happen to make you feel like that?"

I carried my mug to the living room and sat down on the sofa. "Tonight—at the cemetery—that was a very big emotional change. I figured out that I don't want to just exist in a world that's been laid out for me; I want to live in one of my own making. I want to decide what to do with my life, not just sit back and take what comes my way."

He sat down beside me and set his mug on the coffee table. "So, are we dating, or are we in a relationship?"

"You haven't asked me on a date," I told him.

"I thought that the time we spent together in the workshop was a date," he said. "And maybe when we worked on all the tractors together. By my calculations, this is probably our eighth or ninth—maybe even tenth—date."

I set my mug beside his and scooted over closer to him. "I have never gone out with anyone eight or nine or ten times."

He cupped my face in his warm hands and looked deeply into my eyes. "Then I guess we've gone past friendship and just casual dating, and we're now in a relationship."

"I guess we are," I whispered and moistened my lips.

His eyes fluttered shut as he moved in slowly for the first sweet kiss.

For a split second, the idea that we might be moving too fast chased through my mind, but I squashed it, and I leaned in closer to him for the next one.

Chapter Twenty

I am a grown woman. I own this place. I do not have to sneak around. I kept silently repeating those words over and over as I dressed in a hurry, slipped out of Devon's bedroom, and tiptoed down the short hallway.

I was putting my boots on when the door opened, and Jesse came into the house. There was no hiding or pretending. "Hey, Jesse," I said with a smile.

"Are you coming or going?" he asked with a grin.

"I'm going." *Busted,* I thought, but I didn't blush, even though it was an awkward moment.

He handed me my coat from the rack and opened the door for me. "See you in the morning. Have a good night."

"You too," I said as I left behind the warmth—not only of the house but also from spending time in Devon's arms—and stepped out into the cold night air.

I had opened the yard gate when I noticed Celeste's silhouette blocking part of the light flowing from the kitchen window. I reminded myself again that a grown woman owned her sexuality. When I walked into the house, Celeste was grinning like that old proverbial Cheshire cat and pointing toward the corner of the mudroom.

"We've got baby kittens. Jesse found them on his way out," Celeste said. "You've got to see them—but remember what Granny told us: we aren't to touch them for a few days or Caramel might move them."

She took me by the hand before I even had time to remove my coat and led me across the room to the laundry basket. Caramel was curled up in a ball around her three babies—an orange-striped one, a solid black one, and a gray tabby.

"Are we really going to keep them all?" Celeste whispered.

"Yes, we are," I told her. "This house is big enough for four cats, don't you think?"

"Definitely," she answered. "Speaking of births, I'm jealous of this new relationship between you and Devon. Y'all are made for each other, and I hope it's more than just a winter fling."

"How do you know it's anything at all?" I held my hands together to keep from reaching into the basket and picking up the kittens.

"You are glowing, girl," Celeste said.

"Why are you jealous?"

"I wish I wasn't so soon out of a marriage," she said. "Jesse is a good man and deserves something more than a rebound relationship, but there's definitely chemistry between us."

"Don't waste time," I said. "I went to the cemetery and took the first step toward peace with my mother and father this evening." I removed my coat and hung it up, then untied my boots and left them by the back door. "Everything happens for a reason. Devon arrived at Meadow Falls because y'all are friends. He brought Jesse here because we needed a carpenter. Fate is working for us, and if it's meant for you and Jesse to be together, it will work out."

"Are you preaching to me or to yourself?" she asked.

I covered a yawn with my hand. "Both of us need the sermon. I'm going up to bed. Good night."

"You ought to take a shower. You've got the scent of Devon's cologne all over you, and Granny has the nose of a bloodhound. If she catches a whiff of that in the morning at breakfast, she'll have a thousand questions," Celeste said.

I waved over my shoulder and didn't even stop at my bedroom door but went straight to the bathroom at the end of the hall. "Thank you for not asking all those questions yourself," I muttered.

❖ ❖ ❖

"Glenda is doing a fine job of cleaning," Celeste said after breakfast the next morning. "And Granny, you and Polly are a big help at getting snacks ready for our break times. I know that every one of us appreciate it."

"This morning, we're making banana-nut muffins," Polly said. "We'd be glad to make lunch and supper if you would let us."

"Shh . . ." Celeste put a finger over her lips. "I'll lose my job around here if y'all don't scoot on out of the kitchen and let me take care of the meals."

"Something is different around here." Mandy frowned and looked right at me. "And it's more than just the remodeling business."

"I went out to the cemetery last night and told my folks that I would forgive them and that I would work on the forgetting part. I can't control what has already happened, but I can control my attitude toward it."

I hoped my face wasn't glowing and that she hadn't picked up on the vibes between me and Devon that morning while we ate our breakfast.

"And," Celeste said, "Caramel had her babies last night."

"And you waited to tell me until now?" Mandy scolded as she stood up. "Where are they? How many?"

Celeste and I followed the two older women from the kitchen and into the mudroom. "They are in the basket in the mudroom, and there are three," Celeste said and then nudged me on the shoulder and whispered, "You are welcome."

I knew exactly what she was talking about. "Thank you. I owe you."

She nudged me again. "Yes, you do."

Mandy reached inside the basket and stroked Caramel's fur from head to tail. "Such pretty babies, but we won't touch them until they're a little bigger. You just take care of them and be a good mama."

"One little orange one," Polly said, "and one solid black one, and a gray one—and there's a white one with an orange tail and then a cute little calico that looks to be the runt. I count five, not three."

Mandy straightened up and smiled. "You girls need to go back to school and learn some more arithmetic."

Celeste and I were both hovering over the basket right along with Mandy and Polly. "Looks like we do."

"I named Caramel, so y'all get to name the kittens." Maybe that would keep Mandy's mind off what was different in the house for a while.

"I'm calling dibs on naming the black one," Celeste said. "Its name is Rebel, no matter if it's a boy or a girl. That leaves two for each of Granny and Polly to choose names for."

That should keep them busy for a day or two, I thought.

I was passing right by the old wall-hung phone in the kitchen when it rang, and the noise startled me so badly that I jumped sideways and almost knocked Celeste down.

"Answer the thing," Mandy demanded.

"Meadow Falls, Angela Marie speaking," I said, just like my mother had taught me when I was a little girl, but the words sounded strange coming out of my mouth.

"Hello, this is Jeannie Thomas, president of the North Texas Peanut Co-Op," the voice on the other end said. "How are you today?"

"I'm fine," I answered.

"I realize that Harrison has just passed away recently," she said, "but with his passing, an opening on our board of directors has come up. We would like to offer that position to you, Angela Marie. Harrison often told us that he was so proud of you and that you were the smartest person in the whole state when it came to raising peanuts. We would sure like to have your expertise on our board."

"My father said that?" I asked.

"Yes, he bragged on you all the time at our monthly meetings," Jeannie answered. "Would you be interested in filling the position?"

"Can I think about it for a few days?" I asked.

"Of course," Jeannie said. "I'll give you a week and then call back. Again, we would love to have you help us out."

"Thank you." I was surprised that a single word could come out of my mouth.

I hung up the phone and stared at it for an hour—or so it seemed. But I'm sure that only a few seconds had passed when Mandy tapped me on the shoulder and asked, "Your father said what?"

"That he was proud of me and that I was smart," I whispered, still not believing what I had just heard.

"That's a good thing," Mandy said. "Tuck it away in your mind and drag it out when bad thoughts come in to haunt you."

"Jeannie Thomas wants me to sit on the co-op board of directors." My voice didn't even sound familiar in my own ears.

"That's a big responsibility," Mandy said.

"And Jeannie is a delegator. Because you're a new member, she'll pile all kinds of work on you," Polly advised. "She's all up in everything all over this whole county, and she loves to be the big queen bee, but she doesn't do diddly-squat in the way of work. But whether you sit on the board or not is up to you."

"Jeannie Thomas used to be Jeannie Lawson," Celeste said. "I remember her from high school. She was a couple of years ahead of me. She was the president of just about every club back then. She got me to join the committee for the school Christmas dance. We worked on fundraisers and decorations for weeks; then only she got a citation from the principal for all the hard work."

"I remember that time," I said with a nod. "I was a freshman and went out to help you sell cookie dough to everyone in town." My mind was made up in an instant, but I didn't intend to tell Jeannie to find herself another workhorse until she called again.

Was she the reason my father was so involved with everything around these parts? Had he needed to be away from the farm so much that he'd let a woman manipulate him?

No way in the universe, I thought. *Not Harrison Duncan.*

More than likely, he was the one who talked her into being the president of the co-op so *he* could manipulate *her.* Poor Jeannie probably got hoodwinked into filling that position so that my father could keep his hands as clean as his white shirts. She would get awards and citations, and he would always get exactly what he wanted.

Celeste tapped me on the shoulder. "You're doing it again."

"What?" I asked.

"Going off into another world," she answered.

Polly and Mandy were at the table with an open cookbook in front of them. I heard names for the kittens being tossed around right along with whether to make oatmeal cookies or blueberry muffins for break time.

"What did I miss?" I whispered.

"Nothing important," Celeste responded. "But I'd sure like to know what you were thinking about so hard."

"My father," I said and went on to tell her exactly what I had been thinking about.

"You probably got that right," she agreed. "But I've got a feeling there's more going on in your world than you not wanting to work your butt off."

"Yep, you are so right," I told her in a low voice. "I've got a farm to run and a new relationship to take care of. Plus, I want to spend time with you and Mandy. I was groomed to be a peanut farmer, not a socialite. I would rather have an hour of free time to spend with my family than any recognition I might get at a rubber-chicken dinner for sitting on the co-op board of directors."

A brief knock on the door took all our attention away from what we were doing. Then I heard Jesse say, "Y'all come on in. We're just getting started."

"Where is Angela Marie?" Bennie asked. "I'd sure like to borrow Glenda today, if she's all right with that. We work well together when it comes to the finish work after the drywall is all hung up. She does such a fine job that you'll never see a single seam."

"What do you think?" I asked Celeste.

"She's got the upstairs all cleaned, and I was wondering what to tell her to do today, so that's great," Celeste answered. "Pretty good deal we've got going here. Glenda can clean, and she can remodel, too."

I raised my voice as I crossed the kitchen and went through the dining room. "That will be fine, Bennie."

Glenda met me halfway across the foyer and handed off a stack of letters. "Andy Joe was just putting your mail in the box at the end of the lane. Thought I'd save you a trip and bring it to you."

"Thank you." I was glad that I would have to sign for the DNA package when it arrived and that it would not just be left in the mailbox. I liked Glenda, even after the incident at the musical. She was a hard worker, and I hoped that she and Bennie both would be permanent help at Meadow Falls. But that didn't change the fact that she loved to tell everything she knew, and until I knew for sure if Celeste and I had the same father, I'd rather not have Glenda spreading rumors.

Chapter Twenty-One

*I*s that all there is to it?" Celeste asked as she shoved the DNA stick down into the tube and capped it off. "It's a bit anticlimactic, isn't it?"

I took the tube from her and put both of our tests in the little return box. The UPS man was scheduled to pick up the package at five thirty that afternoon. The results would show up in my email inbox in a few days. Until then, it was a matter of waiting.

"*Wait* is a four-letter word, and you know how Mandy felt about us using dirty language."

"She would make us stand in the corner," Celeste said with a giggle. "But what made you think of that word today? Are you that anxious to have all kinds of relatives come knocking on our door, wanting to move in with us?"

"If there's too many of them, we will put a gate at the end of the lane and get us one of those fancy buttons for folks to push and ask for permission to enter the premises," I joked. I didn't tell her that this test was a familial one just to see if we were half-sisters.

I sealed the box and set it on my dresser. "What are you doing the rest of this evening?"

"Jesse noticed the waterfall picture that your great-grandmother painted. I told him the story, and now he wants to check out the place to see if there's some photo opportunities around it. So we are taking a walk to the creek," she answered.

I raised both eyebrows and widened my eyes. "Be careful. You know that old willow tree is like an aphrodisiac."

She had started out of my bedroom, but she whipped around at the door. "Have you been out there with Devon?"

"Not yet," I answered. "I'm waiting for you to go with Jesse first to see if the tree still has magical powers."

"From the way you are smiling all the time, I would say that you don't need any more magic," Celeste said and slipped out into the hallway.

I let her have the last word, mainly because she was right. I opened the balcony doors and stepped outside. From there, I could see Devon's house. Funny—or maybe the word should be *strange*—how the house I had always referred to as Mandy's could so easily turn into Devon's in only a few weeks.

"Maybe that's an omen, too." I went back inside, patted the box as I passed by, and hoped that Celeste was truly my sister.

But how was she going to feel about that? She would have to face the fact that Harrison had known he was her father and wouldn't acknowledge her. Would knowing cause her even more emotional distress than all the stuff she'd gone through with Trevor? Was I being selfish in wanting her to be my sister?

Mandy and Polly were in their bedroom with the door cracked open so Caramel could come and go as she pleased. According to Mandy, all mothers—including cats—need a moment or two away from the young'uns every now and then.

I peeked inside to find them both propped up on their beds and watching the television we had moved over there from the living room. I recognized Blanche's voice from *The Golden Girls* saying something about the night before being wonderful, and Mandy giggling.

I grabbed my coat and hat and slipped out the back door. Stars were shining brightly when I looked up at the sky and thanked God for Polly coming to stay with us for a while. She really brightened up Mandy's days and gave me and Celeste both a little time for ourselves. I had my head down, making sure I didn't step in a hole in the path, not paying much attention to anything else, when suddenly Devon was standing right in front of me.

"Well, hello there," he said with a wide grin.

"Where are you going?" I asked.

"To see if you'd like to come out to my place and watch a movie. Jesse has gone for a walk, and I'd sure like some company," he said.

"Are you asking me for a date?" I asked.

"Yes, ma'am, I am—and I will even walk you home afterwards if you'll promise me a good-night kiss." He was definitely flirting.

I slipped my hand into his. "What are we watching?"

"You can choose from anything that's on," he answered. "Oldies that are being replayed, or we can rent one online."

"Would it be all right if we just have some hot chocolate and talk?" I asked. "I would love to have your opinion on something."

"Something personal or professional?" he asked when we were on the porch.

He opened the door for me and then helped me remove my coat.

"I guess it's a bit of both," I answered.

He led me over to the sofa, and we sat down together—side by side, shoulders touching. He tucked my hand into his and said, "Shoot. But remember, I'm honest when it comes to giving opinions. But before we get into that, I want to say that I like the way your hand fits in mine and the way you fit so perfectly in my arms. It's like our bodies were made for each other." He dropped my hand and draped his arm around my shoulder.

"I bet you say that to all the women."

"Only the super-beautiful ones," he whispered softly in my ear. "But like I said, I'm honest. I've never said that to another woman, and it's not a pickup line; it's the truth. I feel like I've known you forever and that we've been dating for years. I'm that comfortable around you, and I hope you feel the same way."

I cupped his cheeks in my hands. "I do, Devon. I really do. We've known each other for less than a month . . ."

"But we've spent almost every day together during that time," he reminded me. "And I've loved every second of that time, even when you were so angry you slashed a sofa all to pieces."

For only a microsecond, a doubt that he was more interested in the farm than he was in me flashed through my mind, but I blinked the idea away. "I feel the same way."

He pulled one of my hands away from his cheek and kissed the palm. The touch of his lips on my cold hand sent warmth swirling through my whole body. "My mama said that I had to eat my peas before I could have dessert. I want to kiss you right now, but you said you wanted to talk first. So peas first and then dessert."

"I'll swallow them whole"—I winked—"because I want to kiss you, too. Here's my dilemma . . ." I went on to tell him about the offer to sit on the co-op board of directors. "What's your opinion?"

He leaned over and kissed me on the cheek. "I think you've already made up your mind after what Mandy, Celeste, and Polly told you."

"Yes, but I'm second-guessing myself," I told him.

"Never doubt your gut feelings," he said. "You've told me the cons. Are there any pros? Other than being able to say you were on the board of directors? Can you do as much without being a member of the co-op?"

I believe I fell in love with him that very second—as in real love, not lust or just like. "That sure clears the muddy waters. Thank you."

"Anytime, darlin'," he said. "And now, let's make that hot chocolate."

"Sounds good—but first, I've eaten my peas, and I don't even like peas. So now I want my dessert." I pulled his face to mine for a long, passionate kiss. "That's the best dessert I've ever had!"

"Me too, and I wouldn't mind a second helping," Devon said as he brushed a strand of my hair back away from my face.

"Let's just forget the hot chocolate and have hot dessert in the bedroom," I suggested.

He stood and then scooped me up in his arms. We heard Jesse and Celeste coming into the house about the time he closed his bedroom door with his foot.

❖   ❖   ❖

The hands on the clock sitting right beside me on the nightstand flipped to the ten o'clock mark when I glanced over at it. "I should be going," I whispered.

Devon wrapped me up in his arms even tighter. "I wish you didn't have to. I would love it if the first thing I saw every morning was your beautiful face."

"Give me time," I whispered and then kissed him on the cheek. "I've been processing so much lately that I don't want to rush into anything. And that's as much for your sake as mine."

He sat up, and I was sorely tempted to give in to temptation and stay the whole night. "How is it for my sake?"

"I never want you to think you are just a . . ." I couldn't find the words.

"That I am just an outlet for all you are going through?" he asked. "I don't feel like that, Angela Marie. What we have is real and special, and it's one of those things that a lifetime relationship is made of, not a fleeting fling."

I slid off the bed and started getting dressed. "That is the most romantic thing anyone has ever said to me—and I feel the same, but we should go slow."

"Darlin'!" He flashed a smile so brilliant that it lit up the semidark room. "*Slow* went out the window a few hours ago."

"I guess it did, but do you ever wonder what will happen to our relationship when we have our first big argument? The one where I say that I never want to see you again, and you tell me that you feel the same? Do you think we can work past something like that?"

"What we've got is so good that it can endure even a big argument," he assured me. "Want to have it right now and get it over with? If so, let's fight about you not being confident enough in your own sexuality to spend the night with me, no matter what anyone thinks about it."

"I'm too tired to have that fight tonight," I told him. "Let's save it for a later date."

He slid back down into the bed and laced his hands behind his head. "See you in the morning. I'm going to close my eyes now because I don't want to see you leave, and then I'm going to dream of us growing old together and watching our great-grandchildren get all excited about digging up their first peanuts."

I blew him a kiss and slipped out into the hallway. I came to a screeching halt in the living room, where I found Jesse asleep on the sofa and Celeste grinning at me from a chair in the corner.

"Shh . . ." She put her finger to her lips. "He fell asleep during the credits on the movie we were watching. I figured I'd just stick around and we could walk home together. There won't be so many questions that way if Granny and Polly are having a late-night snack."

"You are a lifesaver." I handed her coat to her and then put mine on. "I owe you one."

She eased the door open. "Don't you mean *another* one?"

"Two, then," I agreed. "And you better get out a calendar because I'll owe you even more before planting season."

"I've got the memory of an elephant," Celeste told me when we had cleared the porch. "I don't need a calendar. You need to give me some details on the way to the house."

"I'll tell you one little thing that you should have already noticed," I told her. "I'm still not cold, even though the wind is freezing and about to blow us both all the way to the Gulf."

"Whew!" She whistled through her teeth. "That makes me jealous. Even at the first, I never had that feeling with Trevor."

"For real?" I asked.

She picked up the pace, and I had to do double time to keep up with her.

"Have you ever still been this warm before or after any of your flings?" she asked.

"Nope," I answered. "Do all real relationships feel like this?"

"No, ma'am," Celeste said as she stomped snow from her boots on the back porch. "That feeling is special, and I intend to have it if I ever get married or even get into something serious again. I thought that what you are obviously feeling was just what authors write about in romance books—pure fiction."

Mandy's and Polly's voices floated across the kitchen and the mud-room, and I was grateful that Celeste was with me. *Maybe I should double the number of favors I owe her.*

"Have you girls been out for a walk?" Polly asked.

"Yes, but we didn't get far," Celeste answered.

"There's homemade salted-caramel hot chocolate on the stove," Mandy said. "Don't matter if you just walked to the edge of the yard; you'll be freezing cold, so help yourself. The leftover snickerdoodles are on the table. They go real well with the chocolate."

"We were just talking about how lucky we are that Glenda and Bennie are working out," Polly said. "I had no idea that Glenda was such a hard worker."

"She knows her way around the business of bedding and taping as well as she knows her way around a broom and mop," Mandy said. "I think y'all should hire her and Bennie as full-time help and give them the same benefits that Luis and I got."

I poured myself a large mug of hot chocolate and joined Mandy and Polly at the table. "Let's give it to planting time and then make that decision. By then, I hope to have the remodeling done. It's going faster than I could have imagined."

Celeste brought her chocolate over to the table and sat down beside me. "That sounds like a good plan to me. Like you said before, there's always work to be done on a farm this size, and you will need a couple of dependable supervisors."

"You mean, in addition to Devon and Jesse?" I asked.

Mandy finished off the cookie she was eating and snagged another one. "They should be made dual foremen. Devon can take care of all the mechanical repairs and upkeep; Jesse can help him with that when he's not busy doing anything that requires a carpenter or plumber. Then they can both supervise all the peanut business. That would take a load off your shoulders, Angela Marie."

"And exactly what will I do?" I asked. "I've worked from daylight to dark my whole life."

"You *could* get married and have some babies for me and Mandy to spoil before we die," Polly suggested.

Celeste shot a sly wink my way and then said, "Granny, Angela Marie and I are capable of having a family and still putting out a day's work. You set a good example in that for us."

"Well," Mandy scolded and waved her finger to take in me and Celeste both, "you could get on the ball with that baby business. I'd like to know that there is another generation coming on this farm before me and Polly have a talk with Saint Peter about opening up those Pearly Gates."

"Not me," Polly said. "I don't want to just know there's babies on the way when I step over into eternity. I want to hold them in my arms a time or two."

"Me too," Mandy agreed. "And on that note, you two know what you have to do to make us happy. We'll expect to see some progress toward that in the next few months. Sure wouldn't want y'all to feel guilty if we pass away all sad because we didn't get to see those new babies."

"You've got baby kittens," I reminded them. "Have you gotten them named yet?"

"Peaches is the orange one. Honey is the little calico," Mandy said.

"Tabby is the gray one, and the white one is Sheba," Polly said, finishing up the list. "And as much as we'll love playing with them, they are not human babies. Don't disappoint us."

Mandy pushed back her chair. "You girls can clean up and talk about names for your babies, which we will expect by this time next year."

"Granny, I'm just barely divorced," Celeste groaned.

"But you are, so now it's time to move on," Mandy said over her shoulder as she and Polly left the kitchen.

Celeste buried her face in her hands. "There's no pressure here, is there?"

"I kind of like having that deadline. I may throw away my birth control pills," I told her.

Chapter Twenty-Two

*O*f there were prizes for procrastination, I would never have won a single one. Putting things off just caused me to stress, and that caused me to sink into my own little inner world. On Tuesday morning, during our midmorning break time, I called Jeannie at the peanut co-op. Bennie, Devon, and Jesse had gone back to work, putting up the last of the drywall in the living room. Glenda, Polly, Celeste, and Mandy were still polishing off the last of their coffee and muffins.

"I'm so glad you called this morning, Angela Marie," Jeannie said, her voice sounding cheerful when she answered the phone.

"How did you—"

"Your name popped up on my caller ID," she answered before I could get the last words out. "I'm glad you called because your first job on the board of directors is to organize the dinner that we will have on Valentine's Day. I've got notes from past dinners to help you, and when you come into the office this afternoon, we can discuss the budget. Of course, if you want to spend some more of your own money and make it really nice, I wouldn't complain. Your father said that you were very good at planning parties and dinners."

Mandy looked up at me with a frown. I hit the speaker button and laid the phone on the table. "Are you sure that my father said that about me? It sounds more like something he would say about my mother."

"Like mother, like daughter," she said with a giggle. "I'm sure Sophia taught you all of her tricks, and we are so lucky that you are willing to take on the responsibilities of—"

"Whoa!" I practically shouted into the phone. "I'm not calling to accept your offer. I thank you for it, but my answer is no. I do not have the time to devote to that office—and even if I did, I wouldn't do it."

The silence was deafening, and I finally looked at the phone to see if the screen had gone dark. "Did we lose the connection?" I asked.

"No, I'm here," Jeannie answered. "I just can't believe that you are turning down such an amazing opportunity to improve *your* status and show the community, especially the other peanut farmers, that you are standing behind them."

"So, you think my status needs improving?" I asked.

"I-I didn't mean it that way," she stammered.

"Then please, explain," I said. "Why would my 'status'—as you called it—need anything to make it better?"

"I just meant that you haven't been visible in the community. You've kind of let your dad do all the social work, and—"

"Visibility in the community is not important to me," I said.

Glenda was holding a hand over her mouth to keep from laughing out loud. Celeste eased out of her chair and took off in a run toward the mudroom. Mandy and Polly were smiling so big that I just knew their cheeks would be aching the rest of the morning.

"You won't ever make it as a peanut farmer if you don't put out some effort," Jeannie snapped.

"Am I a member?" I asked.

"Of course." Jeannie's voice was so cold that I could almost feel a chill. "You have been on the roster for years. Harrison paid your lifetime dues more than a decade ago."

"Then I'm sure I will serve the *community*"—I fought the urge to air quote that last word—"as well as a member as I do as a board member.

You do send out an email or a letter telling each one of us when the monthly meetings are, don't you?"

"I was hoping that you would take on that responsibility," she said. Her voice had turned from cold to more than a little bit whiny.

"Sorry but thank you for asking me. I have too much on my plate to do anything other than make a few meetings each year. Can I do those on Zoom? You have a nice day now," I said and ended the call before she could say anything else.

Mandy laughed. "I guess you poked a pin in her balloon."

"Now she may even have to do something other than sit in her office and bark out orders," Glenda said. "She hired me to do some part-time work—answering the phone, filing, and that kind of thing. I lasted three days before I quit, and there were words said that might keep me from even getting an up-close-and-personal visit with Saint Peter. You are smart to never even start. She would have you running in circles while she spends her time on the phone or driving to Lubbock to get her fingernails done or have blonde streaks put in her hair."

"I had no idea that you worked at the co-op," I said.

"It was about six months ago. And, honey"—she lowered her voice—"your father spent a lot of time in the office with her. Not that they had hanky-panky stuff going on; I could see right away that Jeannie was just his puppet. She's not smart enough to run the co-op without him. And if lying sends a person to hell, then that woman has done bought herself a seat right in front of Lucifer's throne."

Had my father really said those things about me, or had she just been manipulating me into bending to her will? I would never know, but it sure didn't sound like the Harrison Duncan I knew, so the doubts would always be there.

"Thanks for telling us all that," I said.

"I'm just speakin' from what I saw with my own two eyes," Glenda said. "And for your information, I think Harrison was too smart to get involved in the bedroom with that woman. She would have blackmailed him if he had."

His words *She just wasn't my type* came back to my mind. If he had truly loved Summer and Roxy, then I could see where Jeannie wouldn't be his type, either, with her fitted suits, high-heeled shoes, and perfectly styled hair.

"'What's done is done and can't be undone,'" I said, quoting one of Mandy's old sayings.

"What are you talking about?" Glenda asked.

"Just something that I've heard before," I answered.

"That's right," Mandy agreed. "And it came from me. Now, you girls need to get on in there and help them boys. Don't you know that behind every good man is a woman pushing him to get the job done? Me and Polly will clean up the kitchen, and then we've got a mind to make a chocolate cake for supper tonight."

"Oh," Glenda gasped. "Will you save me a little piece? That's my favorite."

"We sure will," Polly said. "Now, get on out of here so we can talk about all of you."

"Polly!" Celeste scolded.

"It will all be good, I promise." Polly crossed her heart with a finger.

"That's her promise, not mine," Mandy declared.

I was surprised at the laughter that bubbled up out of my heart. I'd just found out that my father had most likely never said anything nice about me, and it didn't matter—not one bit.

❖ ❖ ❖

"Do you remember that big fight we were going to have?" I panted as I snuggled down closer to Devon and laid my head on his chest. His heart was pounding just as hard as mine; the whole room seemed to be our own private little bubble.

"I can't think of a thing"—he stopped to catch his breath—"that we would"—another deep breath—"be arguing about right now."

"It was about whether I was secure enough in my sexuality to spend the whole night with you despite whatever repercussions that might bring from the family," I reminded him.

Devon moved away from me and propped himself up on an elbow. "Are we going to have an argument right now to see if our relationship can endure such a thing? Before we get into it, I want you to know that I'm not rushing you into something that is uncomfortable. I'm ready when you are, but the time and date is totally up to you."

I traced his lips with my forefinger. "I just want you to know that subject is not going to be our first big fight."

He cocked his head to one side. "Are you saying . . ."

"Yes, I am," I answered him as I slid back down into the bed. "If the invitation to sleep over is still good, I'm staying with you."

"That invitation has no expiration date," he whispered and repositioned his body so that he could wrap me in his arms. "Good night, darlin'. Sweet dreams."

"Good night," I mumbled as I closed my eyes.

The next morning, I checked my reflection in the bathroom mirror while I pulled my hair up into a ponytail. The same old Angela Marie stared back at me. My eyes had not changed color, although they did seem a little brighter and a whole lot livelier these days. My red hair was still as curly as it had always been. When I smiled, I understood how much I had changed, and Devon could take the credit for most of that.

"I'm in love," I whispered. "I don't just love Devon—I'm *in* love for the first time in my whole life."

Is this what my father felt when he was with Summer? I wondered. *Was he constantly looking for a replacement for the love that had made him so happy in their together days?*

I didn't dwell on the questions, because I had learned that some-times there were no answers. Still, it seemed to give me a deeper under-standing of why he'd acted the way he had.

I knew there would be questions when I got to the house. I was ready for them, and I didn't care what anyone thought. I was living, not existing.

Mandy and Polly might—or might not—give me grief over my decision to spend the night with Devon, but I was a grown woman, and I would remind them of that. Glenda would gossip about it when she found out, but I didn't care who knew. Celeste would understand, so there were no worries there. I opened the bathroom door to find Jesse leaning against the doorjamb.

"Good mornin', Angela Marie," he said with just a hint of a smile.

I stepped out around him. "Mornin' to you. See you at the house in a few minutes."

"Yes, ma'am," he answered.

I just followed my nose to the kitchen, where Devon was making coffee. "Good mornin', again. I'm going to the house to help Celeste with breakfast."

He stopped what he was doing and wrapped me up in his arms. "Do you want a cup of coffee to wake you up before you leave?"

"Better not," I said.

He kissed me on the forehead. "If you'll give me five minutes to get dressed, I'll go with you."

"I would like to do this alone," I told him.

"I'll be glad when—"

I pulled his lips to mine to stop him from finishing the sentence. "Me too," I said when the kiss ended.

Most mornings, Celeste and I were up before dawn, and Mandy and Polly didn't come out of their room until breakfast was almost ready. Not so that day. Caramel greeted me at the back door and rubbed around my legs while I looked at the kittens. Their eyes still weren't open, but they had filled out and were five little balls of fur.

"You've got pretty babies," I told Caramel.

"They are pretty," Mandy chimed in.

"But not as pretty as a little red-haired girl scattering toys all over the new living room would be," Polly said.

Celeste peeked around the edge of the door and raised her eyebrows. "Or little blond boys playing with their trucks or building blocks?"

"Either one or both would be wonderful," Mandy said.

I drew in a long breath and marched into the kitchen. "I spent the night with Devon. If anyone has something to say about that, let's get it out before the guys arrive for breakfast."

"I just got one thing to say and then we don't have to talk about it anymore," Mandy said.

"And that is?" I got ready for a lecture on being sure about what I was doing, about needing to remember the reputation of the farm, and about whatever else Mandy could throw at me.

"It's about damn time," Mandy said.

"Is that all?" I couldn't believe what I had just heard.

"Yep. Now, why don't you get to cooking. It's been a long time since I had a night like you just had, but I do remember that it sure made me and Edward real hungry the next morning."

Polly sighed. "Ahh . . . Just to go back and have a few more of those nights."

"At our age, we'd need one of them how-to books." Mandy laughed.

Celeste handed me a wooden spoon. "You can stir the gravy while I whip up some eggs to scramble. The biscuits will be done in a few minutes." She lowered her voice to a whisper. "Well done, Angela Marie. Well done."

Chapter Twenty-Three

I'd never realized how happiness could make time speed by so fast. The living room was finished the first week in February. The ceiling was a pristine white, and the walls were a soft yellow. White blinds covered the windows, and there were simple white valances at the top. I stood in the middle of the empty room that morning and turned slowly. In an hour, a huge truck would arrive with the new furniture I had picked out, but I wanted to savor a job well done for just a little while.

Glenda and Celeste joined me, and for a moment, they didn't say anything at all.

"It is beautiful," Celeste said.

"Do you regret giving all that gorgeous furniture away?" Glenda asked.

"Not one bit," I answered. "I don't even care what y'all do with it. Sell it, donate it, or burn it. I'm just glad it's stored in your barn and not in one of mine. This room represents me."

"How so?" Celeste asked.

"It is free of all the past and ready to be filled with happiness," I said.

"I always thought living here would make for the happiest people in the whole state of Texas," Glenda said.

"Not so much," I admitted. "It was like living in a cold museum. Thank goodness for Mandy and Celeste, or I might have drowned in the tension we had most days."

"My granny used to tell me that we are today what yesterday made us. Remembering the past can make us better or bitter. All three of us have had our problems, and we might do well to remember that," Glenda said.

"I'm choosing the better instead of the bitter," I told her. "How about you, Celeste?"

"Absolutely," she replied with a nod.

"Me too," Glenda agreed. "But right now, we need you to come pass judgment on how to add two bathrooms upstairs. The guys have talked it to death and need us women to show them what to do."

We paraded up the stairs and found Devon, Jesse, and Bennie staring at a plan that Jesse had drawn up on a long piece of butcher paper.

"Tell me what I'm looking at," I asked.

Jesse started to reply, "I'm trying to keep the cost down by—"

"I don't care how you do it," I jumped in. "And I don't care about the cost. I want there to be three bedrooms with a bathroom and closet for each one. Tear out walls or make the bedrooms a little smaller if you have to."

"Okay, then," Jesse said. "We'll arrange things to make the plumbing easier and run the pipes down through the foyer wall."

"That sounds great," I told him.

"That leaves us with only six bedrooms," Celeste said. "Maybe we could turn a couple of them into sitting rooms."

"Nope. I've got plans for them," I told her and then headed back to the empty living room. I wanted just a few more minutes with it before we filled it up with comfortable, brand-new furniture. The whole room smelled like new carpet, and I pictured children learning to crawl or even walk across it in their bare feet. It would be so much warmer than the cold hardwood we had covered up.

"What other plans?" Devon asked as he came up behind me and wrapped his arms around my waist.

"What do you imagine when you look at this room?" I asked.

He answered with one word: "Kids."

"And where will those children sleep at night?" I asked.

He turned me around. "Are you telling me something?"

"Not yet, but that's part of my plan," I told him. "I want a houseful of kids."

"Four bedrooms full?" He gave me a kiss full of passion and promise.

"No, just two," I answered when the kiss ended. "One for boys, one for girls. They need to learn to share."

"What's the other rooms for?"

"That side is for Celeste and her family," I said. "But don't tell her right now. She needs to heal from the divorce and learn to trust again."

"My lips are sealed," he promised. "Tell me more about the side where your kids are going to share rooms."

"Well . . ." I couldn't have kept the smile off my face if I'd sucked on a green persimmon. "I really like this guy I'm in a relationship with, but the information you want is classified."

"When does it become unclassified?" he asked.

"You'll have to ask him," I answered. "I hear a truck coming up the lane. Our furniture has arrived. Tonight, we can sit in the living room."

"I kind of like the bedroom out in my place better," he whispered.

"Me too," I said and rushed to open the door.

Mandy and Polly came out of the kitchen. Everyone else hurried down the stairs to see what Celeste and I had picked out when we had gone furniture shopping a few days before. I told the men where to arrange the big, soft charcoal-gray sofa, the matching rocker-recliners, and the coffee table in front of the fireplace. They placed two settees with pop-up footrests at the other end of the room. Throw pillows in bright turquoise, yellow, and red were brought in and tossed onto the sofas, and then the deliverymen set a few end tables around so we would have places to set our coffee or sweet tea.

When the delivery guys had left, Mandy sat down in one of the recliners and popped the footrest up. "Now, this is livin' high on the hog." She grinned. "But it still looks a little bare in here."

"Later I plan to use pictures of Meadow Falls and the family to decorate the walls," I told her. "Polly, come on over here and take this other recliner for a test run. I bought them special for you and Mandy."

"For us to rock babies in?" Polly asked as she settled into the other chair and set it to rocking.

I shot a look over at Devon, who was smiling.

"Maybe someday," Celeste answered.

"Okay, all the rest of y'all have a seat and tell me what you think." I motioned toward the rest of the new furniture.

Glenda and Bennie claimed the sofa. Celeste and Jesse headed for one of the settees on the other end of the room. Devon took my hand and led me to the other one.

"Yes," I said when we sat down, side by side.

"'Yes' what?" Celeste asked.

"Yes, this is exactly what I wanted. Comfortable, practical, and cat friendly," I answered.

And kid friendly. Let the children run and play in the house. When they need you, stop whatever you are doing and hug them or kiss their boo-boos or sit on the floor and read a book to them. Let them crawl into your bed when they are scared of a storm. Do all the things that Mandy taught you. Fill this place with love and laughter, and don't look back or let the past define you, my mother's soft southern voice whispered ever so softly in my head.

Devon threw an arm around me and pulled me over closer to him. "I love this little sofa. It seems to have been made for just the two of us, darlin'."

"Yes, it was." My phone pinged, and I slipped it out of my shirt pocket to find an email from a laboratory. For a second, I thought it was a telemarketer, and then I remembered the DNA test. I almost opened it right then, but I didn't. I wanted to be alone when I saw whether Celeste was my sister by blood or just by the heart.

"Something important?" Devon asked.

"Yes, but it can wait," I answered. "Right now, I just want to sit here with you and enjoy *this* moment."

Chapter Twenty-Four

Devon gave me a quick peck on the cheek that evening when I walked him outside. "See you at the house in a little while?" he asked.

"Not tonight," I answered. "The DNA test results are in, and I need to spend the evening here."

"Have you looked at the results yet?"

"No, I was afraid I'd be so disappointed that I would cry in front of everyone, and Celeste and I need to be together when I open up that email. I'm afraid that she will be really upset when she learns that Harrison is her father and he literally abandoned her as badly as Roxy did—maybe even worse. Maybe I should just tear up the results and never look at them. I don't want to cause her pain." I wrapped my arms around his neck. "Tell me what to do, Devon."

"I can't, darlin'," he whispered. "I'd like to, but this has to be your decision." Devon grinned as he tipped my chin up with his fist.

As usual, my knees became weak, and my pulse jacked up so high I could feel every beat of my heart in my ears. Maybe I could put off opening that email until tomorrow. That thought lasted about five seconds, and then I realized that I would lie awake all night and worry if I didn't get it over with. No matter the outcome, Celeste and I needed to know.

"Good night, darlin'," Devon said ever so softly in my ear. "If you need to talk after you and Celeste open the results, just text me or come on over."

I sighed as I watched him disappear into the darkness and wished I were going with him. Luck was with me when I went back into the house. Polly and Mandy were looking at picture albums in the living room. They looked so comfortable on the new sofa and were having so much fun that I just stood in the shadows and watched them for a few minutes. I was procrastinating, but seeing them together—like sisters—calmed my trembling hands.

How was Mandy going to feel about that? Would it be a pleasant surprise, or would it break her heart to know that her great-grand-daughter had been treated like trash?

"I intend to make it right, no matter what the outcome," I muttered to myself as I made my way up the stairs. From the light coming across the hallway, I could tell that Celeste's door was wide open. My bedroom and hers were the only two that hadn't been torn up from remodeling. Mandy had declared that no one was touching her room until they took her out of Meadow Falls feet first. I decided on the spur of the moment that to keep her spirit alive in that room as long as possible, we might not redo it for years and years.

I knew I was procrastinating—again. I took a deep breath and held it so long that my chest began to ache. I let it out in a loud whoosh and stopped by my bedroom and got the pictures of Roxy and Summer from my dresser drawer.

I tucked them into my pocket with my phone. The hallway seemed a mile long, but step by nervous step, I finally made it to Celeste's open door. She had pushed back the curtains covering the door out to the balcony and was staring out of one of the twelve glass panels.

"Something interesting out there?" I asked.

She jumped like she had been caught doing something that she shouldn't be. "You scared me, Angela Marie."

"Sorry about that. I thought I was the only one in the family who got so lost in my own little world." I sat down in the rocking chair at the end of the dresser, not sure if she had caught my meaning.

She took a couple of steps over to her bed, plumped up a pillow against the headboard, then kind of stretched out in a sitting position. "Long story, but I was wondering if you were going to do something different with the door out onto the balcony."

"We can change up this room however you want it," I answered. "But I've got a feeling you were thinking about something far more serious than balcony doors."

Still putting off what you came for. I wasn't sure if I was listening to my mother's or Mandy's voice in my head.

"I'd like to keep them just like they are, but I'll be glad to have the paneling taken off and to have my own bathroom and a bigger closet," she answered. "And you are right about my other thoughts. I was wishing that I was as far along as you are, but I'm not."

"In what?"

"In your life. You've moved on, and I'm trying so hard to follow in your footsteps. I was looking out toward Devon and Jesse's place. Figured you would be going home with Devon like you've done for the past week, but then I saw him walking out to his place alone. Did y'all have an argument?"

"Nope." My mouth was dry, and my hands were trembling as I took my phone out of my shirt pocket.

"Then what . . ." Her green eyes grew wider and wider. "The results from that test are in, aren't they? Have a dozen relatives already contacted one of us?"

"They're in, but I haven't looked at them yet." I dreaded having to confess that I'd sent for a familial match, not one to find our ancestors.

"Well, let's see if we're related to royalty," she said with a smile.

"First, I need to tell you something important," I pulled the two photographs from my pocket. "You've seen one of these pictures but not the other one. Look at both of them, please." I handed them to her, and she glanced down at them.

"It's the same person . . ." She frowned and cocked her head to one side. "No, it's not. This one is Summer. You showed it to me and Granny. But this one is Roxy, isn't it? I sure never saw a picture of my mother with that tattoo. I wonder if Granny knew about it?" She drew the pictures up closer to her face. "They look like sisters. I wonder why Harrison had them—"

I butted in before she could finish. "Mandy told us that Summer was the love of his life, but I think he and Roxy had a fling. You have to remember there was only six years difference in their ages. She would have been about eighteen when that picture was taken, and my father would have been twenty-four."

"O . . . kay . . ." Celeste couldn't take her eyes off the picture.

"With that in mind, and after Mandy told us about how upset Roxy was at my father and mother's wedding . . ." I wanted her to make the connection on her own, but she just frowned. I had seen the same expression on my father's face too many times to count. "All right, I'm going to open up the email now."

I found the message and touched the screen on my phone.

"What does it say?" she asked.

"I only sent in the tests for a familial match," I said as I opened the email, then held my breath.

"Well?" Celeste's tone left no doubt that she was impatient.

I exhaled and read the results. "It says that . . ." I glanced up at her. "It says that you and I are half-sisters. The tests are a twenty-five percent match with what they call the cMs—I don't know what that means, so don't raise your eyebrows at me—of DNA falling in a solid place for siblings that share the same father. You are Harrison Duncan's daughter just as much as I am."

She scowled at me. "That's not funny. You don't joke about things like that."

My hands were trembling so badly that I almost dropped the phone when I handed it to her.

"Harrison was . . . *is* my father, and he just let me live here without ever saying a word?" she whispered as she stared at the results.

"Mandy said that Roxy was wild, so maybe he had doubts."

"Even if he did, he could have . . ." She threw the phone on the bed. "He knew. I know he did because Roxy cried when he married your mother. He just wouldn't marry her or claim me because he was ashamed of her. Remember what she told Granny? She and the love of her life had lain under the stars together, but he only wanted to be with her to relive his days with Summer."

"Please don't be mad at me," I pleaded. "I wanted you to be my sister so badly that I prayed that we'd get these results. I'm so sorry now that I've caused you more pain."

She dropped down on her knees. "Oh! My! God!" She slapped a hand over her mouth. "How are we going to tell Granny?"

I sat down beside her on the floor. "I think that's why all those pictures of the two of us are still sitting on his dresser. He knew that you belonged to him, but he was punishing his folks for making him stay here on Meadow Falls."

"It's too much to take in," she said. "All those years I wondered who my father was, and he was right here."

Tears welled up in my eyes and flowed down my cheeks. I pulled a fistful of tissues from the box on the nightstand for myself and handed the box to her. "I never could let you cry alone. That should have told us both that we were more than just best friends. As my sister, half of this farm belongs to you. Our father might not have done right by you, but by damn, your sister will."

Celeste tossed the pictures aside and wrapped me up in her arms. With our cheeks pressed together, our tears mixed. "You don't have to give me half of anything . . ." She hiccuped.

I pushed away from her and shook my head. "I'm seeing the business lawyer next week. We'll talk some more, but I've already made up my mind. Sisters share. End of discussion—and, honey, I agree with you."

"About what?" she asked.

"We don't need to do an ancestor search. Having you is enough for me," I said.

She blew her nose on a tissue and tossed it in the nearby trash can. "Yes, but now answer this: How are we going to tell Granny?"

"I guess I'll just blurt it out, like I always do," I said.

Celeste stood up and paced the floor. "Do you think that she ever suspected?"

I did the same. "We look like little girls playing follow-the-leader."

"Which one of us is the leader and which one is the follower?" she asked.

I laced my fingers through hers and walked beside her. "Neither. We are a team."

"I should be angry with you for not telling me what you suspected and for springing this on me out of the clear blue sky." She looked down at me. "Sweet Lord, we've got the same eyes. Why did I never notice that before?"

"And the shape of your face and hair color is the same as our father's was," I said. "Can you imagine what his mother would have said or done if he had claimed you? I can, without even thinking about it. She would have thrown him out on his own."

"Talk about a dysfunctional family." Celeste sighed. "Maybe there *is* a curse on Meadow Falls."

"*Was!*" I protested. "If there ever was a curse, I declare that it is hereby ended. Together, you and I have ended it, and we are going to be sure that from now on, this is a happy place, not one full of hidden secrets. Now, let's go tell Mandy because neither of us is going to be able to sleep a wink until we do."

Celeste let go of my hand and nodded. "Polly is with her. Do we ask to talk to her alone or just say it in front of Polly?"

I led the way out of the room. "What's that old saying about truth?"

"The truth will out?" Celeste asked.

"That's it, and believe me, once I tell the lawyer, the news will spread over Terry County like wildfire," I replied. "We can tell Glenda tomorrow morning just to get the news rolling."

We had made it to the bottom of the stairs when she stopped dead in her tracks. "Are you sure you are ready for this? I don't want you to have regrets."

"I've been ready my whole life," I answered.

Mandy and Polly had moved from the sofa to the two recliners and were watching the original *Parent Trap* movie on television—the show about twin sisters who had been split up when they were just babies. One went to live with the mother, leaving the other behind with the father. Just like me and Celeste, those girls had spent all those years without knowing they had a sister. But they had lived apart, not together on the same peanut farm. Missing those good childhood years Celeste and I had had.

"Them watching that movie sure seems like a sign to me," I whispered to Celeste.

"I agree," she muttered.

Mandy glanced over at us and narrowed her eyes. "I can tell by the way you are skulking around that you two are up to something."

Polly used the remote to pause the movie and cocked her head to one side. "They kind of look like they did when they stomped in the mud puddles and came in your freshly mopped kitchen. They must've been about two and three back then."

"Spit it out," Mandy said.

I moved the last two picture albums from the sofa to the coffee table. Celeste and I sat down at the same time. The picture of the twins telling their parents they had figured out who they were at summer camp was frozen on the television. That Polly had paused the show right at that exact moment sent cold chills down my spine.

"I . . . w-well . . ." I stammered. "I had a hunch . . ." I took a deep breath. "And I sent away for a DNA test for me and Celeste last week . . ." I sucked in more air. "And the results came back today."

"And who are you kin to? English royalty?" Polly's smile deepened the wrinkles around her eyes.

"No, ma'am, but . . ." I glanced over at Celeste.

"Granny, Angela Marie and I are half-sisters," Celeste blurted out.

Mandy tilted her head. "So that means Harrison is your father?"

"Looks that way," Celeste answered. "Are you okay? The news isn't going to give you a heart attack, is it?"

"As I've told you before, Roxy would never tell me who your father was," Mandy said, "but when you were born, I suspected it might be Harrison. For a little while, he had been as happy like he was when Summer was here, and then you looked a lot like he did when he was a baby. I thought he might come forward and claim you, but he had married Sophia a couple of months before you were born so he could keep his inheritance to Meadow Falls. Inez would have never let him marry Roxy, and I'm not sure it would have been the right thing for him to do anyway. Harrison had one love in his life, and that was Summer. Roxy deserved better than that."

"Why didn't you say something?" Celeste asked.

"What good would it have done? It would have made you bitter, and like I've told you girls many times, hate and love can't abide in the same heart," Mandy answered. "Now, you two get on to your bedrooms and get your homework done." Her brows drew down, and then she almost smiled. "You aren't kids anymore, are you?"

"No, we're grown women," Celeste answered.

"After all the worry and waiting, that was sure enough anticlimactic," I said. "You don't act surprised, Polly."

"Mandy and I have talked about the possibility for years. Now that the cat is out of the bag, what are y'all going to do about it?" Polly asked.

"Be sisters," we both said at the same time.

"You've always been sisters," Mandy reminded us.

"Yes, we have," I said. "And from now on, we are going to share this farm."

Mandy's blue eyes welled up. "I always wanted to see the day that good would come to Meadow Falls."

"It has arrived," I told her, and glanced across the room again at the frozen picture on the television. "There will never again be a curse on this place. Someday, children are going to slide down the banister and chase the cats, and laughter is going to fill this house."

Mandy wiped the tears away with the back of her hand. "Come on over here and give me a hug. I need one tonight."

"Me too." Polly opened up her arms. "I hope we both live to see that prophecy of yours come true, Angela Marie."

"You will," I promised as Celeste and I stood up at the same time to give each of them a hug. I hoped that what I'd said would become a fact, not just a prophecy.

Chapter Twenty-Five

The adrenaline rush finally left my body sometime around midnight. I was in my own bed for the first time in more than a week, yet sleeping alone didn't feel right anymore. Thoughts kept jumping around in my head like a sugared-up seven-year-old on a trampoline. That reminded me of the year I'd asked for a trampoline for my birthday. Celeste and I had talked about it for weeks, and we were going to have so much fun on it, but instead of what I'd asked for, my present had been new overalls and boots.

"Stop it," I muttered. "Stay focused on going to sleep."

I went from thinking about doing tricks on the trampoline that I never got to the argument I would most likely have with the lawyer when I told him I wanted to deed half of Meadow Falls over to Celeste, and if I died first, then she would inherit the whole place. He would tell me not to make rash decisions for a year after my father's death. I played the scenario out in my head when I also told him how I wanted to provide for Mandy and Polly both if I should pass away before they did.

"That's tomorrow's problem," I scolded myself.

No matter how many sheep I counted or how many times I sang "Twinkle, Twinkle, Little Star," I could not sleep. Finally, I threw back the covers and went over to the window to stare out across field after field of plowed ground that had never had dual ownership. A stream of light flowed from the living room window at Devon and Jesse's place.

The door opened, and Devon stepped out onto the porch. He faced the main house for a full minute before he went back inside.

I didn't even take time to get dressed but instead tiptoed downstairs just as I was, in pajama pants and a faded T-shirt. I pulled on my coat and stomped my bare feet down into my boots. I crossed the foyer, dining room, and kitchen as quietly as possible. Caramel looked up from her basket and meowed, so I stopped and gave her a little attention. I remembered what Mandy had said about never waking sleeping babies, and I did not pick up a single one of the sweet little kittens to love on.

When I was about halfway to Devon's house, the light in the living room went out, but the one on the porch came on. I picked up the pace and found the door unlocked. I eased inside and found Devon standing in the middle of the dark living room. He opened his arms, and I walked right into them.

"I couldn't sleep," I whispered.

"Me either," he said.

"Celeste is my sister," I said.

"That's good, right?" He took my hand and led me to the bedroom.

"Very good," I answered as I sat down on the edge of the bed. "I don't like sleeping alone anymore."

He dropped down to his knees and removed my boots, then took off my coat and tossed it over on a chair. "I tried to sleep, but it just wasn't happening. All these years I've slept by myself, and now it's impossible. I believe that means that you and I belong together."

"Are you proposing to me, Devon Parker?" I asked.

"Not right now, but later on down the road, I plan to do just that," he answered as he stretched out on his side of the bed. "I fell in love with you the first time I laid eyes on you, Angela Marie. You said we have to have our first big fight before we can really commit to each other, so I'll wait to see if you still want me in your life forever after that happens."

"We don't have to rush anything, do we?" I snuggled up against him and laid my head on his chest. This was where I belonged—beside Devon for the rest of my life.

"Tonight, I'm just grateful to have you in my arms," he said and then yawned. "The rest of the steps in our relationship can go as slow or as fast as you want. I just don't ever want to lose you."

"Why?" I asked.

"Because you make me happy," he answered.

"I love you, Devon," I said.

"I love you, too. That love is just going to grow forever in both of us," he told me.

Epilogue

Two years later

Time passes quickly when you are having fun. I had heard that all my life, but that Friday morning before Mother's Day, I gave it a new twist when the thought came to my mind.

"Time passes quickly when you are happy," I said to my reflection in the mirror. I wanted to slow down every moment and savor the happiness and the love rather than watch it speed by.

"Yes, it does." Devon slipped his arms around me from behind and leaned to the right so I could see both of us in the mirror. "These past two years have been the best of my life."

"And every day is going to just get better and better." I turned toward him and looped my arms around his neck.

He kissed me, and there was just as much passion in it as there had been in the beginning of our relationship.

"One more of those scorching kisses, and we'll be late for the first big meal at the Parker family reunion, and my mama will scold us for not getting her new grandchildren down there on time." Devon chuckled.

"We've just got one more thing to do before we go," I reminded him. "Celeste and Jesse packed their RV last night, and all we have to do is put the baby stroller in ours."

Devon laced his fingers through mine, and together we started down the stairs. Glenda was entertaining Amanda and Henry, our twins—named for Mandy and Devon's grandfather—in the living room.

"I'm going to miss these babies. Y'all don't let them forget me while you are gone," Glenda said as she put Amanda in one side of the double stroller.

Devon picked up Henry and buckled him into place. "Just yesterday, they were tiny babies, and now they are seven months old. You're right, Angela Marie—time flies when you are having fun."

Jesse chuckled as he and Celeste pushed a stroller into the living room with Edward—Eddie for short—strapped in. "We're burnin' daylight."

Edward had been named after Celeste's great-grandfather and Mandy's husband—the love of her life. Our twins were as different as day and night both in looks and attitude, but they shared their father's brilliant blue eyes. Henry had his father's dark hair—and bless Amanda's heart, she'd inherited my curly red hair. Eddie was the spitting image of Jesse.

"It's going to be a beautiful weekend," Devon said as he and Jesse pushed the strollers out the back door.

"Yes, it is," Celeste agreed, "and I for one am so excited to take the babies to their first Parker family reunion."

Jesse fell in beside Devon when we were outside. "Me too, but y'all do know they are going to get really spoiled these next few days."

"Two good fathers," Celeste whispered.

"The best," I agreed.

"This is our first Mother's Day without Mandy and Polly," Celeste said, her voice quivering.

"Our first Mother's Day, period," I said. "WWMS."

Celeste frowned. "What does that mean?"

"It stands for *What Would Mandy Say?*" I answered.

"That if we shed a single tear, she will rise up out of her grave and haunt us," Celeste said with half a giggle. "They got to rock the babies before they passed on, and that's what Granny wanted to do. We even got pictures of them holding the kids. I'm glad that Polly agreed to move in with us. She was like a second grandmother to us both." There was a hint of sadness in my half-sister's eyes.

"Today, we agreed that we would remember the good times and the good memories, and all the things Mandy and Polly taught us," I reminded her.

We went to the Duncan family cemetery first, and I laid four roses on my mother's tombstone. One for me, one for Devon, and one for each of the twins.

"Amanda and Henry aren't walking yet, but they will be by harvesttime this year, and you'll have another grandbaby sometime around Christmas. Meadow Falls is filled with laughter, kids, and cats these days. And, Mother, if you've got any connections up there"—I looked up toward the cloudless blue sky—"you might use them to give Celeste the twins this time and just let me have just one baby."

"Don't listen to her, Sophia!" Celeste argued. "Give her triplets for even thinking such a thing."

"I'll take them," Devon said.

I whipped around and air-slapped him on the arm. "Whose side are you on?"

He chuckled. "Well, darlin', we said we wanted a big family, didn't we?"

"Then I'll just pray for another set of twins and ask the universe to give Celeste triplets so that we'll each have four," I said with a smile.

"That's a pretty good start," Jesse said with a nod, then kissed Celeste on the forehead.

"I believe four kids might be a pretty good end," Celeste argued.

The guys went on ahead of us, and I closed the gate when we left. "It's hard to believe that our next due dates are about the same time, too."

"It's what sisters do," Celeste said.

When we reached the smaller, less-fancy cemetery, Celeste and I knelt in front of Mandy's grave. Memories flashed through my mind at warp speed, and in each one, Mandy was laughing or telling us a story. I could never thank her enough for what she had done for me. She was the true backbone of Meadow Falls—not the boss but the love. A soft breeze moved through the leaves on the old scrub oak tree not far from her grave. I took that as a sign that she was telling me everything was all right.

"She was the heart and soul of Meadow Falls," I said.

"You know what she would say to you right now, don't you?" Celeste seemed to be talking around a lump in her throat.

"Yep, I do," I answered as I laid four roses on her headstone and Celeste added three to them. "Live for today—not yesterday because it's gone and not tomorrow because it might never come."

Celeste draped an arm around my shoulders. "We both do."

We stood up, and this time we led the way and our husbands followed us with our babies. We couldn't bury Polly right next to Mandy, but there was a spot not far away. We stopped in front of her headstone and laid seven roses on it.

"You were so good to us," I said, "and we made such wonderful memories with you."

"WWPS," Celeste said. "Mandy would tell us to go make more memories at the Parker reunion, but what would Polly say?"

"The exact same thing," I answered.

When we got back to the house, Glenda was waiting on the front porch. "Y'all enjoy the weekend, and don't worry about a thing here. Bennie and I will take care of everything."

Bennie waved. "See y'all on Monday morning."

Devon strapped the twins into their car seats, one on either side of the small table in our brand-new RV. Jesse and Celeste pulled out ahead of us—but then, they only had one child to get ready for the ride to a little park near Post, Texas, where the weekend-long reunion would be held.

"Have I told you today that I love you?" Devon asked as he started the engine. "And that I'm so proud of our family and that I've never seen Jesse so happy?"

"Yes, about three times, but I never get tired of hearing it." I leaned across the console and kissed him on the cheek. "And I love you. Now, as Mandy would say, 'Let's get this wagon train rolling.'"

"Yes, ma'am." Devon smiled.

I sent up a silent thank-you to God, the universe, and fate for sending Devon into my life and for bringing Jesse into Celeste's. And also, for Mandy, who had truly been the lifeblood of Meadow Falls, and whose teachings still lived on in my and Celeste's hearts.

Dear Readers,

It's never easy to write *The End* at the finish of a story. But this book was very cathartic for me, so saying goodbye to Mandy, Celeste, and Angela Marie was doubly tough. I dragged my feet on the last chapter, but they assured me that they have their own lives to live now that we've all found peace, and they have promised to pop into my mind periodically to let me know how things are going. It's not easy to leave my characters behind, because I spend so much time with them that they become real to me. I hope that you feel that way when you reach the last page and that they have touched your emotions.

As always, I have many people to thank for helping me get this book from a simple idea to the finished product that you hold in your hands today. My thanks to my agent, Erin Niumata, and my agency, Folio Literary Management, for everything you do; to my Montlake editor, Alison Dasho, and my entire team there, from copy and proof editors to cover artists and all those who work so hard at promotion—thank you for continuing to believe in me; to my developmental editor, Krista Stroever—please know that I appreciate your advice and suggestions so much; and to all my readers who continue to support me—hugs to every one of you for buying my books, reviewing them, and telling your friends and neighbors about them! And last but not least, to my family, who understands that deadlines often have to come first—thank you for everything you do so I can live out my dream.

Until next time, happy reading.

Carolyn Brown

About the Author

Carolyn Brown is a *New York Times*, *USA Today*, *Washington Post*, *Wall Street Journal*, and *Publishers Weekly* bestselling author and RITA finalist with more than 130 published books. She has written women's fiction, historical and contemporary romance, and cowboys-and-country-music novels. She and her husband live in the small town of Davis, Oklahoma, where everyone knows everyone else, knows what they are doing and when, and reads the local newspaper on Wednesday to see who got caught. They have three grown children and enough grandchildren and great-grandchildren to keep them young. For more information, visit www.carolynbrownbooks.com.